THE BOTANIST

Anne Wedgwood

First Published in 2020 by Blossom Spring Publishing
The Botanist Copyright © 2020 Anne Wedgwood
ISBN 978-1-8380982-8-5
E: admin@blossomspringpublishing.com
W: www.blossomspringpublishing.com
Published in the United Kingdom. All rights reserved under
International Copyright Law. Contents and/or cover may
not be reproduced in whole or in part without the express
written consent of the publisher.
Names, characters, places and incidents are either products
of the author's imagination
or are used fictitiously.

Thank you to all who have read and encouraged me along the way, and especially to three fabulous children – Esther, Hannah and Peter; to Chrissy, and, most of all, to Bruce.

Chapter 1

Am I a psychopath? It's not my specialism, but I've never thought I fitted the profile. It's a shame, it could help keep me out of prison if they arrest me. Only they won't find out. If there's one thing that's not going to happen, it's me going to jail.

If you met me, you'd never guess what I've done. I'm one of the invisible. Women of a certain age, conventionally dressed, going about their business, shopping, gardening, on their own after spending years looking after aged parents, nothing to catch your eye. You'd never look at me and wonder if I was a killer. It was a long time ago, mind you, and I don't dwell on it. I was a different person then, in crisis, and when you're in crisis you get on and do what needs to be done. And if what needs to be done is murder, you do it. I don't like to think about it now, even though it all made perfect sense at the time. I put it behind me a long time ago and got on with life. I had enough to keep me occupied with a full-time job and a small child to look after, and then Mother to take care of. They're both gone now of course, and all that keeps me busy is the garden and the crossword.

Like it or not, I've had to think about it again since

the letter arrived about the gas pipes. They're going to dig up the garden, and there's nothing I can do to stop them. And I know what they'll find when they do. I thought about moving it, but it's too heavy for me now and digging it up could give me a heart attack. I've had to make other preparations, and that's what I've done. Six weeks they said, before the men come. Seven days to go and I've one last job to do.

***

A sense of dread, of premonition. It's a beautiful September morning, but there's a black cloud in my mind that the early sun can't shift. It's not like me to be jittery, but I couldn't decide what to wear when I got up, and I feel as if I've had four cups of coffee rather than just the first sip. I'll feel better if I'm in control so I put on my gardening clothes, knowing exercise will help to clear my mind before I get on with the final preparations.

A soft wind's blowing in the garden as I walk round, deciding which plants to cut back. When I reach the orchard, I find a pair of doves perched on the bird table waiting to be fed. Mother loved this spot. A worn iron bench with a view over the Westwood pastures. She said it freshened her up for the day, and I think of her every morning when I sit here with my coffee. It does me good to remember her in the place she loved best. I could linger, listening to the birds and savouring the view along the path towards the house, but I'll feel better if I get on with things. Now my plans for the garden are settled, I turn my mind to the other big job for the day, mentally ticking off all the items I'll need, and feeling better for doing so.

I'm walking down the path towards the house when I hear the rumble of a truck approaching. I wonder what it's doing here, before it hits me. Surely not. They said next week. I know they did, because I've been reading the letter almost every day. It must be here for some other reason. But no, the doorbell rings as I put my mug in the sink. I can't believe it, but I know there's no other reasonable explanation. They must be here early. My mind racing, I hunch my shoulders and answer the door with a deliberate lack of haste. I can do this. I just need to adapt my plan to the situation. It's important to establish the right impression from the start, and at least I'm wearing my gardening clothes. They'll give me a nicely dishevelled look. The police are bound to ask them about me, and I don't want them saying I'm anything other than a sweet little old lady. I open the door with a puzzled expression on my face to find a burly workman standing on the step, in overalls with Northern Gas written on them and clutching an ID card. There's a kind look about his middle-aged face, and even though I'm in a panic, I feel sorry for what he's going to have to witness. A similarly dressed, lanky younger man is getting out of the cab with an uncertain air. I hope it's the older one who'll be operating the digger.

'Morning, love, we're from Northern Gas. Expecting us, were you?' I'm used to being everyone's love, you can't avoid it round here. I don't make a thing of it, although it would be nice to get a bit of respect now and then.

'No, I wasn't. The letter said you'd be coming next week.'

'Oh.' He stops in his tracks and unbuttons his outside pocket. 'Well, they told us to come today. Look, here it is, written in black and white. We have to do what the boss says or it'll muck up the whole schedule. They must have finished a job early last week and brought yours forward.' He pulls out a creased sheet of paper which I can see has today's date written on it, together with my address. I could make a fuss and tell them to come back next week, but I know this would only arouse suspicion later on, so I give in.

'I suppose you'll have to get on with it now you're here. What do you need to do first? I've never had anything like this happen before. I hope it won't make a lot of mess. I'm very proud of my garden, you know.' I put on my best fussy old woman act and it looks like I've made his day. He can't wait to be helpful and reassuring.

'Don't worry, love, we'll be careful. I can't guarantee no mess, but we'll do our best, and that's a promise. Now, we can bring the digger through the front garden and down the side of the house if you want, but I'm guessing you'd rather we took down a bit of fence and came through the back from the Westwood? We'll put it all back together afterwards, good as new.'

'Yes please, that does sound sensible. Do you know where you're going? I don't want you trampling down more of my garden than is really necessary.'

'Oh, yes, we've got a plan and Mr Grey from the council's here to make sure we get it right. He's a surveyor, real clever. They've sent him along today 'cos it's complicated. You know, with the pipe going under your property. Doesn't happen often, you know.' He sounds rather pleased with himself, and I wouldn't mind betting he thinks he's been specially chosen for this complex job.

'Oh, all right, I suppose that's a good idea. Shall I put the kettle on? I know how you workmen like your cups of tea.'

'Now that would be great. Mine's a tea with two sugars, and young Patrick likes a coffee, white no sugar. I don't know about Mr Grey, but I expect he'll let you know.' Mr Grey is approaching, although he's not dressed to suit his name. It's what they call 'smart casual', and he resembles Prince William in one of those family pictures they like to take to make them look normal. He's clutching a clipboard and doesn't seem interested in making eye contact while he's got that to look at.

'Good morning, er, Dr Templeton, isn't it? I'm Matthew Grey, council surveyor. I've got the plans of your property and the pipe system, and I'm here to make sure we cause the minimum disruption possible. We'll make good afterwards, new fence, turf and so on.'

'That's kind of you, but it's not helpful of you to have

arrived without any notice, and I don't think you'll be able to replace my wild garden very easily. It's been left to its own devices for over thirty years. You won't fix that in a hurry. I suppose it's too late to ask if there's really a need to do all this?' He looks up, startled at my abrupt tone, and his expression suggests he might be about to make more of an effort.

'I'm afraid it is too late, Dr Templeton. We don't dig up people's gardens without good reason, and if those pipes aren't replaced soon, they could leak and cause an explosion. You wouldn't want that, now, would you?'

I'd warmed to him for using the correct title, but his patronising tone is already annoying me. Does he think my brain's gone soft because I'm retired? I decide not to offer him a drink after all and stomp off to the kitchen. He's left looking surprised on the doorstep, not sure what to do next. Good.

Matthew Grey eventually follows me through, and I point him in the direction of the garden. He's quick to get his bearings, and it's not long before he's waving at the workmen over the back fence to show them where to go. My heart sinks a little as I see it's exactly where they had told me it would be. I've not been able to prevent myself from hoping they had it wrong and all my worry and plans were for nothing. But they hadn't got it wrong. It's exactly where they said it would be. The gas pipe runs under my garden. Under my precious wildflower garden. And under the body.

I turn back and decide to wash up the breakfast things and give the kitchen a bit of a clean before putting the kettle on. It will give them time to get started and me a chance to think. I don't think I've said or done anything unusual in the circumstances, and I need to stay calm. There's some banging first, which must be the fence coming down. I run the water in the sink ready to give all the surfaces a good wipe down and put the radio on to drown out the noise. Once the washing up bowl is full, I leave the radio to chunter away to itself and go to the living room and the desk where I do my paperwork. I take out the little pouch and the small book and place them inside a brown envelope. I don't want to leave them where policemen might look and decide they're best off in my handbag for now. Once that's done, I return to the kitchen and clean every worktop until it shines. I'm tempted to have a go at the oven while I'm at it, but I have to acknowledge that if I leave it any longer, they'll be coming in to ask where their drinks are.

I'm getting out the teabags and instant coffee – I was never interested in fancy kitchen appliances, and don't go for clever coffee machines or teapots – when the digger starts. I keep my hand steady as I get milk from the fridge, pour water from the kettle, stir in the sugar. I hesitate before taking it outside. I don't want to spill it from shock, but it's more than half an hour since they arrived, and I know it will look odd if I don't go out soon. I'm halfway down the path when I hear the shout. It's not too alarmed so I don't have to drop the mugs, which is good as I'd not thought to use old ones, and I carry on towards the chaos that used to be my wildflower garden.

The fence is down and there's a big hole stretching halfway across the width of the garden. The older one is climbing down from the cab of the digger, looking cross.

'What's the matter? What are you shouting at me for?' He's yelling at Matthew Grey, as he comes around the back of the machine from the far side. The surveyor isn't yelling back though, he's gone pale and is pointing at the earth in front of the digger.

'What is it? Don't tell me we've hit the pipe? We're only going in shallow to start with like I told you. It's all a lot of fuss...' He trails off as he sees the surveyor's face. 'Hey, sorry, I didn't mean to yell. What's the matter, mate?'

The younger one, Patrick, has already climbed down and is standing by the digger.

'Jim, there's something there. In the earth. Look.' Jim finally sees it. Caught in the digger's teeth is a wad of plastic, the end of a bigger piece of plastic. And tipping out of it, as if to wave hello to us all, is a human hand.

***

'Come along now, Dr Templeton, sit yourself down and you'll soon feel better.' Matthew Grey has been quick to take charge and is responding perfectly to my agitated state.

'Oh, thank you Mr Grey, it's so silly of me. I've seen enough dead bodies in my time, but it's not at all the same when it's your own back garden.'

'Of course, please try not to distress yourself. Put your head down between your knees if you feel faint, Dr Templeton.' He's lucky the circumstances aren't different, or I'd have been tempted to hit him at this point, but I nod gratefully and take some deep breaths for good measure.

Jim and Patrick are hovering outside the kitchen door, the latter as white as a sheet. I hope he's not going to throw up all over my nice clean kitchen floor, and barely manage to stop myself jumping up to get him a bowl.

'Er, would it be all right if young Patrick sits down, love?' Jim asks. 'I think he's feeling a bit woozy. It's the shock, you know.'

'Oh yes, come in, come in,' I say. 'There's a bowl in the cupboard over there if you think you might need it, dear.'

'Thank you, Miss,' he says, sitting down with a shudder. 'I'll be OK, but a glass of water would be nice.'

'And maybe some strong sweet tea,' Jim says. 'That's what you're supposed to have, isn't it? For a shock?'

'Yes, yes,' says Matthew Grey. 'All in good time. We need to call the police first, don't you agree?'

'Yes, of course.' I keep my voice weak and wobbly. 'I don't suppose you could do it, could you, Mr Grey? I really don't feel up to calling them myself. I'm afraid I'm in too much of a state to know what to say to them.'

'No problem, only too glad to help.' He seems delighted to undertake this important task. He goes into the garden to make the call on his mobile and then returns to fuss around the kitchen making sugary tea and rooting out the biscuit tin. I hate sugar and I don't much like tea, but I decide it's best to drink it in the circumstances. As I take the mug from the surveyor, I consider whether I should let him take over entirely. I'd not anticipated having someone so competent in the house. It could be an opportunity to reinforce my innocent little old lady status. On the other hand, I'm desperate to see the body. What state is it in? Is there any hope of it being too decomposed for identification? I'm furious with myself for not having removed the plastic sheet before burying it. Why did I leave it on? I wasn't in a panic at the time, so maybe I simply forgot. Or perhaps it seemed neater not to have to dispose of it? It's so long ago that I can't remember.

I decide my perceived helpless is more important than my need to see the body. I'll just have to wait to find out about its condition. I could always ask – tremulously, of course. So when the bell rings, I don't stir, but stare into the distance with what I hope is a shocked expression and let Matthew Grey answer the door. He's back quickly with two uniformed policemen who go out to the garden and then come back at once, saying now they've confirmed that there is in fact a body on the premises, they'll call in the detectives. They must have been waiting on standby because the bell rings a second time less than twenty minutes later and Matthew rushes to answer it again.

He doesn't come back for a while. Perhaps the police are asking him questions already. Are they asking about me? They must be. If they were talking about anything else, they'd come through at once. I try to imagine how he might be describing me. An ordinary old lady, I hope, not that I regard myself as old, but I must be the same age as his parents, which would make me elderly in his mind. My being a doctor didn't stop him being patronising, and with luck the police will be the same. I suppose he'll say I've got my marbles but I'm in shock right now. It's true, in a way. I knew what was going to happen, but it's a strange feeling now it has. The tea doesn't taste as wrong as it should, and I was grateful for Jim's clumsy efforts to protect me from the 'horrors' as he put it. I almost feel like the person I'm pretending to be. I suppose that's good, isn't it?

The surveyor's talking officiously as they come through to the kitchen, explaining about the gas pipes on the way.

'Yes, it's unusual for them to run under a private property. That's why I'm here, and a good thing too. The council will want a full report, I'm sure.' He almost sounds pleased about it, and stops talking abruptly, as if acknowledging the inappropriateness of his tone. He's followed by two people who must be the police, although they aren't in uniform. They look young to me, but I'm not going to assume any lack of expertise on that account. The woman comes in first. Either she's the superior or the tall man behind her is uncommonly polite.

'Er, this is Dr Templeton, the owner of the property.' Matthew Grey seems pleased to have something less sensitive to talk about. 'And this is Jim, and Patrick, they're the ones who were operating the machinery at the time.' It almost makes me smile, wondering how long he'll be able to avoid using the word 'body', but I don't respond, maintaining my stunned and distressed expression.

'Thank you, Mr Grey.' It's the woman who speaks first, so she must be in charge. She turns to me.

'I'm sorry to have to meet you at such a distressing time, Dr Templeton. I'm Detective Inspector Ronnie

Twist and this is Sergeant Luke Carter. We'll have to ask you some questions, but first we need to see the body.' So she's not afraid to use the word. I suppose she's used to it. I nod vaguely without looking at her, and she turns back to Matthew Grey.

'Would you be able to show us what you've found, please?' she says, calm as you like, as if it's nothing more than an archaeological curiosity and she's a museum director.

'Oh, yes, certainly.' He sounds taken aback, but I don't know why. He was keen enough to take over before so he can hardly be surprised when they ask for his help. The three of them leave the kitchen and Jim looks around, at a loose end.

'Would you like another cup of tea, love? I'm sorry, I don't know where the things are.' Exasperation brings me out of my semi-stupor, and I get up and make more tea. I even dig out a teapot so as to make enough for all of us and give Patrick a glass of water.

It's not long before the sergeant comes back in. He says his boss is making some calls and the uniformed constable will take Jim and Patrick to the police station to make a statement. The digger will have to stay where it is for now, but they should be able to retrieve it in a few days' time.

'But what about the pipe?' says Jim. 'We're supposed to replace it this week. And what about the digger? When can we have it back?'

'I'm afraid I can't say,' the sergeant says. 'It's a crime scene for now, but we'll let the council know when we've finished with it.'

'Well you'd better call my boss, that's all I can say,' Jim says. 'He won't be pleased, I can tell you. We've a strict schedule to keep to. If I know him, we'll be on another job tomorrow and we'll not be able to get back here for weeks. Sorry, love,' he says, turning to me. 'Looks like you'll have a hole in your fence and a mess in your garden for a while.'

'Never mind,' I say. 'It can't be helped. I'm sure you'll let me know when you're ready to come back?'

'Course we will, love, now you take care, eh?' He grabs Patrick by the shoulder and drags him out before anything else can happen to disrupt his day, leaving the sergeant and me in the kitchen.

'Tea?' I ask. 'There's plenty in the pot.'

'Oh, why not.' He sits down and gets out his

notebook, which is of the electronic variety, while I pour.

'I need to ask a few questions, Dr Templeton, is that OK? We can do it here for now, there's no need to take you to the station just yet.' He has an open face, the sort that can't lie. He's big in the wooden kitchen chair, looks like he could be a rugby player. Young but not too young, no rings on his fingers or holes in his ears. Conventional, you might say. Decent. That's good. Maybe I'll remind him of his granny.

'Yes, of course dear, go ahead.' The tea's poured and I sit opposite him at the table.

'You're the only occupant of this house, is that correct?'

'That's right, dear. I had my mother with me until she died, and my daughter moved away some time ago, so yes, there's only me.'

'And for how long have you lived here?'

'Now let me see, it was nineteen seventy-four when I married Reg, so it would be…Oh, can you work it out for me, sergeant? My mind's still in a bit of a spin.'

'That's forty-five years, Dr Templeton.' He's quick to work out the sum, so he's got a brain. I'll have to remember that.

'I presume Reg is – was – your husband?'

'Yes, that's correct.'

'But you live here alone, so did he die? Or are you divorced?'

'Neither, I'm afraid to say. Reg went missing not long after we married. He's probably on your missing persons' list, if it goes back that far. Or maybe he won't be now. I had to have him declared dead in the end.' I suppose I shouldn't be surprised to see his hand hover uncertainly as he takes this in, but he keeps a straight face and merely taps away on his screen.

'And your mother? When did she die?'

'Late last year, dear.'

'I'm sorry to hear that. Had she lived with you for long?'

'Oh, yes, she moved in soon after my daughter was born. She lives in London now. Joanna, I mean.'

'It seems like a big property to take care of on your own. The garden must be nearly an acre. Do you look after it all yourself?'

'Almost. I have a man in to do the heavy work, pruning the trees and cutting the hedges you know, but I do the rest myself. And Mother did too, until she fell ill.

It was she who designed it. Gardening was her passion, right until the end.'

'Do you mind my asking what she died of?'

'Oh, she had been diagnosed with Parkinson's but soon after that she passed away in her sleep, lucky lady. I came in with her tea one morning to find she'd gone. She was ninety-four, so she'd lived a good life. I hope I go the same way.'

'I suppose we all do.' He smiles kindly at me. Yes, I'm falling nicely into the granny category.

'I'm sorry, but I have to ask, Dr Templeton. Do you know anything about the body in the garden?' He makes it sound like an Agatha Christie title but he's probably too young to realise.

'I most certainly do not. What sort of question is that?'

'It's the sort of question we always ask in these circumstances, Dr Templeton. There's a body in your garden and you're the sole owner of the property. There's no one else we can ask.' There's an awkward pause.

'Well the answer's no. I don't know anything about it. It's all extremely upsetting. First they come and dig up my lovely wildflower garden, and why anyone put a gas pipe under it in the first place is a mystery to me. And then they go and find a body. It's enough to give me a heart attack.'

'So, can I confirm that you are stating that you have no previous knowledge of the presence of a deceased person in your garden?'

'Yes, you can, sergeant. And now, unless you're about to arrest me or put me under caution or whatever it is you do these days, I'd rather not talk about it any more. I'm upset enough as it is. I'll make some more tea if you don't mind.'

'Please do. I'll see how my boss is getting on. I'll be back soon.' He sidles out of the back door while I put the kettle on and wonder how much tea it's possible to drink in a morning. I know he's gone to report what I've said about Reg and Mother to the detective inspector. They'll be thinking it's Reg in the garden, even though they can't know how old the body is. That's fine with me, let them think what they like. They can't stop me denying everything, which is what I'm going to do.

He's back soon enough with the inspector and Matthew Grey, who, to his inadequately disguised disappointment, is also told to leave, and to report to the station to make a statement before the end of the day. It looks as if this has been the high spot of his career, and it occurs to me that he may well think it worth repeating at the office or even reporting to the local paper.

'Will this be in the papers, do you suppose?' I ask before he has a chance to leave. I want to know what the police have to say and for him to hear it too.

'I daresay the media will find out soon enough,' says DI Twist, careful not to look directly at the surveyor. 'But I can't say how much interest there'll be, with all the current fuss on about the new bypass. I suggest we inform them ourselves and say there'll be no further information given out while the investigation is underway. That might keep them happy for a few days at least.'

'Yes, that sounds sensible. Thank you, Inspector,' I turn to Matthew Grey. 'Goodbye Mr Grey, and thank you for your help.' He looks surprised to find himself dismissed so abruptly and leaves in a deflated fashion, his future as the source of a major criminal investigation apparently curtailed. Both detectives follow him out and it's a couple of minutes before they return to the kitchen. I suppose they're working out what to ask me next, and I make sure I've got a distressed expression on my face.

When they come back DI Twist sits at the table and tells me they can't be sure yet if the body is a man or a woman. They'll be joined soon by a forensic anthropologist and a photographer, and they'll know more after they've been. She's professional but kind, dealing with an old lady in shock. I use the opportunity to take a good look at her while she's telling me things I already know. She's dressed like a detective should be – smart and unfussy. Her wispy ash-blonde hair is pulled back in a bun and her baby blue eyes have a faraway look to them. Her resting features are self-contained, calm, almost placid, giving her the look of a mildly interested sheep. She's not communicating any emotion at all, and this is not a good sign. I'm reminded strongly of the wolf in sheep's clothing cliché. I don't think she'll be as easy to play as her sergeant and I remind myself to stay meek and mild.

'Thank you for explaining everything, Inspector. I'm afraid this has all put me into a bit of a spin. It was bad enough them digging up my precious garden, but for this to happen....I don't know what to say. In fact, I'm feeling a bit faint, do you mind if I go and lie down for a bit?'

'Not at all, but there are a few questions I need to ask you first. We'll leave you alone once the team arrive and you can have a rest then. Shall I pour you some more tea?' So not a pushover yet. I agree to the tea and she pours it out for me, thankfully not adding even more sugar.

'Sergeant Carter has filled me in on your conversation with him so far,' she says as she nods to him to carry on taking notes. 'But I need to go over some aspects that you've already covered. Just to be clear. I'm sure you understand,' she gives me a perfunctory smile as she passes the mug – no rings, I notice.

'Yes, I understand.' I try to sound as weary as possible. 'But this has been a dreadful shock, Inspector, and I'm quite exhausted by it all. I hope it won't take too long.'

'We'll do our best, Dr Templeton, but we can't ignore the fact that a dead body has been found in your garden, and we need to gather as much information as we can without delay.' I can't see what the hurry is, when he's been there over forty years already, but it wouldn't be helpful to say so, and I hold my tongue.

'I understand, Inspector. I'll do my best to help you.

What do you want to know?'

'You've told DS Carter that you live here alone, and previously with your mother and daughter. We'll need full details for them both, but DS Carter can go through those with you later. You have some help, I believe, with the garden. Is there anyone else who visits the property regularly? Cleaners, workmen of any kind?'

'No, I do everything else myself.'

'We'll need the name and number of your gardener before we leave. Does he spend much time here on his own?' I guess she's wondering if he might have something to do with the body. I hadn't considered this as a possibility and see no need to hold back from letting her pursue this pointless trail.

'Yes, I tend to go out when he's here. He prefers it if I let him get on with things without interfering. He doesn't come every week, only when a big job needs doing, pruning the trees or cutting the hedges. He's here for a few hours when he does that, so I usually go out for the day to avoid all the noise and the mess.'

'Does he have keys to the property?'

'No, but I think he knows where I keep the spare.'

'Hmm, we'll need to interview him later. Now, I need

to ask you more about your husband. Reg. You said he went missing, I believe. Can you tell me about that, please?'

'There isn't much to tell. He just disappeared one day. I never knew where he went, and I had him declared dead in the end.'

'That must have been difficult for you.' She runs her finger round her mug of tea, but I notice she's not drinking it.

'Yes. I don't like to talk about it. It made for a trying time. You know how people can be with their gossip.'

'And you were left to bring up your daughter on your own. Is that why your mother moved in – to help with the baby?'

'Yes. Joanna was born six months after Reg left and Mother moved in shortly before the birth. I went back to work, and she looked after the baby for me.'

'And I gather you looked after her until she died. She must have been glad to have been able to stay in her own home.'

'I suppose she was, yes. I retired sooner than I'd planned to make sure of it.'

'Let me get this right,' says DI Twist, looking directly

at me for the first time. 'You and Mr Templeton married and moved into this house in which year?'

'We were married in February nineteen seventy-four. And he wasn't Mr Templeton. His name was Blake. I hadn't changed my name before he disappeared, and I saw no need to when he'd gone. It was easier professionally as well.'

'And your daughter? Which name did she take?'

'She's a Templeton. Reg hadn't come back when she was born, and by that time I didn't want his name in the house.'

'And he… disappeared, you said. When, exactly?'

'Three months after we were married. The May of the same year. Do we really have to talk about this now? It's all rather upsetting.'

'I'm sure it is, and I'm sorry about that, but you must realise, Dr Templeton, we have to consider whether the body in your garden might be your husband?' Ah. It didn't take her long to come up with that, did it? I wait for a moment before replying, while a shocked pause hangs in the air and I muster my indignation.

'You think…that…that <u>thing</u> out there is Reg? But he…they said…Oh, dear, this is all too much. How could he have got there?'

'We don't know who it is yet, Dr Templeton, and it's too soon to consider how the body got there. I just want to you understand why we need to know everything you can tell us about Reg. Was it a happy marriage?'

'What do you need to know about that for?' I hadn't expected questions like this. I thought I'd prepared myself for anything, but apparently not.

'Answer the question please, Dr Templeton. Were you and Reg happy together?'

'Of course we were, we were newly-weds, not long back from our honeymoon. Why wouldn't we be happy?'

'Oh, there are all sorts of reasons for young couples to have difficulties at the start of married life.' She looks at the ceiling as if reading from a list, and I almost find my own eyes drifting upwards to see what it says. 'Tensions can arise so quickly when people live together for the first time. Not having much money is a common cause, or a baby being on the way before both parties are ready to be parents. Might that have been the case for you and Reg?' Now this is more helpful, I can use this idea.

'Well, I don't think Reg had expected to become a father quite so quickly, it's true. Money wasn't a problem as I was earning a good salary, but that wouldn't have lasted if I'd had to give up work. And although we hadn't discussed it, I'm sure it's what Reg would have expected me to do. They weren't problems in my mind, but they could have been worrying him, I suppose.'

'Was he faithful? Might he have gone off with another woman?'

'Oh, I can't pretend there wasn't talk of it at the time, but there was never a hint of who it might have been. I don't know, I've wondered often enough. Maybe there was someone and I was too naïve to realise. I was very trusting of him. I never questioned him when he said he was late home because he'd been in the pub with his friends. Maybe he was having an affair.'

'What about his friends? Did the police talk to them at the time? Did any of them have any ideas about where he might have gone? Or what could have happened to him?'

'They may have done, but I didn't hear anything about it. I didn't know his friends particularly well. He never brought them home with him and when we went out it was usually just the two of us.'

No doubt they'll find out that this isn't strictly true at some point, but if they don't identify the body they might not need to. Best not to give too much away for now.

'Did he have any enemies? Anyone who might have born him a grudge?'

'Not that I was aware of. There was some talk of a shady deal with a building contractor. I didn't like the sound of it, but I kept out of it. He didn't like me interfering with his work. That might have had something to do with it, I suppose.' I hope this is enough to get DI Twist off my back whilst feeding her enough of interest to think she has something to follow up on. I suppose she has her boss to keep happy back at the police station.

'And the garden? The area at the end has a wild look about it. It's quite a contrast to the rest of the plot. Can you tell me why that is?' Despite myself, my stomach clenches. They're asking far more questions than I'd anticipated, and behaving like a helpless old lady is starting to come more naturally than I would like it to.

'Why do you need to know about that?' I allow my voice to tremble now, in the hope they'll stop for a bit.

'Because that's where the dead body is, Dr Templeton.' The vague expression has gone, her voice has taken on a hard edge and she looks more like a hawk than a sheep. I feel a prickle under my skin and the sense that this is going to be harder than I had thought. 'We need to know everything about your garden and who has had access to it over the years, and once we know how old the body is, we'll need to know even more. There will soon be scene of crime officers arriving to go over every inch of your garden, so if there's anything you haven't told us, it will be better for you if you do so now.'

That's all very well, I think, but as far as I'm concerned, you've had enough for the present. Why don't you spend some time working out if it's Reg in the garden or not and leave me alone for a bit? I decide the time has come for this interview to end – tearfully.

'I've told you everything I know. There's nothing more to say. I'm afraid I really must go and lie down now. If you've got any more questions, you'll have to ask them later.' I push myself up unsteadily from my chair and head for the door before she can say anything more.

***

No one follows me as I make my way slowly up the stairs, clinging tightly to the bannister in case they're watching. I lie down on the bed, to be on the safe side, and listen to the comings and goings beneath me. After a while it's clear I won't be disturbed, and I creep to the window. I can see down the length of the garden but the arch obscures my view of the far end, as I knew it would. I always keep this window open, so I can hear their voices, but not clearly enough to catch what they're saying. I lie down again and let my mind drift back to my last proper conversation with Mother, before the forgetting began.

'What will you do when I'm gone, Lilian? Will you stay here? It'll be a bit big for you on your own. It's a bit big for the two of us, to be honest.'

'I know, Mother, but it's suited us, hasn't it?'

'Oh, yes, it's certainly suited me, you know it has. I'm so grateful, Lilian. I want you to know. I know I'm ill, I know I won't always be able to say it to you, so I'm saying it now. I'm so grateful to you for bringing me here, to this house, and the garden. You know that, don't you?'

'Oh, Mother, it's me who should be grateful. All those years looking after Joanna for me – how would I ever have managed without you?'

'You'd have coped, Lilian, you always do. But you turned my life around. If it hadn't been for you, who knows how I'd have ended up?'

'Well, we both ended up all right, didn't we, that's the main thing. Joanna too, even though she's in London now.'

'You could go there, you know. After I'm gone. To live nearer Joanna. She'd love it if you did.'

'Let's not think about you being gone, Mother, it's a long way off.'

'I know it is. I wish it weren't. I don't want to lose my mind. The wobbles are bad enough, but I don't want my mind to go too. Isn't there something you can do to stop it?'

'Try not to worry, Mother. Who knows, maybe you'll fall asleep one day and not wake up in the morning.'

'Now that would be lovely, Lilian, just lovely. I've had such a good life here with you, I'll be ready to go whenever the time is right. As long as you don't put me in one of those homes.'

'It's a promise, Mother. Don't worry, I'm sure the time will be right before there's any chance of that happening.' I patted her knee, and she gave me the sweetest smile in the world.

Whenever the time is right. Who can know when that is? It's easier than you might think as it happens, as I've found on more than one occasion. It was certainly right for Mother. But what about me? Has the time come for me to leave this house as well? First Joanna, then Mother, is it my turn now? I have to face up to it – maybe it will be soon. I let my mind relax, thinking of all the places I could go, and before I know it, I've slipped into sleep, despite my best intentions. I'm woken by a shout from the bottom of the stairs and find to my surprise that over an hour has passed.

'Dr Templeton? Are you all right?' It's the young sergeant, too polite to come upstairs, I'm glad to note.

'Yes, I'll be right with you.' I come down to find them waiting in the hallway.

'DS Carter and I have finished in the garden for now,' says DI Twist. 'It's quite something, your garden, Dr Templeton.' I can't help but feel a swell of pride. It is a wonderful garden and I'll always be proud of what Mother achieved in it.

'Yes, Mother designed it. It was her pride and joy, and now I try to keep up the good work for her.'

'I'm sure you do a great job,' says DI Twist. Is she trying to be nice? This is definitely a change from her previous tone.

'Thank you.'

'You have an impressive greenhouse,' Sergeant Carter says. 'My grandad's always been a bit of a gardener and I couldn't help but notice it. I didn't go in, but you have a lot of plants in there for the time of year. Are they hothouse plants? I assume they're not seedlings?'

'No, it's where I grow my rare species. Mother designed the garden, but the greenhouse has always been mine. I've been growing rare plants since I was a girl, and the greenhouse protects them from the elements.'

'Oh, yes, I see.' He's losing interest and DI Twist is showing signs of wanting to leave.

'As I said, we're finished for today, Dr Templeton. However, there's still a lot of work for the scene of crime officers to do, so we'll need to ask you to move out for a night or two while they complete their work.'

'Is that necessary? Moving out, I mean? Won't they be finished by the end of the day? Can't I come back for the night?'

'I'm afraid not. They'll be searching the whole garden, and possibly the house as well. We really do need you to vacate the property. It'll protect you from the press for a while as well. Is there somewhere you can stay nearby? With a friend perhaps? And would you like to ask your daughter to come up and stay with you?'

'No thank you, I'll be fine. I'll call Joanna, but there'll be no need for her to come all the way up here. And I don't have any friends I would want to stay with. Where would you suggest I go?'

'There's a local bed and breakfast we use in these circumstances,' says DI Twist. 'If you pack a few things, Sergeant Carter can take you there on his way to the station. We'll be in touch tomorrow but give me a call in the meantime if you think of anything relevant or have any questions.' She hands me a business card. 'DI Sharon Twist' it says. Ah, I was wondering where she got Ronnie from. That's one question answered.

'Thank you, Inspector, I'll go and get my things,' I say as I turn back up the stairs. Once in my room I take some time to sit on the bed and wait for the shaking to stop. It hadn't occurred to me that they'd make me leave the house. And I realise now that their search could easily extend beyond the wildflower garden. She said it would take a couple of days to complete. How long will it take for them to work their way down to the greenhouse? And how long to find out exactly what I've been keeping in there?

***

When we get to the bed and breakfast, I decide it won't do at all. I make a fuss to the sergeant and insist on being taken to the Beverley Arms hotel. I tell him I'll pay for myself, but I need privacy and I won't get it in the cosy little house they had in mind, with Mrs Bloom or whatever her name was fussing around me. I insist on a ground floor room at the back of the hotel and breathe a sigh of relief when they confirm that one is free. I've got two out of three potentially incriminating items in my bag, and I'll deal with the third tonight.

The room is even better than I'd hoped for, with a door leading onto a tiny porch outside. I'd come prepared to climb out of a window, and I'm pleased to find that this won't be necessary. I know I'm fit for my age, but it would have been a challenge. I pass the time by ordering from room service, having a shower, and calling Joanna. She's shocked, of course, but I tell her there's nothing to worry about and not to come up; I know she's always busy at the start of term.

When one o'clock comes, I step onto the little terrace

and check there's no one around. Beverley is all but deserted and I use the back streets to take me to the house, jogging whenever a car passes so as to look like a runner. There aren't many about at this hour, which is a relief, and I've caught my breath by the time I turn into my road and edge along in the shadows where I won't be noticed. I can see police tape and a policeman standing at the entrance to the drive. I hadn't thought of that. I'll have to go around by the Westwood path. I creep back down the road and round to the one running parallel to it, where there's a gate leading onto the pastures. I open it slowly, slowly so it doesn't squeak and walk as quietly as I can along the track.

I can just make out another policeman standing about twenty feet away in the yawning gap in the fence. He's bent over his mobile phone, its blue light lending his features a ghostly sheen. There's a small gate set into the fence at the near end. It's hidden on both sides by the ivy which I've allowed to grow wild. I've always found it reassuring to know I could get in this way if I forgot my key, and nobody can tell it's here. I judge that the policeman's absorption in his phone and the rustling of the leaves in the nearby trees will provide sufficient cover if I'm careful. I push the ivy gently aside and open the gate, praying there won't be more police in the garden. Once on the other side, I stand still and survey the devastation that used to be my garden. To the far left and just within sight, I can see inappropriately cheerful pink plastic netting breaching the gap in the fence, and a huge trench surrounded by black and yellow striped police tape. The fairground atmosphere is completed by a dozen bright orange bollards positioned around the hole, presumably to prevent clumsy constables from falling in. A few forlorn poppies dip their heads as if searching for the absent body. Closer to hand, there are holes all over the rose garden and orchard, and the flowerbeds are a tangled mess. I have to stop myself from gasping and try not to think about the work it will take to restore the garden to its former state. There are more important matters to focus on right now, and I make myself concentrate on the task ahead.

I wait in silence for a minute to make sure there's no response from the policeman. The air stands still around me, and I feel his absence in the pit of my stomach. How could it have meant something that he was here? I didn't care about him when he was alive, so why should I now?

Memories of that night rush into my brain, confused and competing for attention. My head spinning, I turn quickly and tiptoe down the path to the greenhouse. Despite my racing heart, I find a temporary calm among the orchids. I force myself to focus as I trail along the tables, glancing their soft petals with my fingertips, and my mind gradually quietens. It wasn't him unsettling me, it was the inevitability of change that screamed up at me from the hole. Nothing can stay the same now, even if I do succeed in deceiving those detectives. Mother's gone, there's no denying it, even though my mind hasn't wanted to accept it, and without her, what's the point of me being here anyway?

I've reached the end of the greenhouse, the locked-off section. Built to resist Joanna's inquisitive little fingers, it later kept Mother safe from the dangers within. I smile to myself as I consider the irony of this thought. It's time to dispose of its most incriminating resident. I can't let the police find it, and I'll have no use for it now in any case. Or will I? Maybe it would best to make a final preparation. Just in case. I get my thick gloves and a plastic garden sack. I put the whole pot in the sack and tie it securely, then ease my way out of the gate and back onto the Westwood. The policeman's still glued to his mobile. Thank goodness for the wonders of modern science.

It's not far to the allotments, but every step is infused with dread that someone will see me, even though I've worn black clothing and stick to the side streets and bushes. The pot is heavier than I'd expected, and there's no possibility of jogging this time, even for a few feet. I'm panting by the time I reach the field, almost dropping the key as I fumble it out of my pocket. I eventually unlock the gate after what seems to be an age of grappling with the chain, go to my shed and put the bag and gloves inside. I'd like to stop and catch my breath, but I don't dare delay any longer. Before leaving I pull out the envelope from the front zip-up section of the backpack and pop it into an empty pot.

My getaway plan and the one thing that might incriminate me are now both safely tucked away in a place the police don't even know exists. As I make my silent way back to the hotel, I decide that all things considered, it's round one to me.

Chapter 2

Silence. Lilian stood still and counted to a hundred, childhood memories of games of hide and seek calming her fears in the moonlight. Not a sound, and why should there be at this time of night at the end of a long, quiet street? The warmth of the late spring day had worn off and she shivered as she turned towards the house, hooking back the French doors as she went.

At first glance the room looked unremarkable. Shabby furniture, out of date television, threadbare carpet, and a single small bookcase. No pictures, or anything else to suggest anyone had the time or inclination to make it homely. She'd not had a chance yet to bring it to life, but she would soon. The coffee table was bare. She'd cleared everything away while she waited for night to fall completely, and there were no signs of coffee, cake, or bucket. It was just an ordinary, not particularly welcoming, living room. Except for one thing. The dead man on the sofa.

There was no need to check. He was definitely dead, and Lilian carefully wrapped first the rug and then the plastic sheet beneath it around the body. The plastic crackled, and she hoped it wouldn't make too much noise once she was outside. She bound it up tightly with clothesline in half a dozen places to make it more manageable and then paused briefly, going over the plan in her head.

Lilian went outside and wheeled the barrow up through the French doors. It would be easier to transfer the body if the barrow was right next to it, and she knew the sofa was too heavy for her to move. As expected, the barrow brought in dirt from the garden, and she noted with approval its neat tracks across the old linen sheet covering the carpet. This time, she thought with satisfaction, she had considered things properly. Not like the last time, when panic had caused her to make the errors that had led to this night and this ghoulish task.

Lilian pushed the barrow up hard against the sofa. Her work in the accident and emergency department a year or two ago had given her a good knowledge of how to move heavy weights efficiently. She'd had a whole team to help her there, and she'd be on her own tonight, so she was glad he was slim and not too tall. He looked surprisingly small now he was dead, and she realised the force of his personality had given a distorted impression of size. That was something at least. She was going to need as much luck on her side as possible. Start with the feet. Then she wouldn't have to look at the outline of his face, even through the sheet and the plastic. The barrow started to roll away from her as she lifted his feet and she had to put them back and wedge it in place with a brick from outside. She heaved his feet, legs and buttocks into the barrow, and then steeled herself for the head and shoulders. The legs and torso took up most of the room, and his head flopped queasily over the front edge, but she didn't have the strength to rearrange him. It would have to do.

Lilian bent at the knees, remembering her training in heavy lifting, and not wanting to pull her back. Her arms strained as she lifted the handles and manoeuvred her load slowly towards the doors. It was much heavier than she had anticipated, and the barrow wobbled drunkenly across the shabby carpet. She would have to get to grips with the balance of it. She couldn't conceive of any of getting him back in if he fell out. There was a loud clunk as the front wheel landed on the hard surface a few inches below, and she paused, listening again, but there was no sound other than her own shaky breathing. Lilian readied herself for the long push down the path, knowing she would have to force herself not to stop at every sound. She focused on keeping the barrow straight and level, and she found an angle at which it seemed happy to stay balanced. It rumbled bumpily along the bricks, gathering pace as it passed the overgrown flowerbeds and giving her a modicum of confidence in her ability to keep it upright.

When Lilian reached the grassy area beyond the arch at the end of the path, she realised things were about to get harder. Looking across the unkempt lawn, with its daisies and dandelions, she knew she would not be able to maintain the momentum she had gained on the path; the friction would be too much for her. She lowered the handles carefully to the ground, glad of the excuse to stretch her back, and stood with her hands on her hips, considering what to do next. It was a distance of roughly thirty feet, but it might as well have been a mile; Lilian knew she couldn't get across it with a dead man's body in a barrow. She needed a smoother surface and she racked her brains to think of what to do.

Suddenly she remembered the wood. It was left over from the shelves in the bedroom. Only rough planks and bricks, that was all they'd been able to afford at the time, but they had fallen off the back of a lorry and had been plentiful, and she knew exactly where to find the leftovers. Lilian left the barrow and went to the shed. There was enough light from the moon to see by, and she knew where the wood was anyway, she could have found it by touch alone. It took several trips to and fro, but she soon had an almost smooth path stretching from the arch to the end of the garden.

Despite the improved surface, wheeling the barrow to the hole was the hardest physical work Lilian had ever embarked upon, and she made herself rest every few feet. Having got so far, she couldn't afford to make any mistakes now. She had to take care of herself, after all.

She reached the hole at last, thankful she hadn't needed to dig this herself. Now she was here, she cursed herself for not having thought of using it last time. It would have saved so much trouble if she'd not panicked before. That's what comes of not planning properly, she told herself. Never again would she allow that to happen.

The wooden path led right to the edge of the hole, but when she eventually got there, Lilian saw she had the barrow at the wrong angle. She was standing with the head in the middle of the long side. There was no way she would be able to get the body in from this point. She needed to manoeuvre the barrow to the far end. Cursing inwardly, she set it down once more and retrieved three of the planks from further down the lawn, making a path around the edge of the hole. Heaving the planks down the length of the garden had not helped her energy levels; remembering her medical training, Lilian took several deep breaths, getting as much oxygen into her lungs as she could. The barrow nearly toppled as she turned it to follow the path round the hole, but she kept it steady and held it firmly in place as she turned the final corner at the end. One last turn and she was there.

With the barrow in place, she hesitated. She had a nasty feeling that if she lifted the handles now the body would land head first, leaving her to tip it heels over head in order to lie flat. The alternative was to get into the hole herself and drag it in, and Lilian didn't think her muscles were up to the job. She would have to tip it. By this time, she was getting frustrated with the whole procedure, and her anger gave her a renewed spurt of energy. In you go, and good riddance too, she thought, I've just about had enough of you. She lifted the barrow with all her might and the body slid, slowly at first and then in a rush, into the pit below. She stepped forward to see that, as she'd feared, the head was at the near end of the hole, with the feet sticking up as if the body were doing a headstand. She jumped in quickly and pushed on his chest before the head had time to lodge in the earth. He toppled over, gravity helping her at last, although the body was a little too long and she had to bend the knees to make it fit. Lilian knelt briefly on the damp soil, allowing her body to fold in exhaustion. She couldn't allow herself to rest for long though, and after only a few seconds she picked herself up, clawed her way out and lugged the planks back to the shed.

Picking up her spade, she returned to the hole. She knew the chances of anyone seeing the body out here were remote, but she couldn't risk a late-night walker on the Westwood looking over the fence. She went round to the mound of earth on the other side and started shovelling. It had been covered with weeds until yesterday, and she had put in several hours' work breaking it up, so it was ready to be moved. Even so, it was gruelling work after all she had already done, and she had to force herself to shift every spadeful, ignoring the blisters growing on both her hands. When the mound was at last reduced to a modest heap and the surface was flat in front of her, she looked up to see the dawn inching its way into the sky. She let out a deep sigh. It was done. She was safe at last. She could plan for the future, and for the baby.

Chapter 3

I dream about that night. Not one of my normal jumbled dreams, forgotten by morning. A clear, sickening recollection of the night I buried him. So vivid I can smell the honeysuckle as I wheel the barrow under the arch. I'm glad it's not flowering now, or I'd want to tear it down. Maybe it was inevitable, but it's disturbed me. I'm grateful I'm not at home, where even more memories might lurk.

I have breakfast in my room, in line with my professed desire for privacy, and the police call soon after to say they need to talk to me. Would I rather they came to the hotel or I went to the station? I opt for the hotel as I don't like the implications of the station. I'm not a convicted criminal yet, and I don't want them getting any ideas.

'Good morning, Dr Templeton,' says DI Twist, polite as always. It's impossible to tell from their expressions whether it's good news or not. DI Twist is looking as indeterminate as before and Sergeant Carter is quick to make himself at home in one of the comfy armchairs. I leave the other for the inspector, sitting on the more upright desk chair myself in the hope its formality will give me an advantage.

'Good morning, Inspector. I don't suppose you've come to tell me I can move back into my home, have you?'

'I'm afraid not. The SOCOs are still busy there but they are hoping to be finished before the end of tomorrow. No, we've got some more questions for you following our preliminary inquiries yesterday, and discussions with the Chief Constable.'

'All right.' My heart's thumping. Surely they can't have found anything of significance already? There'll be no indication of cause of death, I'm sure. And how can they possibly find out who he is after all this time? I know there was no identification on the body. I took everything off him and dumped it all in a bin in London forty years ago.

'Yes, we've made some good progress. But before we go into any details, I have to ask you again, Dr Templeton. Do you have any idea as to how the body could have got there?' Her eyes are wandering slowly round the room as she speaks. It's a bit distracting and makes me wonder what she's looking for.

'No, I haven't,' I say. 'And I really would like this

matter dealt with quickly. All I can say is, it must have been put there before my time. I'd appreciate it if you could stop bothering me about it. I don't think it's good for my heart to be stressed in this way.'

'So you are saying, Dr Templeton, that you don't know anything at all about the body? You're happy for that to go on record?'

'Yes. I said as much yesterday and I'm saying it again today.' I'm sticking to my story whatever they say. Disproving a denial is one of the hardest things to do, I believe.

'In that case, you may be surprised to hear we have strong cause to believe the body was placed in your garden at a time after your arrival.'

'What do you mean? I don't understand.'

'It means you were living in the house when the body was buried in the garden.' She's looking directly at me now for the first time, and the sheep look is sharpening up again, along with her tone. I pour a glass of water for myself from the hotel's supplies and allow my hand to tremble as I do so.

'But that's impossible! What makes you say that?'

'We've been able to date the clothes on the body.

They were sold in a local menswear shop and they were new in for the summer season. The shirt and tie were only stocked from April nineteen seventy-four.'

'But mightn't they have been available at an earlier date somewhere else? Maybe in York, or even London? How can you be so sure they came from the Beverley shop?'

'They use their own labels, Dr Templeton. The clothes definitely came from that shop and at that time.' There's a silence. If the sergeant was writing with an ink pen I daresay we'd hear it scratching, but he's using a tablet and it doesn't make a sound as he taps away at it.

'So you see, Dr Templeton, there's no doubt you were living in the house when the body was put in the garden. Have you genuinely got no idea how that could have happened without your knowledge? Assuming that is, you don't have any information to share with us about it after all?'

'No, detective, I don't have any information to share, as you put it. I can only imagine someone put it there when I was elsewhere. On an overnight shift at the hospital, perhaps. Or away on holiday. Maybe you'd like to check the records? If they still have them, of course.

The old hospital's gone now, and I don't know whether the new one will have kept them.'

'Yes, it's something we'll look into,' says DI Twist. 'I would like you to think back, Dr Templeton. To when your husband went missing. Can you remember much about that time?'

'You mean other than being on my own, pregnant, and abandoned by my husband? No, not much. It was all rather stressful, and I've tried not to think about it. I coped, it all worked out, and that's the end of it as far as I'm concerned.'

'I admire your resilience, it can't have been easy to manage in those circumstances. But I'm afraid it's no longer the end of it. We're waiting for test results to come in, but in the meantime, we have to explore all lines of inquiry.'

'Oh, yes, and what might those be?'

'There's just one at the moment. As I mentioned before, until evidence arises to the contrary, we have to act on the assumption that the body is your husband, Reginald Blake.'

'Reg? You think it was Reg in the garden? How could it be Reg?' I hope I'm not sounding too naïve, but I know

I ought to sound surprised.

'We don't know how the body got there, and we don't know it was Reg,' DI Twist says, an impatient edge to her voice. 'But he went missing at a time that matches the clothes on the body and he's never been found, which leaves us with no option but to consider that it might be him. You're an intelligent person, I'm sure you understand.'

'I suppose I do. I'm sorry, I didn't mean to be snappish, it's all very trying and I daresay I'm not handling the strain especially well.' I need to back down if I want her sympathy, and I aim for a conciliatory tone.

'Tell me about your husband, Dr Templeton. What did he do for a living?'

'There's not much to tell. He was an estate agent. He did well for himself, bought this house, even though it was on a big mortgage, and we came to live in it. I got pregnant, then he disappeared.'

'And this was in May of nineteen seventy-four, is that correct?'

'Yes.'

'What happened, exactly? Was there a row?'

Her voice has softened a little , but I don't trust it and

concentrate on getting my story straight.

'No, nothing like that. I had come back from a night shift at the hospital. I had a nap and woke in the afternoon. Reg usually came home at around six o'clock. I prepared a meal, but he never arrived.'

'What did you think had happened to him at that point?'

'I didn't worry at first. I thought he must have gone to the pub with one of his friends. He did that sometimes and he didn't always remember to let me know. I was worried when it got to ten o'clock, but I didn't want to make a fuss. He'd have been furious with me if I'd gone to the police. I decided he must have stayed over with a friend and I went to bed. He still had a single man's habits in many ways, and I couldn't think of any other explanation. I was up early in the morning for my shift and didn't get back till seven thirty. When he still wasn't there, I started to get worried.'

'What did you do then?' She's sitting very still, not looking directly at me but completely focused, nonetheless. Sergeant Carter is tapping away at his screen, eyes down.

'I looked in his drawers and the wardrobe. I realised

some of his clothes were missing and his suitcase too, the one we'd taken on our honeymoon. Oh, dear, it's all coming back to me now, I've tried not to think about it for so long, and it really is very painful to do so.' I stop and look for a handkerchief, sniffing for good measure and thinking it time I had a little sympathy, but she carries on regardless.

'And once you knew the clothes and suitcase were missing?'

'I checked the desk drawer. Reg liked to keep his savings in there, he wasn't keen on banks for some reason. It was gone.'

'Was it a lot of money?'

'A few hundred pounds. It doesn't sound much now but it was a lot in those days.'

'What happened next?'

'I knew he'd left me then. I've been thinking it all through since we spoke about it yesterday, going over and over it in my mind, and I realise now Reg wasn't as pleased about the baby as I'd expected. He still liked to live the single life, you know, go to the pub with his friends, off to the races, that sort of thing. I do wonder if there was someone else, but it was so soon after our wedding that I can't believe it. Looking back, I don't think he was ready for marriage, and certainly not for fatherhood. If I'm honest, I have to admit it was a bit of a whirlwind romance. Maybe we weren't suited, and he saw it first. I was wrapped up in my job and perhaps he wanted a more conventional sort of wife. I don't think he knew what else to do but leave.'

'Did you report him missing?' She's speaking quietly now, perhaps not wanting to interrupt the flow of my story.

'I did in the end. I was too embarrassed at first. I was terrified about what people would think of me. A person in my position, a respected professional, abandoned by her husband only a few months into her marriage? The gossips would have had a field day. Well, they did have a field day, but not until I was ready for it. I waited a week, hoping he'd come back, but he didn't.'

'Was this when you reported him missing to the police?'

'Yes, it was a week later, as I said. I told them everything I've told you today. There's probably a record of it somewhere. They couldn't do much, though. They said it looked as if he'd just decided to leave, and people who did that usually didn't want to be found. If there was no sign of foul play and no crime had been committed, they couldn't put out an alert. They told me to contact all our friends and relations to ask if anyone had heard from him but there wasn't much else they could do.'

'I see. It must have been a difficult time for you.' The words sound understanding, but her expression hasn't changed, and I don't suppose for a minute she's feeling kindly towards me.

'Yes, it was. I got through it, though. I let the news leak out on its own. By the time most people knew, I was heavily pregnant, and I think they felt sorry for me. Mother came to live with me, to help with Joanna. I carried on working, and we made a life here, the three of us.'

'And you never heard from Reg?'

'Never.'

'Did you try to find him?'

'Not at first. I was angry with him. If you want to leave, then leave, I thought. If he didn't want to be with me then I didn't want to be with him either.'

'But later on?'

'Yes, I did later on. Joanna was about eleven and she

was asking and asking about her father. It was distressing her, so I said we'd try to find him. I went back to the police, but they weren't any better that time around, so I hired a private investigator.'

'Did you now?' She seems surprised, but I'd have thought it's what a lot of people do in such circumstances.

'Yes, why not? It was to placate Joanna. I didn't want him back, but I thought if he turned up it would settle her mind. Either he'd want to get to know her or he wouldn't, but at least she would know.'

'Did he get anywhere? The investigator, I mean.'

'No, not a whisper. It was a relief to me; I didn't want him back after all that time. But it was hard for Joanna. I had him declared dead then. I didn't want any problems if I ever came to sell the house. It was in his name, you see.'

'I understand. What about his family? Didn't they want to find him?'

'They never bothered with him much. They lived out past Driffield and they seldom came as far as Beverley. They were farmers, and they were cross with him for not taking the farm over from his parents. I only met them the once, at the wedding. I don't think they liked me much and they never came to visit. When he disappeared, I went out there to ask if they'd heard from him, but they hadn't. They didn't seem particularly worried. They said they were sure he'd turn up in the end, but they'd lost interest in him long before then.'

'I see. So, during that year and the year or two afterwards, what sort of state was your garden in?'

'The garden? I'm sorry, what do you mean?' I know exactly what she means, of course, but it won't look good if I show it.

'Your garden, Dr Templeton. It's extremely beautiful and nicely laid-out now, but has it always been like that?'

'Oh, yes, I understand. Well, no, it hasn't. When I was first married it was mostly a big field. It was better looked after near the house, beds on either side of the path, you know, but there was no lawn or rose garden. There were fruit trees where the orchard is now, but the rest of the land beyond the arch was little more than a meadow. I didn't go past that point for a long time, years maybe, when Mother said it was a waste to have so much land and not to use it properly.'

'So you established the wildflower garden?'

'Yes, Mother wanted it. She loved the butterflies and other wildlife it attracted. And we couldn't have coped with any more formal gardens once we'd put in the roses and the lawn. It was enough work keeping on top of what we already had.'

'Am I right in thinking that before the landscaping took place, you wouldn't have noticed if anything had changed in that area? If a patch of ground was disturbed, for instance?' Good. This is my chance to encourage the idea that someone else put the body there.

'No, I never went down there, as I've said. And the fence wasn't a tall one like it is now. It was barely more than waist high. It was to keep the cows out more than anything else. We didn't worry about intruders in those days, you know. I only had the taller fence put up when we landscaped the whole plot.'

'So anyone could have climbed into that part of your land?'

'I suppose they could. I'd never thought about it before now. Are you saying someone could have put a body there during that time? Before the garden was finished and the fence was raised?'

'I'm not saying anything,' says DI Twist. 'I'm

considering possibilities. I'm also considering how, if the body is Reg's, it got there without your knowledge. And if so, where his suitcase and clothes went. Do you know if he had any enemies?'

'No. I told you yesterday that I don't, and I still don't today. I have to say, I'm rather tired and stressed by all this, Inspector, and if you don't have any new questions to ask, I'd like you to leave now. I'm sure you understand.' I get up and open the door. They don't look pleased, but they must have run out of questions after all because DI Twist gives the sergeant a small nod and they get to their feet.

'We'll be in touch soon, Dr Templeton,' she says. 'With news of when you can move back into your house. And with further questions.' She makes it sound like a promise, although I know it's closer to a threat, and I don't thank her as they leave.

When they've gone, I sit down in one of the comfy chairs and heave a sigh of relief. Not because I believe for a minute they won't be back, but because at least it's over for now. I make myself a cup of coffee and wonder what to do with myself. I realise I've been so preoccupied with my night wanderings I've forgotten to look at the news to see if there's been any fuss. I didn't think to pack my laptop, but my phone has a link to the internet, and I log on to the hotel wifi. It doesn't take me long to find the Hull Daily Mail website, and there it is, the first thing to pop up on the screen: Beverley body baffles police. A typically alliterative headline. I suppose I shouldn't be surprised. There's not a great deal more; DI Twist hasn't had much to tell them, and she's made it clear that identifying the body could take some time. They've named the road, and whilst it's a long one, there aren't many houses in it. I wonder if there are reporters and cameramen stationed outside the house, and although I'm not tempted to go and see for myself, I can't stop myself turning on the TV news. There it is; all over the flat hotel television screen. The latest update on the protest about the bypass comes first, but there's no getting away from it. Everyone in Beverley will know where the 'baffling body' is located. The reporter's standing at the end of the road, a few short yards from my front door, naming the road and saying the house is empty at present. There's a small crowd gathered on the pavement. It's mostly made up of people who look like they're media, with a few more ordinary-looking onlookers.

It's a strange feeling, looking at my house on the screen. It makes me feel like a character in a TV drama, even though they haven't named me. Yet. I wonder how long it will take. Should I stay at the hotel for longer? Will they get tired of waiting and go away? I want to avoid having to talk to them, but I'm desperate to get back to the house and deal with things. My mind flits between confidence that the police won't find out anything and the certain fear they'll unearth everything, and I'll have to make a quick getaway. Prepare for the worst and hope for the best, Mother used to say. But it will be hard to prepare for the worst with a crowd round my door.

I make myself calm down and remember the bypass and DI Twist's assessment. She didn't think it would take long for people to lose interest. If I make it clear I'm not going to talk to them, hopefully they'll go away. I force my mind back to the television. Eventually last night's exertions catch up with me and I fall asleep in front of a home improvement programme.

***

The reporters were here when Sergeant Carter brought me back yesterday , but I followed his advice and made a short statement saying I was sure the police were doing a good job with the investigation and I had nothing to say. I'm not picking up the phone when it rings, and I put in an online supermarket order from the hotel which arrived this afternoon. It seems this has sent the message that I won't be coming out again for some time as they haven't bothered knocking on the door.

I don't ask if they've searched the house; it would look suspicious if I did. But it's obvious they have. They didn't make a mess, but everything's a little out of place. I can't tell for certain if they've searched the desk but I'm glad I got its contents out before they had time to do more than destroy the garden.

I know it will only be a matter of time before the police are back again with more questions. I need to get back to the allotment as soon as I can, and it will be best to go when it's dark. I don't think they're suspicious enough to be following me yet, but I need to act quickly in case they change their minds. A surreptitious peep through the landing curtains in the late afternoon confirms interest has been quick to fade, and I know I'll be able to go out tonight.

I've been putting off going in the garden. I don't want

to look at the 'scene' again as they call it, but I'll have to if I'm going to make a bonfire. I tell myself to get a grip and go outside.

I do my best not to look at the churned-up beds and pitted lawn, and I turn instead towards the business end of the garden, where the musty smell of the shed is comfortingly familiar as I pull the door open. They might have looked through here as well, but if they have it doesn't show. I put on my thickest gardening gloves and, keeping my eyes firmly above ground level, cut back the climbing roses and the ivy in the orchard. There are a few apple trees in need of pruning, and before long I've got enough for a small bonfire. I build it up in the metal bin ready for the final addition and go inside to make something to eat.

The hours to midnight don't pass easily. I'm in constant fear of something, but I don't know what. I tell myself the police won't come before tomorrow, and even if they do, why would it be a problem? They'll hardly have gathered enough evidence to arrest me, will they? And even if they do and they search the house, there's nothing dangerous for them to find now. To make myself feel better, I get my backpack out ready for the trip to the allotment and check my bicycle tyres are in good order. I make myself watch television for an hour, even though there's nothing on except the news and soaps. I've finished my library book and none of the volumes on my shelves appeal, so I make a mental note to go to the library soon. I cook a time-consuming meal and watch some historical documentaries on the television but it's still only ten o'clock, and I can't bear to watch any more. I make a cup of tea and think over the events of the past few days, considering what might happen next. Then I get out my laptop and look for criminal lawyers. Just in case.

When it's finally time to leave I find I've calmed down after all. I take my time dressing in dark clothes and stroll down to the front gate to make sure there's no one there. The road's deserted, so I put on my backpack and wheel the bike out of the garage. It only takes ten minutes to cycle through the silent streets to the allotment, speeding along the route which made me feel so exposed last night. My hand doesn't shake at the gate this time, and I walk confidently to my plot and the shed. The plant's too big for the backpack as it is, so I cut off the taller stalks, stuff them into the sack beside the pot and lower it into the backpack together with the gloves. I take a last look round the shed in case there's anything else I need. I don't want to come back more than necessary. If the police found out about this place, I'd lose my greatest advantage. No, I've got everything at home. It's time to go.

Back at the house I take the backpack into the garden. There's no wind tonight, and the silence is absolute. The moon is up, and something about the air reminds me of the night I buried Harry. Perhaps it's the last hint of roses taking me back. It must be coming from the briars on bonfire. My mind seems to want to dwell on the past, but this is hardly the time for it, and I get down to work.

Putting the thick gloves on first, I make certain there's not an inch of bare skin showing, take the stalks from the backpack, place them in a sealable plastic box and put it on the kitchen step. I turn back to the pot and carefully prise the root bowl out. A second plastic box sits ready and waiting, but I can't fit the lid on, so I hold it at arms' length as I return to the fire bin. I tip the contents of the box in quickly and slam the lid shut. The soil clinging to the roots will damp it down a little at first, but it will all burn through in the end. I wash down the pot and the box with bleach and put them in a garden sack which goes into the green general waste container. I'll light the bonfire first thing in the morning. Then at least one piece of evidence will be out of harm's way.

I'm tired after all the exertion and reward myself with a coffee before turning my attention to the contents of the first plastic box. I may be a poor cook, but there's one thing I do know how to make, and I'll prepare one final brew before going to bed.

***

It starts to feel as if life is getting back to normal. After collapsing into bed and sleeping more soundly than I can ever remember sleeping before, I wake feeling refreshed. My first task for the day is to burn some evidence. Dressed and washed, I head into the garden with the firelighters from the living room. As I approach the bin, I have a sudden attack of doubt. What if the police come back now? Won't they think it suspicious for me to be lighting a bonfire? Might they put two and two together and realise I've something to hide? I slow to a halt on the path, the firelighters clutched in my hand. Should I take it inside and burn it in the living room fireplace? It would be quicker, and no one would see. But no, if the police did come, they'd be bound to smell the woodsmoke, it always lingers for days. And they'd be sure to wonder what I was doing lighting a fire so early in the year, especially when the weather's been so mild. No, a bonfire's more plausible, and the quicker I get on with it the better.

I poke the firelighters into the bin and light it with the long matches. A watched fire never takes any quicker than a pot boils, so I go back inside and make myself a coffee. By the time I come back it's burning nicely. And if anyone asks, I've been making a start on tidying up the garden. It's made for a lot of rubbish, and what could be more normal than a garden bonfire in September? At the end of the day I'll pour sand into the bin and put the ashes and my cooking equipment into the rubbish with the sack, ready for the bin men tomorrow.

Taking stock of the situation, I'm pleased with myself for ensuring the items necessary for a potential getaway are out of the house. The single incriminating item still here is well disguised, and I'm not quite finished with it yet. Come to think of it, I may not have much advance notice if I do need it. I could use it neat I suppose, but cake has always worked perfectly in the past, and I see no reason to change now. I decide it's time for an afternoon in the kitchen.

I've always enjoyed baking. It started in my teens when I first asked Mother to teach me. She loved to cook, and there were always cakes and biscuits waiting for me when I got back from school. I was more interested in plants, but she managed to pass on her favourite recipes to me in the end, and Joanna is an excellent chef, when she has the time. It feels good to get out the ingredients and butter the tins, and I can feel the tension in my shoulders receding as I mix the batter. I don't need a recipe for this one – it was the first one I learnt, and it's always been my favourite.

While the cakes are cooling, I check on the bonfire and do some tidying up in the garden. It's good to be out in the fresh air, and when I call Joanna at the end of the day, she says I sound better.

'Better than what?'

'Oh, Mum, you know, better than you have been. I've been worried about you, with the dreadful body in the garden business. You've sounded – I don't know – distracted, I suppose. But you seem back to your old self today.'

'Yes, I feel like it too. Getting out in the garden has done me good.'

'Do you think it's all over now? Have the police come back yet?'

'No. I hope when they do it'll be to say the case is closed. I really don't see what they can find out after all this time.'

'I know I've asked you this before, Mum, but do you think it might be Reg?' She's never called him anything else, other than for a few weeks when we hired the investigator.

'No. I don't. I think it's someone we don't know, put there by someone else we don't know. I think somebody took advantage of the low fence and buried a body when we were away. They might have been watching the house for a while and known the end of the garden was neglected. Who knows? But I'm certain it's not Reg.'

'I'm glad. I'm sorry to have asked again, but it's been preying on my mind. I don't know how I'd handle the thought of his being there all those years while we were living in the house, and with me playing in the garden. It's bad enough thinking of a stranger's body being there.'

I can hear her shudder on the other end of the line, and I feel sorry for having brought this on her.

'I know. I'm trying not to think about it, and so must you.'

'I know, Mum. But do you think you can stay there now? Knowing what was there all those years? I'm not sure if I could.'

'It's something I'll have to think about,' I say. 'Maybe it is time to think about moving on. I've loved living here, but it's not the same without your Granny.'

'No, you're right, it's not. It feels different to me and I'm not even living there. I can't imagine what it must be like for you. Oh, didn't she just love her garden? I'll always remember her out there, pruning her roses, picking apples, helping me in my little patch.'

'She was happy here, wasn't she?'

'Oh, yes, Mum, so incredibly happy. And it's so good to know she didn't have to leave. You know, to go into a home. I thought she'd have to when she started to get worse, but it seemed like she knew when she wanted to die. Is that a silly thing to think?'

'No, Jo, it's not. She knew exactly when she wanted to go, and she did. I hope I'll be able to do the same thing.' I say this knowing it's more than wishful thinking. I wish I could warn her that she might lose me sooner than she'd like, but I can't.

'Don't we all? Oh, let's not get gloomy. Things are looking up, aren't they? You'll soon be back to normal, they'll replace the gas pipe, and you can plant seeds there. It will all look lovely again in no time. I'll come up for half term as planned, then. Are you sure you don't want me to visit sooner? I could come for the weekend if it would help.'

'I'm sure. Don't worry about me. You'd better get back to the marking, hadn't you?'

'Thanks for the cheerful reminder, Mum. Take care – bye.'

It always does me good to talk to Jo, especially now I'm on my own. Even though I can't share all my worries with her, she cheers me up. The house feels less empty for a while and I think I can afford to be optimistic. I tell myself the police haven't come back because they haven't made any progress, and they never will. The forecast's good for tomorrow, and I decide I'll go for a bike ride in the morning.

The next day, they're back.

I'm finishing my coffee and considering which route to take to Cottingham avoiding main roads when the doorbell rings. It takes me by surprise, and I think it must be the postman with a package. I'm trying to remember if I've ordered anything online recently as I open the door to find the detectives in front of me.

'Oh,' I say. 'It's you.'

'Yes,' says DI Twist. 'I hope we've not called at an inconvenient time, Dr Templeton. Could we come in for a chat?' Her tone's relaxed and friendly, nothing sinister about it to my ears. I feel hopeful they've come to tell me there have been no developments and they're closing the case.

'Of course, please come in. Can I get you a drink or anything?'

'No thank you, we're fine.' Is this a good sign? Telling me it's all over wouldn't take long enough to need a drink, would it? We seat ourselves in the living room and Sergeant Carter gets out his tablet.

'We've come to let you know about the latest developments in the case,' says DI Twist.

'Oh, yes?' My heart's beating like a drum. This isn't

what I was expecting.

'Yes, we've made progress in identifying the body. Good progress, in fact. We're as certain as we can be that we have a definite identity.'

'Oh, yes?' I can't think of anything else to say. 'Who do you think it is?' I can't believe they've identified him. How have they done it?

'We believe it's a man named Henry Johnson, commonly known as Harry Johnson. He went missing at around the same time as your husband.' She seems to be waiting for me to respond, and I say the first thing that pops into my head.

'How did you find out it was him?' I make my voice sound normal, interested even, but it takes all my self-control to do so.

'We were able to get a DNA sample from the body, and it was a partial match to a local person already on the database. When we talked to the family, they told us a story about a long-lost uncle. His sister is still alive, and she was able to fill us in on the details. The time at which he went missing ties in with the period during which the clothes were sold. We think this is sufficient evidence to suggest it could be him. We're still looking through other partial matches of course, and we'll follow up any new lines of enquiry should they arise.'

'And have you been able to find out how he died?' Don't tell me they've worked that out as well.

'We don't have a conclusive answer to that at present,' she admits, and my heart slows down a little. 'There's no sign of trauma – knife wound, gunshot, that sort of thing. In fact, there's nothing to indicate he died of anything other than natural causes.' Thank goodness. I'm pretty confident there wouldn't be traces of the poison after all this time, but I wouldn't have liked to bet on it.

'We're working on the theory of it being either poisoning, which would probably be undetectable after all this time, or natural causes, although the latter is unlikely.'

'Why would that be?'

'Because if he died naturally, why would he need to be buried in your garden?' Fair enough, I suppose, I can't argue with her.

'Well, this is all very interesting,' I say. 'It's amazing what you can find out these days, isn't it?'

'Quite. Anyway, Dr Templeton, we need to ask you if you knew the man.'

'Oh, yes, I suppose you do. What did you say his name was?'

'Harry Johnson. Do you remember anyone of that name?'

'I don't think so, Inspector. Did he live locally?'

'Yes, he lived in Hull. He was in touch with his sister, Dora, who as I said is still alive. I don't suppose you knew her by any chance?'

'No, I don't recognise her name either, although if she had lived in Beverley, I might have known her by sight. It's a small place in many ways, as I expect you've found yourself, Inspector. Was it she who reported her brother as missing?'

'No one reported him. Dora was in her teens when he vanished, and she didn't have the confidence to report him missing herself. Her parents were ashamed of him, she says, because he'd got involved in some dodgy deals, and they wouldn't have anything to do with him.'

'That's a shame. It must have been hard for her to keep in touch with her brother under those circumstances.'

'Yes, although he took her out from time to time in his fancy cars. He was a bit flash, she says, and cagey about where his money came from. He didn't tell her much about his social life, and we don't know a great deal about his acquaintances yet. Was he one of your husband's friends by any chance? Or do you remember anyone who sounded like him? As far as we can tell he was a good-looking man with plenty of charm for the ladies.'

I can't help thinking that they're telling me a lot. Is it normal for the police to divulge so much information to someone who they might be considering as a suspect? It occurs to me that they may be doing it as a means of tricking me into revealing my own knowledge, and I remind myself to be careful.

'I didn't know many of Reg's friends. My shifts at the hospital stopped me socialising like most people do, but I don't think so. The name doesn't sound familiar to me, and I don't remember anyone of that description.'

'Well, let us know if anything does come back to you, won't you?'

'Of course, Inspector. Can I ask what this means for the case? And for my garden? I would like to put things to rights again, and there's still the gas pipe to be replaced.'

'Oh, we've completed our work in the garden now. Someone will get in touch with the gas company and let them know they can resume their work. Hopefully, it won't take too long.'

'Does this mean you've finished with me?' I ask. 'I suppose you'll have other avenues to explore now you know who it is?'

'We do have new avenues, it's true, but I don't think you've seen the last of us, Dr Templeton.' She turns her gaze fully onto me and her tone hardens. 'I still find it surprising your having no knowledge of the body. It's interesting that you never had cause to disturb that section of the garden. The body wasn't buried deeply, and it wouldn't have taken much to have unearthed it, even without a big digger. It's quite a coincidence your choosing precisely that section of the garden to leave wild all these years.'

'What are you insinuating, inspector? Are you still suggesting I knew something about the body?'

'I'm simply saying it's a coincidence. And in my experience, coincidences aren't as coincidental as they might appear. The body may not be your husband, Dr Templeton, but there's no reason yet to dismiss a connection, particularly in view of the fact that Reg and Harry Johnson went missing at the same time.'

'Is it? In what way, may I ask?'

'In a way that makes me wonder if Reg might have known Harry Johnson after all. And if he could have killed him, buried him, and run off to avoid any inquiries about him. It also makes me wonder if he might have had some help from his wife.'

'You can wonder all you like, Inspector. I don't know anything about the body, and no number of coincidences is going to change that. Is that all for today?' I stand up in the hope this might encourage them to leave.

'Yes, for today,' says DI Twist. 'We'll see ourselves out, thank you.' She whisks herself out of the room, her startled sergeant scuttling in her wake.

I'm shaking as I sit down. I hadn't expected this. I never thought they'd get DNA from the body, let alone find a match. Harry can't have been the only one in his family with a tendency to stray from the straight and narrow. I shall have to think carefully about how to take it from here. Things are becoming more complicated than I had anticipated.

Chapter 4

He was waiting for her. Her heart thumped into her stomach, but she knew she couldn't let him see, and she put a smile on her face as she wheeled her bicycle towards him.

'Good evening, Harry, what brings you here?'

'It's the lovely Lil! Home from work, are we?'

'Yes Harry, as you see, home from work. What are you doing here?'

'Come to see you, what else? Can I come in for a bit?'

'I'm rather tired, Harry. Is it urgent?'

'Not urgent perhaps, but.... pressing, that's what I'd say. Yes, pressing, I think. Can I come in, then?' He's turning on the charm as usual, thought Lilian. He'd made sure to look his best, not a single dark hair out of place, and dapper as always. You'd have thought he was off for a posh night out, not just coming around to Lilian's house. Come to think of it, maybe he was off for a posh night out after this. As long as he didn't think he'd be taking her with him. She couldn't believe even Harry could think that, not at a time like this.

'All right, come in, I'll put the kettle on.' Lilian sighed as she put her key in the lock.

'Now that's the ticket,' he said. Why does he always have to talk like someone in a forties musical, she wondered. 'A nice cup of tea would be lovely, and maybe a bit of that sticky ginger cake you make?'

'All right,' she said. It had always been hard to resist his flattery and she was more than ready for a coffee herself. Lilian let Harry follow her through to the kitchen, where she made the drinks in silence, not wanting to encourage him. She got out the ginger cake and they sat opposite each other at the kitchen table as if squaring up for a fight.

'So, Harry, what's up? Is there a problem? You didn't come back the other night, so I assumed everything was all right. Isn't it?'

'No, nothing's wrong. It all went as smooth as you like,' he said. 'No, I just thought we didn't have time to discuss things properly then, it was all a bit of a rush.'

'Yes, I suppose it was a rush. What did you want to discuss, Harry?'

'Terms, Lil, terms.'

'Terms? What do you mean?'

'Well, I did you a big favour, didn't I? It's only right to expect something in return, fair's fair you know.' He smiled winningly as he bit into his cake, but it didn't reach his eyes. Lilian used to think they were as blue as the sky, but now they were more like gimlets. She wondered what he wanted. Money, most likely. Well she had plenty of that, but if he thought he was having all of it he could think again.

'All right, Harry, let's not beat about the bush. How much?'

'How much what, Lil?'

'How much money do you want? I assume there were some – overheads? Incidental costs? I suppose you need me to cover them, is that right?'

'It's good of you to get straight to the point, Lil. How about ten thousand?'

'Ten thousand pounds? You have to be joking, I've not got that much. Be reasonable.'

'Oh, but I am being reasonable, Lil. I've been working it out. You've been earning doctor's wages for how long – five years or more? You've been living at home, so no rent to pay. And you moved into this house that Reg bought, so no spending needed on your part. I reckon you've got at least ten grand tucked away. Where is it, Lil? Under the bed? Shall we go up and have a look together?' He reached across the table to take her hand as he said this, and she got up quickly, snatching it away as she did so.

'For goodness sake, Harry! Look, you're right, I do have some savings, but they're in the bank, so you can stop your dirty jokes right now. I could give you two thousand pounds; would that be enough? I agree I should pay you something, and that's a lot of money.'

'Ah, but the job's not the only thing you're paying for, is it, Lil?' Still the snaky smile on his face, which turned her stomach. How could she ever have found him attractive?

'What do you mean?'

'It's the keeping quiet. You wouldn't want me telling people where Reg is, and more to the point, how he got there, now would you?'

'Of course not, but you'd hardly be doing yourself any favours if you did, Harry. All I'd need to do is to say you killed him yourself.'

'Maybe you would, Lil, but you'd still be an accomplice. It wouldn't look good for you, would it, a nice respectable doctor involved in the murder of her own husband?' He wasn't going to give in easily, she could see.

'It wasn't murder, I told you, it was self-defence!'

'Call it what you want Lil, you killed him. You know it and I know it, and so will the police if you can't do better than two thousand.'

'How about five thousand?'

'Make it six and I might be happy.'

'All right. It'll take some time to get it for you, I can't take it all out of the bank at once. You'll need to come back in a few days.'

'That sounds fine to me, Lil. Good to do business with you.' He grinned at her over his coffee cup but made no move to go.

'Well now that's settled, I'd be grateful if you could leave, Harry. I've had a long day and I'd like to make something to eat now.'

'You're not inviting me to join you, Lil? Or, even better, why don't I take you out for dinner? To celebrate our agreement?'

'No, thank you. Funnily enough, I don't see it as a cause for celebration.' Lilian could tell Harry was trying to think of a witty reply to this, but for once he seemed to be lost for words. He stuffed his last piece of cake into his mouth, swigged back his tea and got up from the table at last.

'All right Lil, I'll be off. I'll see you in a few days – shall we say Friday? And when I come back, we can discuss our future arrangements.' Lilian's heart plummeted. She was already wondering if she was going to be lucky enough to get away with a single payment, and it looked as though she was right to be wary.

'Future arrangements?'

'Yes, Lil. We both know Reg won't be coming back, don't we? Which leaves the way clear for me, so to speak. You know you've always been the only woman for me, don't you? I stood aside like a gentleman for Reg, but now... There's nothing to stop us getting married, is there?'

'Married? To you?' Lilian couldn't help herself, and it came out as a cross between a splutter and a choke.

'Yes, Lil. Married. To me. You see, it doesn't really matter how much you give me now, it's only to tide me over. Once the fuss has died down you can declare Reg dead, and we'll be walking down the aisle together. Now won't that be lovely?'

***

It was fortunate she was too shocked to speak. If she'd found her tongue, she knew she'd have said something she would later regret. As it was, she simply told him it was an interesting idea, and she would look forward to discussing things in more detail on Friday, and how about nine o'clock as she would be late back from the hospital that day. Harry seemed pleased by her acquiescence and she was too relieved to see him walking away to be insulted by his arrogance.

She bolted the door behind her and went outside to clear her head. It was a warm evening for May, almost balmy, and she walked down the path as far as the arch. The garden wasn't tamed yet, and she couldn't wait to see her mother get started on it. She'd be full of ideas and schemes, Lilian knew it. She smiled as she thought of this, and how happy her mother would be at last. Then she remembered Harry. She couldn't see him welcoming Grace into their home if she was married to him. She couldn't marry him. He was cunning and cold and very big trouble. It wasn't going to happen. She regretted ever asking him for help and she vowed never to put herself in such a position again. Everything would be carefully planned this time.

Even as she surprised herself with the thought, she knew there was only one solution. She would have to kill him, and she knew exactly how to do it. She still had the little bottle tucked away with the plant, hidden amongst the orchids in the greenhouse in her mother's tiny garden. She could collect the mixture tomorrow and put it in a cake the following day. Harry couldn't resist her ginger cake, and it disguised the taste perfectly.

The problem was the body. Where could she put it? If she'd had a solution to this last week, she wouldn't be in this mess now, and it wasn't a question that was easily answered. She looked up at the sky and the Black Mill on the horizon. The tall trees of the Westwood swayed gently in the breeze, and the glow of the evening sun drew her towards them, under the arch and across the tangled lawn. In her short time in the house she'd not ventured beyond this point, she'd been busy with other things, but she knew the plot was large. It was the reason for her being here, after all. She decided to walk to the boundary, picking her way through the weeds and wildflowers as she made her way to the edge of the garden. The fence was low, easily climbed if anyone should wish, and she made a mental note to put up a taller one some day.

Lilian stumbled as she thought this and looked down to find herself on the edge of a shallow pit. It was less than a yard deep at its central point and extended in an egg-like oval for a length of over six feet. Along one side of it sat a low mound of earth, covered with weeds and apparently the result of the pit being dug. Of course! Lilian remembered now. Reg had told her the previous owners had planned to put in a pond. They'd bought this extra piece of land from the council a long time ago for the purpose, but then the old gentleman had become unwell and they never got around to finishing it. Reg had talked about doing it himself, but Lilian hadn't expected him to make good his promise, and she had forgotten about it. Oh, Reg! Life was simpler when he was around, thought Lilian. She'd fretted about him and planned to divorce him, but he was nothing like as much trouble as Harry. If only she'd taken more care with her hiding place. If only she'd known about this pit, come to that. She could have put Reg in it and that would have been that. Too late now, she told herself. Time to get on with it. With a last look at the glowing sun, she turned towards the garden shed.

***

Once Lilian had decided she had to kill Harry, it was easy. She had three days to plan, more than enough to consider every detail. She had lied about her hours on Friday. She finished at lunchtime, which gave her time to prepare meticulously, as she had never prepared before. You live and learn, she thought to herself. She had certainly lived through enough, and if she hadn't learned something by now, she never would.

Wednesday was Lilian's day off, and she used the opportunity to visit her mother. It would give her a chance to tell Grace about Reg's disappearance as well as to get what she needed. She'd been visiting regularly ever since she got married, to tend to the plants in the greenhouse as well as to make sure her mother was in good spirits. She really must move the greenhouse and its contents to her new home soon. She couldn't risk her mother going in there, even though she'd shown no inclination to do so. She timed her visit for mid-afternoon, and Grace was delighted to see her, as always.

'Lilian, darling, what a lovely surprise!' Lilian smiled inwardly; she often came at this time of day, and she knew her mother would have been hoping to see her, although she would never have wanted Lilian to feel she had to come.

'Hello, Mother.' Lilian kissed Grace on the cheek, and they went through to the kitchen, where Grace put the kettle on and started preparing milk and tea leaves.

'Busy week, dear?' Grace asked. 'You're looking a bit peaky. Is the baby tiring you out? I know I felt dreadful in those first few weeks, but you'll feel better in a couple of months, I promise.'

'Yes, I know. It's nothing a cup of tea won't fix,' said Lilian. She knew it wasn't the baby making her look tired, but she found it easier to agree with her mother.

'Would you like some cake? I've got one freshly made,' Grace reached for the cupboard door as she spoke, and Lilian wondered if it was a ginger cake and whether she'd be able to eat any if it was. As it turned out she didn't need to worry; it was a Victoria sponge, and she accepted a large piece, finding that she had an appetite, despite having not managed either breakfast or lunch.

'How's Reg?' Lilian had planned to tell her mother that Reg had disappeared and she didn't know where, but she couldn't. Her head was too full of Harry to manage it at the moment, and she didn't want to say something which she might regret later on. Least of all did she want her mother coming to the house to help her out in her hour of need.

'He's fine. You know, busy at work as usual.'

'He must be excited about the baby.'

'Yes, he is.' The answers came automatically, and Lilian found herself in a surreal state of mind, watching herself sitting and talking with her mother as if nothing had happened. She needed to take herself in hand, and she got up suddenly, startling Grace as she did so.

'I thought I'd go out in the garden for a bit. Check on the greenhouse, you know.'

'Yes, of course, dear.' Grace looked surprised, as well she might, but Lilian knew she wouldn't say anything – she was too pleased to have Lilian in the house to upset things by taking offense.

'I won't be long, there's just something I want to check on. I don't want to forget about it…' Lilian was through the back door and half way to the greenhouse before she finished her sentence. Once inside, she stood with her hand on her chest, catching her breath. She was surprised to find herself in such a state, and she recognised the feeling from long ago, from the only other occasion on which she had cause to deceive her mother so convincingly. Despite everything she had been through, this unsettled her more than she could ever have imagined, and she felt a sudden and urgent need to get away. She found the cracked flowerpot, grabbed the little brown bottle and stuffed it into her pocket. A quick glance around confirmed that the plants were all healthy, but she watered them anyway for good measure. Back in the kitchen, she gulped down the rest of her tea and told her mother she wasn't feeling well.

'I'm sorry, Mother, I think I need a lie-down after all, and I'll be best off having it at home. It's come up on me all of a sudden. Did that happen to you too?'

'Yes, it did, sometimes,' said Grace. 'Don't worry, Lilian, it's all perfectly normal. But I suppose you know that, don't you?'

'Yes, I suppose I do.' Lilian smiled wanly as she pulled on her coat. 'I'll be back at the weekend, I'm off on Saturday.'

'That will be lovely, dear. Take care of yourself, won't you? And tell Reg he's got to look after you!'

'I will. Goodbye, see you soon.'

The whole exchange with her mother had worn Lilian

out, and she was grateful that she didn't have anything more to do that day. The baking and digging could wait. For now, she would go to bed, pull the curtains and hope to sleep till morning.

***

As Lilian cycled home on Friday she knew she had more than enough time to make all the arrangements. She had come home in time to make the cake the previous evening, still feeling the benefits from her long sleep, despite having worked all day. Afterwards, in the pink evening light, she had tackled the mound of earth. It would be easier for her to fill the pit if the soil was already broken up, and she had wanted to get everything ready before the day itself.

The contrast to last time was so marked that Lilian felt almost giddy with confidence. She made herself calm down. Over-excitement was not going to help her. She needed to be composed, clinical, bring a little of her work persona to bear. She lifted her chin as she wheeled her bike round to the back of the house and told herself to behave like a professional.

Feeling jittery nonetheless, she picked up her spade and dug around in the mound of earth again, ensuring there were no weeds or large lumps to hinder her later on. She collected the wheelbarrow from the shed and placed it on the patio near the French windows. The exercise calmed her nerves, and she made herself a cup of coffee before setting up the living room.

Reg's short-lived enthusiasm for the pond had included the purchase of a large sheet of plastic with which to line it, and Lilian retrieved this from the shed. She laid it on the sofa, tucking it in firmly around the cushions and covering it with a similarly secured rug. It brightened the drab room up more than she had anticipated, and she resolved to get another one once this was all over. She positioned the coffee table within easy reach of the sofa and checked the lamps were working so she could create at least a semblance of cosiness when Harry arrived.

Back in the kitchen Lilian laid out the tea tray with cups, saucers and cake plates and put the cake on a stand. She knew it wasn't dangerous to touch it briefly, but she handled it with plastic gloves to be on the safe side, cutting two slices ready for Harry to help himself. Needing something to do, she cleaned the kitchen, and then made herself a big plate of bacon and eggs. She was going to need her energy tonight.

***

'Harry! My word, don't you look smart this evening!' Lilian beamed as she held the door wide open.

'And you're looking rather lovely yourself, Lil,' said Harry. He seemed taken aback at the warmth of the welcome. No doubt he had expected arguments, anger, maybe bargaining or cajoling, not a wide smile and Lilian dressed up in her best frock.

'Come in, come in,' she said. 'I've set up the tray in the living room. I'll get the coffee, it's nearly ready. And I've made a fresh ginger cake. I know how much you like it, and it goes so well with coffee, I find. It's that mixture of sweetness and spice, don't you agree?'

'Er, yes, I suppose so.' For once, Harry was silenced by Lilian's chatter. She'd never talked to him like this before and she supposed he was starting to wonder what was going on. Lilian suppressed a smile as she left him perched on the sofa, looking around the room with a proprietorial gleam in his eye. No doubt he was planning how to improve it once he had her money to spend. She hoped he was enjoying himself; plans were about as far as he was ever going to get with that idea.

'Coffee!' Lilian breezed in with the coffee pot. It was only filled with instant, but she didn't think Harry would know the difference. 'Let me pour for you, Harry. Do help yourself to milk and sugar.'

'Er, thanks Lil,' Harry said. Lilian sat at the other end of the sofa, which wasn't far away at all, and picked up her cup.

'So, here we are,' she smiled.

'Yes, here we are, Lil.' Harry ground to a halt, seemingly unsure of what to say next. Lilian thought she could guess what was running through his mind. On the one hand, her mood indicated she was ready to accept his proposal, but on the other, this must seem too good to be true. Harry looked uncertainly at Lilian as she crossed her legs decorously and turned towards him with a smile. He had probably expected to be conducting negotiations across the kitchen table, but a more intimate setting was much better suited to Lilian's purposes.

'Don't you want to discuss things? Our getting married, I mean. Oh, do help yourself to a piece of cake, won't you, Harry?'

'Oh, yes, thanks Lil.' Harry took a piece and bit into it immediately, looking thankful to have something to do while he gathered his thoughts.

'So. Harry. I've been thinking about what you said the other day, and I've decided you're right.'

'Hngg?' Harry's mouth was full of cake and he almost choked at Lilian's words. He swallowed, hard. 'You do?'

'Yes. I don't like to talk about what happened to Reg, and it wasn't particularly romantic to try to blackmail me, but I've decided to overlook it.' Harry seemed to be lost for words. It was true he'd blackmailed her, but it was clear that romance wasn't something he'd considered as part of the equation.

'You see, Harry, I did like you. I liked you a lot at one time, but then Reg came along, and things sort of snowballed. I don't know how it happened really, but now I think it must have been meant. More coffee?'

'Yes, please.' Harry's eyes were beginning to lose focus, and a sheen of sweat had appeared on his forehead and upper lip. He shivered and held out his cup. Lilian ignored these signs of distress and carried on talking as she poured the coffee.

'Yes, I've been thinking about it a lot, and, despite everything you said the other day, I've decided marrying you is the right thing to do. Once some time has passed and I've had Reg declared dead, like you said.'

'That's great, Lil.' Harry loosened his collar. 'I'm sorry, Lil, I'm really happy to hear you say all this but I'm not feeling too good. I'll take my tie off if you don't mind. And could I have a glass of water?'

'Of course, Harry, I'll fetch you one. I won't be long.' Lilian went into the kitchen and filled a glass from the tap. By the time she returned, Harry was hunched over on the sofa, looking grey.

'I'm sorry, Lil, I think I might be going to be...' He retched into the bucket which Lilian had fetched along with the water.

'Don't worry, Harry, you're just a bit queasy. It's all the excitement, I expect. Here, lie down and you'll feel better soon.' Lilian stayed with him for an hour, mopping his brow and holding the bucket, until he lost consciousness. Then she went into the kitchen, made a fresh cup of coffee, and waited for it to be over.

Chapter 5

What makes a perfect murder? I suppose it's a complete lack of detection. And by that, I mean no one even knowing it <u>was</u> a murder, as well as the killer not being discovered. I never set out to commit a perfect murder, but it would be nice to think I'd accomplished it. It's not something many people achieve in their lives, and it's hardly something one can boast about. But it would give me a certain satisfaction. Come to think of it, I suppose I have done. It's so long ago I'd almost forgotten about it myself.

Harry doesn't count. He was a perfect murder to start with, but now he isn't. Although if it weren't for the DNA match, they'd never have worked out who he was, and it would still have qualified as perfect. The method works, and that's what matters. The plastic sheet was my downfall, but I wasn't thinking about him being unearthed at the time. It's easy in hindsight; anticipating the unexpected is much more problematic.

I won't need to worry about the long term this time. I don't even know if I'll need to kill anyone else, but I have a feeling I might. If it comes to it, I'll be making a speedy departure, so that's what needs planning most carefully. A delayed discovery would be helpful, but I can't do much about it until I know who it is and where. Now the cake is made, I need to focus on my getaway.

I'm putting on my rubber gloves, ready to give the bathroom a good clean, when the doorbell rings. I know it must be them. No one else comes calling in the middle of the day, or at any other time of day, come to that. I sigh as I pull off the gloves and let them in.

'Good afternoon, Dr Templeton, how are you today?' So it's the friendly approach this time. I'll do my best to be polite. I know I've been a bit sharp on occasion, and it doesn't help matters.

'Very well, thank you, although it's extremely upsetting still having such a mess in my garden. I don't suppose you know when they'll come back to finish it off, Inspector?'

'I'm afraid it's not my department,' she says. 'But we'll see if we can hurry things along. Will you make a note of it please, Luke?' She turns to the sergeant, who nods, a startled look on his face. I'm surprised too. Maybe she's trying to butter me up, but why would she want to do that?'

'I suppose you'd better come in. I've got the kettle on;

would you like some tea or coffee?'

'Yes please, a drink would be very nice. We're both coffee people, no sugar thank you,' DI Twist answers for them both. So they were humouring me with all that tea drinking before. I leave them in the sitting room where they will no doubt have a good look round. Nice old ladies bring in drinks on trays, so that's what I do. I put the coffee in cups rather than mugs even though it's instant, and some slices of ginger cake onto little cake plates.

'I hope you like ginger cake. I'm not much of a cook, as my daughter could tell you, but this is one thing I can be trusted not to get wrong. It was Mother's recipe.'

'Thank you, it looks delicious,' says DI Twist, although I notice she doesn't take any. The sergeant can't resist, and I enjoy watching him trying to find time to eat it in between taking notes. DI Twist waits patiently for him to sort out his fingers before starting to talk.

'We've made some progress with our investigations,' she says. 'And there are some questions we need to ask you.'

'Oh, yes?' I make myself sit back in my chair. I don't want her to think I'm on edge, but my heart is already hammering. What questions? What investigations? Who have they been talking to?

'Yes. Sergeant Carter has spoken to Mr Johnson's sister again. He'll fill you in.' She crosses her legs comfortably and sips her coffee, and I'm relieved. Sergeant Carter has always seemed more manageable and I think I'll be able to handle this, whatever it's about. He leans towards me, concentrating hard on not messing up his interview in front of the boss. I hope he's feeling nervous. It'll make things easier.

'As DI Twist mentioned, we've spoken to Dora Waters - Harry Johnson's sister - again,' he says. 'We've been trying to find out more about his life before he disappeared, and his friends and acquaintances in particular. Mrs Waters has a box of his possessions which she took from her parents' house after he left, and it included some photographs. Can I ask you to look at this please, Dr Templeton?'

My heart sinks as I see it. I had completely forgotten it had been taken, and I would never have guessed Harry had a copy. I suppose it was the only photograph he had of the two of us. I never let him use his camera when we were out, despite him being so proud of it. Even then, I knew it wasn't wise to let him have any evidence of our being together, and I've never liked having my picture taken in any case. I have to think quickly. I hadn't expected this, and it looks as if I'm going to have to tell them more than I'd hoped. I peer at the photograph and make a fuss about finding my glasses to give myself time to decide what to say. I see the two detectives exchange glances. They obviously think they're on to something, and I have to admit they're right.

'Ah, that's better,' I say. 'Now, let's have a proper look at this. Oh, yes, this must be the Beverley Arms, can you see the beer taps? They used to have a lovely bar in the old days. It's all changed now, I believe, although I don't go in there myself.'

'It's the people we want you to look at, Dr Templeton.' Sergeant Carter can't keep a hint of impatience out of his voice, and DI Twist shoots him a frown. 'I expect you can see yourself and your husband in the picture.'

'Yes, of course, that goes without saying.'

'And the others? Do you recognise them?'

'Let me see, yes, there's Frances standing next to Reg. I can't make out the fourth person so well.'

'We'll come back to Frances later,' he says. 'Look again please, Dr Templeton. Are you sure you don't recognise the man standing next to you in the picture?'

'Now let me see… Oh! It's a long time ago obviously, but…. is it Harry?'

'Yes, Dr Templeton, it's Harry Johnson. He seems to have his arm around you. Are you certain you don't remember him?'

'Now I think about it, I suppose I do, although I wasn't at all happy about him getting so close. Look, I don't exactly look thrilled, do I?' He can't deny my expression in the photograph is awkward. You can almost see me pulling away from Harry as if keen to escape.

'You told us earlier that you didn't remember anyone called Harry Johnson,' says DI Twist. 'Why was that?' It's a while since she spoke; she startles me, and the directness of her question reminds me to be careful.

'I'm not sure,' I say. 'I suppose it was because I was in shock, and the name truly meant nothing to me then. It was a long time ago, and I never knew him well. His name had quite literally gone from my mind. Seeing this photograph now brings it all back to me.'

'And what might that be? What does it bring back?'

Sergeant Carter has taken up the reins again and I turn to him with a feeling of relief.

'Not much I'm afraid,' I say. 'I'm trying to get it clear in my head now. He was a friend of Reg's, that's right, but they didn't spend much time together. He was a bit of what they used to call a 'wide boy'. He fancied himself as a cool customer and was always strutting around in his smart clothes.'

'Yes, that ties in with what his sister told us,' says the sergeant. 'As we mentioned to you before.'

'Oh, does it? I'm afraid I don't remember much of what you said before, I've been in such a state. I don't know when I'm going to get over it, to be honest.'

'The sooner we get to the facts, the sooner it will be over,' interrupts DI Twist, rather abruptly in my opinion. 'And the more you can tell us, the quicker it will be. What do you remember about Harry Johnson?'

'As I've said, not a lot. He was Reg's friend. I didn't get to know him well, with us only being together such a short time.'

'So how come he was with you in this photograph? It was taken before your marriage to Reg, wasn't it?' DI Twist sounds very sure, and I can't assume she hasn't found out about Frances. She's hovering in the background, and I assume that's only because they wanted to know about Harry first.

'Yes, it was, and as you can see, Harry was keener to be next to me than I was to be next to him,' I say tartly.

'I'm only asking because his sister said that shortly before he disappeared, Harry told her he had met someone,' the sergeant says. 'Someone who hadn't been interested in him, but who he was confident would marry him now, although he didn't tell her why. Looking at this photograph made us wonder if it might have been you?'

'Well it wasn't! How could it be? I'd only been married a few months when Harry disappeared! All right, he was keen on me for a while. He took me out a couple of times, but I only went to shut him up. He wasn't my sort at all, and I ended it long before I met Reg. Is that good enough for you?' I've done it again, lost my temper with them, and I have to make myself sit back in my chair and sniff into my handkerchief.

'I daresay it's enough for now,' says DI Twist. 'But it isn't helpful if you try to hide what you know from us, Dr Templeton. We're more than likely to find things out in the end.' Oh, you think so, do you? We'll have to see about that. There is absolutely no chance of you finding out everything, young woman, I can tell you that for nothing. I sniff a few more times and consider asking for a glass of water, hoping to break her flow. I know what she's going to ask next, and I could do with some time to gather my thoughts. Sergeant Carter looks at me uncertainly and asks if I'd like some more coffee.

'I expect I can work out what's what in your kitchen,' he says, and I nod gratefully over my handkerchief. DI Twist pauses while there's no one to take notes and gazes around the room again.

'It looks like an old house in here, but the back seems more modern,' she says eventually, just as I'm beginning to wonder if I should break what is becoming an awkward silence. 'Have you had much work done to it over the years?'

'Not a great deal,' I say, glad to be able to talk about something less contentious. 'This part was a farm cottage in Victorian times, and it was added to in the nineteen twenties. I had a new bathroom put in downstairs for Mother but nothing else structural.'

'You've certainly made it welcoming in here,' she says. 'I'd love to have a fireplace like yours, and those watercolours are beautiful. Are they by a local artist?'

'They're my own,' I say. 'I've made a study of plants since childhood. Most are in sketch books, but Mother wanted some for the walls and those were for her eightieth birthday.'

'You must miss her.'

'Yes, but life goes on. She had a good life and I'm glad she didn't suffer.' It's what people always say about death, isn't it? The ordinary platitudes. Don't mention the aching gap in your life, the silence hanging in the air, the loss of a companion who can read your every thought, who loves you, trusts you, no matter what. I brush my eyes to clear the tears that suddenly brim, but she's too busy looking at the paintings to notice. The moment's silence is broken by the return of the sergeant with fresh coffee. He's found more cake too and added it to the plate – maybe this was his motive, and I smile. Everyone loves Mother's ginger cake.

'Now, Dr Templeton.' It's back to business, I can tell by her tone. 'Looking at this photograph again,' she says, picking it up to illustrate her point. 'The fourth person, Frances, what can you tell us about her?'

I hold back a sharp remark about them probably

knowing everything already and decide I had better tell the truth this time.

'She was Reg's first wife, and my good friend. This photograph was taken at their engagement party. I remember it now; she took ages choosing that frock.' I can recall the evening as if it were last week. Frances was excited about her new dress, but she couldn't keep her eyes off her engagement ring. She kept turning her hand to and fro to make it catch the light, and I was pleased for her. All she'd ever wanted was to be married, even if they hadn't found anywhere to live yet. She made me get ready with her and she put my hair up in the latest style and plastered my face with makeup. No wonder I looked uncomfortable, even before Harry put his arm round me.

'Dr Templeton?' Sergeant Carter is speaking gently, and I realise I've drifted off in my memories. Much to my surprise I find tears in my eyes. Maybe it's no bad thing in the circumstances.

'I'm sorry, this must be bringing back some sad memories,' he says, and I nod and sniff again into my handkerchief.

'We understand Frances died not long after her marriage,' DI Twist says after giving me a minute to compose myself.

'Yes, only a year later. It was awfully sad and dreadfully sudden. They said it was a heart attack, even though she'd always been fit and well.'

'And you were married to Reg less than a year later.'

'Yes, that's right.'

'Only seven months later, I believe.'

'I suppose that's correct, yes.'

'It's a very short time between losing one wife and marrying the next. How did it happen so quickly?'

'I don't know! It just did. Reg's sister, Susan, was worried about him after Frances died. He wasn't looking after himself, hadn't gone back to work, wouldn't see anyone. I suppose he was depressed, but we didn't use such words then. Anyway, she asked me to go around to see if I could help him get himself together. That was how she put it. It was my being Frances's friend, and a doctor too, I suppose, that gave her the idea.'

'What happened? When you went to see him?'

'Oh, he was in a right mess. The house hadn't been cleaned since Frances died, and it was more than a month later by then. Every dish in the kitchen was dirty, and there wasn't even a pint of milk in the fridge. I don't know what he was living off. Toast, mostly, I think, and baked beans.'

'And you helped him?'

'Yes. He wouldn't speak to me at first, so I set to and cleaned up. Then I did some shopping, put milk in the fridge, and took round his dinner for a few days. In the end he started talking and I helped him get his confidence back so he could return to work. By the time he was able to cope without me he didn't want to, and I was becoming fond of him, despite everything.'

'Everything? Didn't you like him?' She looks at the photograph as if wondering what was so unlikeable about Reg.

'I never thought badly of him, but we didn't have much in common other than Frances, and I'd not got to know him particularly well.'

'So what changed?'

'As I said, I grew fond of him. It was nice to be appreciated, and losing Frances had changed him. He was different – more considerate. I always thought he took Frances for granted, but he was different with me. He told me I was kind, clever. No one had said that sort of thing to me before.'

'Not even Harry?'

'Oh, Harry! He was a flatterer. I never took anything he said seriously.'

'But you took Reg seriously?'

'I suppose I did. He wasn't in a state to flatter anyone deliberately, and I think he looked up to me. You know, with my being a doctor. That was nice too, I'll admit. And then there was Mother.'

'Your mother? What did she have to do with it?' asks DI Twist.

'She was old-fashioned, you know. In her mind, any woman still single past the age of twenty-five was a hopeless old maid. She'd been on at me to find a husband for years, and to be honest, I thought the time had come myself. I didn't fancy the dating game, and Reg was turning out to be harmless enough, so I thought, why not?'

'It seems a strange reason to be married.'

'I suppose it does, but I was never one for romance. I thought it would be a good idea to settle down, it seemed Reg would suit me well enough, he was keen to get married, and so we did. It was very simple really, even if it seemed hasty to some people at the time.'

'Were you pregnant?' DI Twist asks.

'No, I wasn't! You don't hold back with the awkward questions, do you? No, I got pregnant later as it happens, although I suppose a fair few people thought as you did at the time. It didn't bother me. It's never bothered me what people think, and Reg wasn't in a state to care. He was simply happy to have someone to look after him.'

'And then he left.'

'Yes. And then he left.'

There isn't much more to be said. They leave soon after, saying they'll be talking to Reg and Frances's relations and friends next, and asking if I know any of them. I tell them I don't, and I'm not sure who they'll find to talk to. They'll be back in due course, they say, and I wonder how long it will be. It's bound to take time to locate people, and I hope I'll have a few days' peace now. I'll need it if I'm going to get the next part of my story straight.

Chapter 6

Lilian hadn't wanted to kill Reg. Not in theory or in practice. It was spontaneous to say the least and had never been part of her plan. Looking back later, she would acknowledge she had no alternative once he'd found the diary, although she blamed herself for not having used a more secure hiding place. She didn't dwell on it for long, it wasn't in her nature to do so. And she had achieved her original purpose, even if it did lead to complications later.

It was a Saturday morning. Lilian had a day off from the hospital and Reg was planning to come home from the estate agents at lunchtime, handing over to one of the juniors so he and Lilian could spend some time together. This was not at Lilian's request. The limits imposed on their shared time by the combination of her changing shifts and Reg's office hours was a blessing as far as she was concerned. But Reg liked to be with her, perhaps to remind himself that he had someone to look after him, and since she had found out she was pregnant, he had become irritatingly protective.

Lilian hoped to spend some of the next day with her

mother, and she knew this would not go down well with Reg. She decided to butter him up by playing the dutiful wife, and she was already slicing apples for a pie when he came down for his breakfast. Lilian put her hand on her tummy, wondering when she would feel the baby kick. It was too small right now, but she wanted to feel it. She didn't know if she loved the baby yet, but she knew it would help her to get what she wanted, and she loved it for this.

'Good morning, my darling.' Reg kissed Lilian on the cheek as he came into the kitchen. 'What's going on here, then?' Lilian hated these endearments, but she hoped she wouldn't have to put up with them for too long. If everything worked out the way she planned, Reg would be out of the house in a year's time, and she could have everything precisely the way she wanted it.

'I'm making apple pie for your supper,' she said. 'I know it's one of your favourites.'

'You're too good for me, Lil,' he said, picking up his tea and a slice of toast. 'I'm going to see if I can fix that leak before I go into work. I reckon I know where it's coming from and I want to take a look. Harry will send one of his boys over if I ask him, but I'd rather see to it myself.'

'That sounds sensible,' said Lilian. She had no wish for Harry or any of his 'boys' to be poking around in her home. She finished slicing the apples and put them in a pan with sugar, water, and a pinch of cinnamon. Lilian added a handful of raisins, which she knew Reg would like, and got out her rolling pin before measuring out the flour. Half her mind was on the pie and half on her mother, who she had been worrying about recently. She was also thinking about Reg's shirt, which had a nasty stain on it. Reg was pottering around upstairs, trying to work out where the leak was coming from. It was dripping in beside the window in the dining room, and he'd been cross when he found it the previous evening, because he'd thought he'd fixed all the holes in the roof. Lilian wasn't surprised, they were always finding new leaks in this house. She'd seen the state of the tiles and thought they probably needed replacing, but Reg said they didn't have the money for it, and they'd have to make do with him fixing it. The roof would resemble a patchwork quilt at this rate, Lilian thought as she rolled out the pastry. She was absorbed in considering how to fix the problem properly one day, and didn't notice when the noises above her stopped. The next thing she knew, Reg was coming slowly down the stairs, which was strange as he usually dashed about when he was mending things, trying to look efficient.

'Did you fix it? I thought you would, you're so good at these things,' she said, thinking a little flattery wouldn't go amiss. There was no reply.

'Reg?' she said. 'Did you find where it was coming from?'

'No, Lil. I found this.' Reg walked into the kitchen carrying Lilian's diary. He was flicking through it with a frown on his face. 'What's all this about, then? You've been writing in here about me I see, and a fair bit about Frances too, and there's even a bit about Harry. Why were you writing about Harry? You hardly know him. And why did you hide this under the floorboards?'

Lilian swore inwardly at herself for not paying attention to the location of the leak and its proximity to her diary's hiding place. At the same time, she realised he'd not had time to read it all, although it was certainly possible he'd seen enough to ask some awkward questions.

'It's nothing Reg, only some old scribblings, it does

not mean anything. I was just… just writing down some things about my life for the baby, when it's older, to read about us and what we did before it was born, you know? I thought it would be nice for it to read all about us, don't you agree? Come and sit down and I'll show you what I mean.' She guided him into a chair as she spoke and tried to take the book from him, but he held on. Not wanting to make a fuss, she moved away from him and put the kettle on to boil. 'I'll make us a nice cup of tea and I can explain it all to you.'

'But Lil, why would you need to hide it? And why would the baby need to read about Harry? And Frances? They've got nothing to do with our lives now, and the baby won't be able to read it for years. I don't understand….'

Reg was turning pages randomly, and Lilian's heart was pounding as if it would burst. She knew it was only a matter of time – maybe seconds – before he came to the pages which would tell him everything. Lilian froze, she knew she had to do something, but she couldn't think what. She was unable move, so terrified was she of what he would do when he found out. She made herself put water in he kettle, set it on the stove to boil, spoon tea into the pot, all the while thinking furiously of what she could do or say to stop Reg.

'Come on Reg, give it to me.' She put her hands on his shoulders and tried the softly-softly approach. 'It's not finished yet; I wanted it to be a surprise. I'll show it you properly when it's all done.' But she was too late. She could see he had come to the very pages she had prayed he wouldn't see. Reg sat still as stone and Lilian could almost see his brain working as he processed the implications of what he was reading. A terrible hush hung in the air before Reg rose up from his chair with a roar that must have rattled the glass in the windowpanes.

'You TRICKED me!' he yelled in her face. 'You LIED and plotted and planned and...and...' His face crumpled as he looked at the little book again. 'You're a monster,' he whispered. 'A MONSTER!' He pushed the chair aside, rushing for her and pinning her against the door with his hands around her throat. 'I'm going to KILL you!'

Lilian writhed and struggled, but he was too strong for her. There was a sound like the wind rushing down a tunnel in her ears and she could feel the blood throbbing through her brain. Her eyes went dark and she knew she was teetering on the verge of fainting. She realised she wasn't going to escape his grasp, and fell limp, hoping he'd think she was unconscious. He loosened his hands briefly, giving Lilian the precious seconds she needed to stamp hard on his foot, put her knee where it would hurt him most, and wriggle away while he recovered himself. She dodged around him and snatched up the rolling pin. Reg's back was towards her, and she whirled round to strike him on the back of the head. She thought she'd need to hit him several times, but he crumpled immediately and fell sideways onto the floor at her feet.

Lilian stood absolutely still for what she knew was only a few seconds but felt like hours, hearing nothing but the pounding of her chest and the birds outside as the roar in her head subsided. She was brought to her senses by the kettle whistling, and realised she needed to do something. She took the kettle off the stove and then approached Reg slowly, still holding the rolling pin, not knowing if he might jump up and grab her or worse, but he was completely still, and when she felt with trembling fingers for a pulse, there was none. There was blood, though. Reg had smashed his head on the hard stone floor and there was blood everywhere.

Lilian turned slowly and put the rolling pin back on the counter, then as if in a dream, she picked up the kettle and made the tea. She sat at the table for a moment, then rose quickly and took her cup into the garden, where the rain had stopped, and the birds were singing. It was going to be a beautiful day.

***

Lilian's newly regained composure deserted her as soon as she returned to the kitchen and saw Reg. The sight of the pool of blood brought home to her what she'd done, and she made herself feel for a pulse again, even though she knew she wouldn't find one. Her experience with the grimmer side of death at the hospital and throughout her training meant nothing to her as her mind flooded with pure panic. Gone was the cool, calculating killer of the past. All she could think of was how she was going to get the bloodstains off the tiles. And what on earth was she going to do with the body? There was no way she could pass this one off as natural causes. She would have to think of a plausible story to explain what had happened, and even if she reported it as self-defence, there was no guarantee she wouldn't end up in prison. Even now, she knew she would have to dispose of the body herself. But how? And where?

Lilian forced herself to step around Reg, wash up and put away her teacup. This gave her time to calm down, and she realised maybe there was someone who could help her. She found her handbag and emptied it, riffling through the contents with shaking hands. Please don't say I've thrown it away, she thought desperately. She'd never meant to hang onto it, but she wasn't good at keeping her belongings in order, and she couldn't remember having disposed of it. And she hadn't. For once, her lax approach to handbag management was a fault to be glad of, for there it lay, crumpled and rough around the edges. *'Harry Johnson, Contractor'*, and a phone number in Hull. She'd been suspicious of his job title when he'd given it to her. 'What exactly do you contract, Harry?' she'd asked, doubting she'd get a straight answer. 'That's for me to know and you to wonder, lovely Lil,' he'd said. She wondered why she'd bothered to ask.

Now she was glad of his dubious profession. Frances had always been against Reg spending time with Harry, convinced he was nothing but trouble. What she'd have thought if she'd known Lilian had been seeing him, she dreaded to think, but luckily, she never found out, and nor did Reg. She'd never been quite sure why she did, other than to stop him from pestering her, but he had always had charm, and plenty of money for nice restaurants, which might have had something to do with it. She'd known it couldn't carry on though, and it had been a relief in a way to have to marry Reg. At least it meant she couldn't see Harry any more.

He hadn't seen it in the same way though, and when he'd cornered her one wet Saturday morning shortly after her engagement, she hadn't been able to get away.

'Well now, it's the lovely Lil! Let me shelter you, my dear.' He'd steered her into a doorway with a firm hand on her arm, giving her no choice but to comply.

'I hear congratulations are in order, Lil,' he said. He was holding her close and Lilian flushed with embarrassment, hoping no one would see them standing like this.

'Yes, thank you Harry, they are,' she said.

'Reg is a lucky man, that's all I can say,' he said. 'I'm sorry to hear it, though. I was rather hoping you and I might have got hitched ourselves at one time.'

'Oh, we had some fun, Harry, but I don't think we'd have been suited.'

'Maybe not Lil, maybe not. Mind you, I wouldn't have said you and Reg were an obvious pair, now you mention it. And it's all a bit sudden, isn't it? Frances barely six months in her grave. Some might say it's a bit hasty on his part. Not in the family way, are you Lil?' He gave her a wink and pulled her even closer, which she wouldn't have thought was possible in such a cramped space.

'No, I'm not! It's none of your business why we're getting married, and I'll thank you not to make wild suggestions. Someone might hear, and the last thing I need is gossip.'

'All right, Lil, hold your horses, it was just a joke. I'm happy for Reg, he was in a terrible way when Frances died and I daresay it's you who got him back on his feet. I hope you'll both be very happy. But if you ever need any help – any help at all – give me a call. Here's my card.' He tucked it into Lilian's handbag before she could stop him, and she pushed away from him and out into the street to prevent him saying anything more.

Thinking back to their conversation, less than six months ago, Lilian wondered if he'd meant it. She'd not seen Harry since the wedding, although she knew he'd been trying to rope Reg into one of his schemes. She hadn't bothered saying anything to Reg. She knew Frances had tried to stop him in the past to no avail, and she doubted there was anything criminal going on anyway. Although it would be helpful if there were. Then he'd maybe go to prison and she could divorce him, which would make life easier for her in more ways than one.

But he hadn't had time to do whatever it was Harry wanted him to, and he hadn't gone to prison. He was lying dead on the kitchen floor, his head surrounded by a pool of congealing blood.

Lilian gave herself a shake. If she didn't make the call now, she would have to explain why she had left it so long. Even Harry might notice the blood wasn't fresh when he saw how thickly it lay on the tiles. She picked up the card and took it to the phone in the hall.

'Harry? Is that you?' She was surprised to find her voice was high and shaky without her having to put it on. She must really be in shock, she thought, wondering at the same time how she could be viewing herself with such detachment.

'Yes, this is Harry. Who's this?'

'Oh, Harry, I need your help!'

'Lil? Are you all right?'

'No, I'm not all right, Harry. Can you come to the house? Now? Something terrible's happened and I didn't know who else to call.'

'On my way, Lil. Sit tight, I'll be there in half an hour.'

Lilian used the thirty minutes to go over her story in her mind and to assess whether any tidying up was required in the kitchen. She put the pie ingredients in the fridge and cleared away the dishes. She grimaced as she washed the rolling pin. The blood wouldn't come off completely, but she put it in the drawer, thinking Harry would have no reason to look there and she could dispose of it later on. She left the contents of her handbag on the kitchen table, deciding they would support her story. She was sitting in the kitchen, going over the details, when Harry arrived.

'Oh, Harry, thank goodness you're here!' She pulled him quickly into the house, not wanting anyone to see him, even though neighbours were few and far between .

'Now, now, Lil, what's up?' Harry's face looked as if he couldn't believe his luck, but he managed to compose himself. Lilian decided this was the one and only occasion on which it would be appropriate to throw herself into his arms and duly did so, sobbing into his shoulder.

'Hey, Lil, Lil, what is it? It can't be that bad. Everything will be all right now I'm here. But where's Reg?'

'Oh, Harry, there's been the most awful accident. Reg fell.... and hit his head.... and... I think he might be....'

'Where? Show me!' Lilian pointed to the kitchen door and followed him, still weeping. Harry rushed over to Reg and felt for a pulse. 'Have you checked, Lil? You're the doctor after all.'

'I was in too much of a panic. I still can't believe it happened. I think I must be in shock. But I think he must be, don't you?'

'Oh, come on Lil, you'll have to have a feel. Come here, we'll do it together.' Lilian knelt beside Harry and they both placed their fingers on Reg's neck.

'Nothing,' she said, standing up. 'He's dead.' Lilian sat down at the kitchen table and looked up at Harry as if waiting for guidance. She found her hands were shaking, and she allowed him to fetch her a brandy to settle her nerves.

'Come on Lil, tell me what happened. Was it an accident?'

'Of course it was an accident! What else would it be?'

'I don't know, I'm sorry, Lil. Tell me what happened. Why didn't you call for an ambulance or the police?'

'Because they'd say the same as you. What does it look like? I can't risk going to prison for killing him. You know what these cases can be like – innocent wives locked up for killing their husbands, when it was self-defence.'

'I thought you said it was an accident?'

'Well, it wasn't completely, but it was self-defence, and I didn't mean to kill him!'

'Lil, you're not making sense. Tell me what happened. How did it all start?'

'All right, I will.' Lilian took a swig of brandy and a deep breath. 'It started with me clearing out my handbag.'

'Your handbag? How could a handbag cause all this?' Bewildered, Harry indicated the scene of devastation on Lilian's kitchen floor.

'I'll tell you if you stop interrupting.'

'All right. Sorry, go on.'

'I'd decided to clear out my handbag. I'm no good at keeping it tidy and I couldn't find my lipstick, and Reg said I should sort it out. He was being impatient, so I thought I'd better do it right away, and I emptied it all onto the table. See, everything's still there.'

'All right, what happened next?'

'Reg came in as I was tipping everything out and he was having a bit of a laugh at the mess and looking through everything, asking what I needed old receipts and cinema tickets for, you know.'

'Well, no, I don't know, but go on, Lil.'

'And he found your card.'

'My card?'

'Yes, the one you pushed into my bag the day we met on the street in the rain. Don't you remember?'

'But that was months ago, Lil. I thought you'd have thrown it away by now.'

'Well I hadn't, as you can see. And when Reg saw it, he went mad. He was asking why I had it, and had I been seeing you behind his back, and getting so angry it was frightening. I always knew he was the jealous kind. Frances said so when they were married, and I never told him we'd been out in the past. I knew it would upset him, and I was right, wasn't I? But he wouldn't believe me. He went on and on at me and I eventually had to admit we'd dated a few times and you'd given it to me for old times' sake, and that only made things worse.'

'How worse? What did he do, Lil?'

'He got me up against the door and he had his hands around my throat – look, you can see the bruises.' Even as she wept, Lilian was pleased with herself for having thought to keep this element of truth in her story. 'I thought he was going to kill me, Harry. The blood all rushed to my head and I thought I was going to pass out. I remembered about wild animals playing dead to fool their predators, and so I pretended to lose consciousness and he let go a bit and I gave him a big push. I was hoping to get away from him, that was all, but he stumbled backwards and crashed into the stove, and then he fell on the floor and cracked his head on the tiles, and he didn't get up. I was afraid to check his pulse, Harry, in case he stood up again and came after me.' Lilian collapsed into floods of tears, and Harry moved round the table to hold her in his arms as if he'd been waiting for this moment all his life.

'I couldn't call the police. They wouldn't believe me, and even if they did in the end, I'd go to prison first, I know I would. I can't go to prison, I can't. I've got Mother to look after, and now there's the baby as well. I can't risk gaol, surely you can see that?'

'Baby? Are you pregnant, Lil?'

'Yes, it's only a few weeks, but yes. Oh, Harry, I was so pleased and excited about it. What am I going to do now?'

'Don't you worry, Lil. I'll take care of everything. Leave it to me.'

***

It was the first time Lilian had ever asked anyone for help, and Harry didn't let her down. He told her to stay out of the kitchen until he came back, which he did after dusk had fallen. Lilian agreed it was best if no one else was involved, so it was she who helped him to wrap the body in plastic sheeting and then an old bedsheet. Harry brought in a removal men's trolley, and it was only a short distance to his van, which was parked right outside the door. Lilian was grateful for the tall hedges shielding the drive from the eyes of passers-by, although it was dark by then and even the dog walkers had turned in for the night.

Lilian hadn't eaten all day and she was completely exhausted, but she made herself ask the question.

'Where are you taking him, Harry?'

'Best if you don't know, Lil. I think that's for me to know and you to wonder, don't you?' Lilian couldn't help smiling a little at his well-worn catch phrase.

'All right, Harry. And thank you. I'll never be able to repay you. You've been a hero.'

'Don't worry Lil, I'll think of something.' He gave her a quick grin and left her alone in the gloom.

Chapter 7

I can't stand this feeling of being trapped. The police haven't said I can't go out, but something's been stopping me, and even though I don't know what it is, I've had enough of it. I get out my bike and cycle into town. I'll get a book from the library and some milk, and maybe go to a café for a coffee.

My spirits lift as soon as I'm cycling with the wind in my hair, and I'm feeling almost cheerful as I chain my bike up outside the library. I decide to get the milk and coffee first, so I won't have to carry my books around town. I'm walking past the post office when I hear my name being called.

'Lilian! It is Lilian, isn't it?' I don't recognise the voice and turn just as a large hand lands on my arm.

'Yes.' Who is this person? But before I can ask, she enlightens me.

'It's Susan! You remember, Susan Blake I was, although it's Susan Fanshawe now.'

'Susan! Hello! How are you?' I can't help the false cheer in my voice, it's a response to the shock of seeing her. Does she know? Have the police been to see her? What is she doing in Beverley? I've not seen her since

Reg disappeared and hadn't expected to now. I thought she was safely tucked away on her farm. Or dead.

'Not too good, to be truthful. But let's not stand about in the street. It won't do my old knees any good. Shall we go for a cup of tea? My treat?' There's nothing I can do. Her knees might not be too good but there's nothing wrong with her hand, which still has my arm in a vice-like grip.

'All right,' I say, not ungraciously. 'How about here?' You're never far from a coffee shop in Beverley, and we're practically on the doorstep of one, so that's where we go.

Although I didn't recognise her at first, she's not changed much. She's carrying a knitted bag – maybe she makes them herself? – and wearing a shapeless floral dress and sandals. She takes her time finding her purse amid much rustling of papers, so in the end I offer to pay for us both. Once settled with a pot of tea, there's no stopping her.

'Oh, it's a long time, isn't it, Lilian? I never much liked coming into Beverley, I don't mind telling you, but I've come to live here with my daughter now and I'm a real convert!'

'How nice,' I say, hoping this won't mean she wants to meet up regularly. I can't imagine anything worse than weekly chats with Susan.

'Yes, I've got three daughters and two sons. Quite a brood! My oldest and his wife have taken on the farm. Such a relief to us all. I married Bob not long after... you know, after Reg. He was straight out of agricultural college with no farm to call his own, so Dad was delighted to hand over to him. He's passed away now, and my son needs the farmhouse for his own family, so Lucy said she'd got space and why didn't I come and help out with the grandchildren, so here I am!'

'Lovely,' I say weakly. The woman's like a steamroller. I don't remember her being this voluble before, but I suppose I mostly talked to her when she was worried about Reg. Maybe that had a calming effect.

'What about you, Lilian? Any family? I was sorry to lose touch, but you know how it is. What with the farm and all the kids and my mother to look after, I barely made it past Driffield for forty years!'

'Oh, nothing like yours, Susan. There's just me and my daughter Joanna. She's in London now, teaching. No grandchildren. Joanna never married; she's always been happy on her own. She visits from time to time.'

'It sounds a lonely life, I must say.'

'It's not felt lonely. I had Mother with me until last year, and I'm considering a move now. Perhaps to London to be nearer Joanna.'

'That sounds sensible. It's good to be with your family. Your mother must have been quite an age?'

'Ninety-four.'

'Well I never.'

'Yes, quite.' Isn't she going to mention it? She must have heard about it. Or hasn't she worked out it's my garden? There's an awkward pause. I sip my tea and wait for her to fill it.

'I hope you don't mind my asking Lilian...' Ah, here it comes. 'There was a story on the news the other day. About a body in a garden. It looked an awful lot like Reg's house. You don't still live there, do you?'

'As a matter of fact, I do,' I say, and I put down my cup, wishing I'd managed to override Susan's imperious order of a pot of 'Yorkshire's best' for two.

'Oh, I'd assumed you'd have moved away. It's a big house for such a small family.'

'I suppose so. I never got around to it, what with one

thing and another.'

'So, this body. It was in your garden?' Stupid woman, of course it was.

'Yes. It's been a difficult few days, Susan. I've only come into town for the first time today, as a matter of fact.' Even Susan can't be too dense to realise this is code for please shut up, but no, she carries on regardless.

'The thing is, Lilian, I can't help wondering. I suppose I could go to the police and ask, but I don't like to somehow.' She hesitates, fiddling awkwardly with her teacup.

'What did you want to ask, Susan?'

'I wanted to ask… if it's Reg?'

'Are you saying you think that body's Reg and I put him there?'

'No, I was only wondering if…'

'Well it sounds like you are. And I'm happy to tell you it's not Reg. The police have confirmed it. So now you know.' Susan is silent for once, and I take advantage of the fact to gather my belongings.

'I'll say goodbye to you now, Susan. And if Reg does ever get in touch with you, please let me know. I'd be very interested to know what he's been doing all these years while I've been bringing up our child on my own and putting up with malicious gossip from people like you.' Her mouth is still opening and shutting like a goldfish as I walk out of the door, feeling a deep sense of satisfaction, together with dread that I've poked a hornet's nest. I'm trembling as I turn out of the coffee shop, trying to get my bearings, but I take myself in hand and go into the supermarket for the milk. I choose a biography from the library and go home. Despite everything, the outing has done me good and the book will be a distraction. Even though the encounter with Susan was unnerving, it's provided me with some new information. She clearly hasn't been interviewed by the police yet, although I know it's only a matter of time before they talk to her. Is she clever enough to work out the implications of Harry having been found? I don't think so, but her daughter might be.

When I get in the telephone starts to ring. I haven't heard it in the last day or so, and I forget it might be an unwelcome caller. I snatch the receiver up before it diverts to the answering machine, expecting it to be Joanna on the line, and hoping she's all right. I'm startled to hear a loud, male voice.

'Good morning, Dr Templeton. It's Alan Stewart from the Hull Daily Mail. We've been informed that the body found in your garden earlier this week is a Mr Harry Johnson, and he was a friend of yours in the past. Would you like to comment on this? Our readers would be interested to know more about him and why he ended up in your flowerbed.'

'No, I wouldn't like to comment. And he wasn't in the flowerbed.'

'Oh? Where exactly was he?'

'He was in the…' I catch myself just in time. He'll get all sorts of information out of me if I let him, especially if I allow myself to get angry. 'I've no comment to make on the matter.'

'Are you sure? Because we'll be running the story tomorrow and I know what our readers will think if it looks like you're hiding something, Dr Templeton.'

'I've nothing to hide, young man. And don't come knocking on my door either. I've nothing to say to you. Goodbye.' I put the receiver down with a bang, although my hand is shaking. Who have they been talking to, and what will the papers say tomorrow?

Chapter 8

Lilian only just recognised Reg's sister in time. She could barely remember meeting Susan at the engagement party and the wedding, and she had to think quickly in order not to look rude. She looked different, of course. She'd had her best clothes on at their previous meetings, and she was now dressed dumpily in a shapeless cotton dress and sandals, her hair wound in an untidy plait around her moon-like face. She carried a knitted bag that looked like something her grandma had made and she appeared to be hot and sticky in places Lilian preferred not to think about.

'I don't know what to do, Lilian. And you're the only person I can think of who might be able to help. Have you got time for a chat?' Susan stood awkwardly on the doorstep, clearly waiting to be asked to come in.

'I can't ask you in, Susan. Mother's not well. I could come out for a bit, though. Shall we go for a walk?'

'Oh, yes, thank you Lilian. I'm sorry about your mother. I'll wait here while you get your bag.' Susan looked around her furtively, and Lilian wondered what on earth she was doing. Didn't she want to be seen with her?

Lilian called to her mother to let her know she was

going out. There was only a murmured response, which was all she expected. Grace used up all her resources coping with work and spent most of her time at home lying down.

It wasn't the best of days for a walk. The air felt heavy with moisture and there was no breeze to cool them. Even so, Lilian didn't want to bump into anyone she knew, so at her suggestion they walked through town and up onto the Westwood. After exchanging pleasantries on the way, they found a bench near the trees and sat down.

'What did you want to talk about?' Lilian asked, although she hoped she knew.

'It's Reg,' said Susan. There was a pause and Lilian wondered if she was supposed to fill it. She didn't know Susan well, but from what she'd gathered she was like most of Reg's family. Well-meaning but not much else. Still, she'd got herself here from the farm outside Driffield, which was no mean feat.

'Is he all right?' Lilian asked.

'No, Lilian, he's not all right. That's what I've come to see you about. To ask if you could do something for him.'

'I'd be happy to help in any way I can, Susan, but why me? There must be plenty of people who know him better than I do. I didn't spend much time with him, you know. It was Frances who was my friend, not Reg.'

'Oh, I know. But everyone else has tried and we're getting nowhere, and his living so far away doesn't help.' Lilian smiled inwardly at this. Beverley was less than twenty miles from Driffield, and easily reached by bus or train, but it was a world away from the farm in Susan's mind.

'No, I don't suppose it does,' she said.

'We've done our best, but I can only come once a week, and the rest of the family are busy on the farm. They say he'll pick up, but I've been to see him this afternoon, and he isn't picking up at all. The house is in a state and he won't let me clean up for him. He hasn't gone back to work. He just sits there all day staring at the walls from what I can see. And he won't talk to me. I'd ask his friends to try but I don't know how to get hold of them. I doubt they'd make a difference anyway, the way he is.'

'No, I don't think that would help. I wouldn't have thought they'd know what to say to him.'

'But you would, wouldn't you Lilian? You're a doctor after all. You must have had to deal with people in this situation before. Haven't you? Oh, I'd love to scoop him up and take him home with me, but I know he wouldn't come. He says he wants to stay where he is because it's where Frances was. He says he'll never leave that house as long as he lives because it's where they were happy together.'

Lilian's stomach lurched when she heard this, but she told herself Reg was grieving and was bound to change his mind eventually. She would encourage him to go back to Driffield. It was a good idea – probably the best one Susan was ever likely to have. It was obvious at the wedding that Reg's family were put out that he didn't want to take over the farm. They seemed to think he was getting above himself, coming to Beverley and wearing a suit to work. Maybe it was time for him to go home.

Lilian realised Susan was waiting for her to say something, and she gave herself a shake.

'Sorry, Susan. I was thinking about Reg and the best way forward. You're right, I have come across people in this situation before, and I might be able to help him. Would you like me to go to the house and talk to him?'

'Oh, Lilian, would you?' Susan's eyes filled with tears and she fumbled in her knitted bag for a handkerchief. 'I'd be so grateful. Will you try to get him to come home? So we can look after him? Maybe he'll even decide to take on the farm. That would be wonderful.'

'I'll see what I can do.' Lilian patted Susan's chubby knee and asked if she'd like her to walk her back to the station.

'Oh, I came on the bus. It's cheaper, you know. Dad will pick me up at the other end in the tractor. I said I'd be on the three thirty.' She looked anxiously at her watch, plainly incapable of coping if she missed her designated bus.

'Well I'll walk you to the bus station then, it's not much out of my way. Perhaps you could give me your telephone number? So I can let you know how I get on?'

'Oh, yes, that's a good idea.' Susan scrabbled in her bag for a pencil and some paper. Lilian wasn't the best at keeping her own handbag tidy, but she shuddered to think of what Susan's was like if the noises coming from within were anything to go by. After removing a dirty comb, several bus tickets, a battered leather purse and an unsavoury wad of tissues, Susan finally unearthed a stubby pencil and an old shopping list. She wrote the number carefully and laboriously in a rounded hand; Lilian took the paper with her fingertips and put it delicately into her own bag. She didn't plan to use the number more than was strictly necessary, and she had no intention of giving her own in exchange, but if she made a call or two it would at least prevent Susan from turning up on her doorstep again.

Lilian walked home slowly from the bus station, considering her next move. It was good that Susan had approached her. She had been going to call on Reg anyway now a month had passed since Frances's death, and Susan's request gave her a plausible reason to do so. Not so welcome was the news of Reg's determination to stay in the house. Hopefully, it would turn out to be part of the grieving process, but she would need to plant the seeds of the idea of moving as soon as possible. It was what Susan wanted, for which Lilian was grateful.

Lilian knew she had only one chance to make this work. If she put Reg off at the first visit, she couldn't imagine getting a second opportunity. She tried to imagine the scene when Susan went to see him knowing what she did of Susan – even though it wasn't much – she doubted she would have had the force of personality to make Reg do anything he didn't want to. He was her big brother after all, so neither of them would have been accustomed to her telling him what to do. Susan would have been kind and gentle, easily upset if Reg shouted at her, and Lilian was sure he would have done. He must be feeling like a wounded animal, hiding himself away from anyone who might talk to him about Frances, taking whatever comfort he could from being in the place he could remember her best. Lilian didn't know what it was like to have someone who you loved die, but she had read enough books to get the general idea.

She decided a no-nonsense approach would be best. She wouldn't take no for an answer. She'd march in as soon as he opened the door and take charge. She would wear her old clothes, ready for cleaning, and she would take milk, bread and a ginger cake. Everyone liked her ginger cake. Her mother had given her the recipe and it was the only thing she could make with a guarantee of success. She smiled to herself as she thought of the different ways in which the cake had helped her to achieve her purposes in the past. At least this time she could stick to the original recipe.

***

Lilian didn't tell her mother where she was going. There would have been too many questions, and she didn't want to upset her with thoughts of Frances and her untimely death. They had been to the funeral together and it had taken Grace several days to get over it. Lilian didn't want another episode like that. She waited for a day when her mother was working and she had a day off from the hospital and started baking as soon as she had the house to herself. She knew the smell would linger so she made two cakes, one for Reg and the other to share with her mother at teatime. She put the cake in a basket along with a pint of milk, a loaf of bread and cleaning materials, and she was on Reg's doorstep by late morning.

As she knocked on the door Lilian wondered if Reg would be up yet. She knew from bitter experience what the behaviour of a person with depression looked like, and she prepared herself for Reg to answer the door in his pyjamas. Assuming he answered at all. There was no response at first, so Lilian shouted through the letterbox.

'Reg, it's me, Lilian. I've brought you some milk.

Susan asked me to come and I won't go away until you open the door, or she'll be cross with me. I'm going to lean on the doorbell until you do, so you might as well get on with it.' She was prepared to say she didn't mind seeing his pyjamas, but she though it would do him good to get dressed, so she didn't. Lilian put her basket down on the step and leaned on the bell as promised, looking around her as she did so.

She had only been here once before. She hadn't wanted to come, but Frances had insisted, and it would have looked rude not to, so she had. It had been a short visit. Reg had been home and in a bad mood. He had someone coming over and he wanted Lilian out of the way. Lilian thought she could guess who it was, as she'd been out with Harry the night before, and she was happy to take the hint and leave, after a short guided tour from Frances. It had looked run down then, and she couldn't imagine it had improved since. Frances had told her Reg had over-extended himself with the mortgage and they were barely managing to get by. She'd wanted some shelves for the bedroom, but they'd had to make do with home-made ones using some bricks and planks she suspected had come off the back of a lorry.

'Harry gave them to Reg, so I expect they'll have come from somewhere I'd rather not know about,' she'd said. 'But at least I've got my shelves, I suppose.' Lilian felt a small pang of sadness for Frances, who'd had so few of the things she wanted in life. She was probably better off dead, she thought. At least she wasn't living in a run-down house with a jealous husband, no money and even fewer prospects.

It was a quiet road, and Lilian knew it could be a wonderful place to live, with the Westwood only yards away. It was a bit out of town she supposed, but what was wrong with that if you had space and tranquillity? Her thoughts were rudely interrupted by the door opening and Reg scowling at her. She lost her balance momentarily and had to put her hand on his arm to right herself. Interestingly, he didn't brush it off. When was the last time a woman touched him? And how much had he missed it?

'What are you doing here?' he growled, his voice husky from underuse. He had dressed himself, but he looked as if he had done it with his eyes shut, and his face was gaunt and stubbled. Lilian took a step back, trying not to wince at the unwashed smell.

'I told you. Susan asked me to come. Are you going to let me in?' Lilian didn't wait for an answer, but marched through as if she owned the place, brushing Reg to one side as she headed for the end of the corridor, where she remembered finding the kitchen on her previous visit.

'But I don't want you here. Why did she ask you anyway?'

'Because I'm a doctor and Frances's friend. And because she thought I could help. And, Reg, because she was at her wits' end worrying about you.'

'She doesn't need to worry. I'm all right. I don't want people interfering.'

'I'm sure you don't, but you're clearly not all right. Look, I know you don't want people here, but you do need some help. I'm going to clean up a bit, leave you some supplies and then go. You don't have to talk to me, you don't even have to look at me if you don't want to. You can sit in the front room or go back to bed if you want. I assume that's where you've been most of the time?' He nodded, stunned by the flow of words, and, no doubt, by the authority in Lilian's tone. Something she guessed he'd not heard much of since leaving home.

Lilian didn't wait for any further response but set to work, starting with the mound of dishes in the sink. Reg watched for a few minutes and then shuffled off. Lilian didn't know where to and she didn't much care either.

It took her three hours to put the kitchen fully to rights, and by this time she thought she deserved a coffee. She couldn't find any, and had to make do with a few dusty tea leaves, lingering in the bottom of the caddy. She made a pot and sat at the kitchen table to drink it and to eat a slice of the ginger cake. Not wanting to see what the rest of the house looked like, she called to Reg on her way out.

'I'm off now, Reg. There's a pot of tea and a slice of cake for you in the kitchen. I'll be round tomorrow with something for your dinner. Don't make me lean on the bell or I'll leave it on the step for the foxes. Bye.' She slammed the door behind her without waiting for an answer and headed for home, a small smile on her lips.

***

It didn't take long. She hadn't thought it would. She had judged him to be weak and easily persuaded, and she was right. He quickly succumbed to her efforts to feed him, and within a fortnight they had fallen into a routine.

Whenever her shifts allowed - which was at least three times a week – she would take him a meal. It was easy to cook a third portion at home. Her mother wasn't in a state to notice the extra food, which Lilian would take to Reg and warm up on the stove. To begin with she left him to it, picking up the dishes at the next visit. But as time went on, she started to linger, and within a month she was staying on to do the washing up, talking about the weather and other undemanding topics while he ate.

It was Lilian who helped Reg get back to work, and Lilian who taught him how to look after the house, although he never mastered the art of cooking. When she called Susan after the first two weeks, there was plenty of good news to report.

'Well the house is clean at least, and he's eating again. And talking a bit as well.'

'Oh, Lilian, that's wonderful. You're so clever. Have you talked to him about coming home yet? D'you think he will? Has he gone back to work?'

'Not yet, Susan. He might be ready to get back to work soon, but he still talks about the house a lot and how it helps him to be there. I think we'll need to wait a while longer before suggesting he goes back to the farm.'

'All right, I'm sure you know best. You've done wonders already, Lilian. I'm so grateful.'

'You're welcome, Susan, I'm glad to able to help. I'll keep taking him his dinner for a while longer, then once he's back at work I'll suggest he starts using those ready meals they sell in the supermarket. He's got a little freezer in the fridge; I'll fill it up for him.'

'Thank you, Lilian. I will pop in and see him myself, but it's hard to get away right now. The farm's really busy and Mum's not been well.'

'Don't worry, Susan, I'll look after him.'

'And you won't forget to mention coming home, will you?'

'I won't. Goodbye Susan.'

Lilian had as much reason as Susan for wanting Reg to go back to the farm, and she didn't waste time in suggesting it. She waited until Reg was back at work before raising the subject, reasoning he'd be in a better frame of mind to consider a change once this had happened. He was finishing a portion of shepherd's pie when she brought it up.

'Have you thought about the future, Reg? Will you stay in Beverley?'

'Of course I will, Lil. Why wouldn't I?' Lilian hated him calling her that. Only Frances had called her Lil, and hearing Reg do it reminded her too sharply of what had happened. She bit her tongue. It wouldn't help to get cross with him, and it wasn't worth the bother of asking him not to use the name.

'I wondered, perhaps, with Frances gone, if you might want to go back to your family, to the farm. I know Susan wants to have you home. She'd love to look after you herself, and you're so far away from her here.'

'Yes, and that's the way I like it. I hated the farm and I'm never going back. It runs you into the ground, farming does. I've seen what it did to my dad and now my mum as well. The best thing I ever did was leave to go to college and find a job here. Apart from Frances. Marrying her was the best thing that ever happened to me.'

'Of course it was, Reg, and I can't imagine how much you must miss her. But wouldn't it help you to be with your family at such a hard time? Being part of a busy house with plenty of people to talk to might help to take your mind off things.'

'You wouldn't say that if you knew my family. All

they can talk about is the farm. If I went back there, I'd get sucked into it all and I'd never leave. I couldn't stand it.' Lilian thought she knew Reg's family far better than he realised if Susan was anything to go by, and she secretly agreed with him. But she owed it to Susan and to herself to do her best to persuade Reg otherwise.

'I'm sure you're right, Reg, but maybe it would be worth a try, just for a short time? To give yourself a break from having to look after yourself? And it would stop them all nagging you to go home, at least.'

'They're not nagging me any more. I think they've given up on me. Even Susan hasn't come to see me for weeks. It's out of sight, out of mind with that lot. And anyway, I can't leave this house. It would feel like I was abandoning Frances. No, Lil, I'm going to stay here and do it up exactly how she would have wanted it. I know she had her plans. We couldn't afford to do much before she died, we didn't have the money for it. But she would have done. I know she would. And I'll do it for her now, even if it takes me till I die.'

Lilian was silent. There was nothing more to be said. She cleared away the dishes while Reg went into the garden to have a cigarette, and left without saying goodbye.

Lilian walked home across the Westwood. It was a long route, but she needed to think, and she had always found this was the best place to do it. The huge sky against the green of the pasture calmed her, and she sat on the bench around the Black Mill, staring at the minster while she gathered her thoughts.

Although encouraging Reg to go back to the farm was Susan's main purpose, it had been a means to an end for Lilian. It would have been so easy, if he'd agreed to it, for Lilian to suggest she buy the house from him. She'd have given him a good price and she'd have been a cash buyer. She had almost enough in the bank already and could have given him the rest in less than a year. This was clearly not going to happen. There had been steel in Reg's voice, and an undercurrent of anger, even though he'd not fully expressed it. She knew there was no point in raising the subject again.

Lilian had experience of her plans not working out, and she was confident in her ability to come up with a solution to this problem. It was only a matter of time, and she would sit on this bench until an idea came to her. She tried to think logically. Her objective was the house. She had to have it. She had never been more certain of anything in her life. She had planned to buy it from Reg, but that wasn't going to happen. So, what was the alternative? There was no point in killing Reg. If she did, it would pass to his parents as his nearest relatives. Or whoever he'd named in his will. If he had one. People like Reg often didn't bother with such things. Maybe they'd sell it to her? No, it was too complicated. They'd wonder why she wanted it and there would be too many questions, which she couldn't risk. There would also be the problem of covering up Reg's murder. It would look suspicious if he died of a heart attack too, and she didn't know how else to do it. She would have to think of something else.

If Reg had died first it might have been easier to get Frances to sell her the house. It was a shame he hadn't, but she'd never have had the opportunity to get to him like she did with Frances. If Reg had died first…the house would have gone to Frances as his wife. And if Reg married again…the house would go to his new wife if he died. Hmmm. If Reg married again, Lilian could befriend his wife and then kill her, and maybe he'd sell up then. No, that was a stupid idea. There'd be suspicion, and who knew if Reg would ever marry again, and if he did it might not be for…

Lilian's thoughts halted as abruptly as if they'd been a car brought to an emergency stop. Who was the person Reg was most likely to marry? Who was looking after him? Bringing him meals and filling his fridge? Who could get him to depend on her, start to like, and even love her? And who could then get pregnant, have a child, and divorce him, getting the house for herself?

Problem solved.

***

It was like taking sweets from a baby. Once she knew what she had to do, Lilian acted with military precision. She told her mother about Reg, having kept it from her until now. Grace approved of her kindness and even helped with cooking extra food. Lilian didn't tell her where the house was. It might have raised her mother's suspicions, and there was no need for her to know yet.

Lilian went back to Reg's house two days later, behaving as if nothing had been said about his moving out. She continued to visit every couple of days but started to bring the food to cook in his kitchen so as to be with him for longer. She gradually improved her appearance, wearing dresses instead of casual clothes, and applying a bit of make-up. She went to the hairdressers and got her hair cut in a style reminiscent of Frances's. After a few weeks she suggested Reg give her a spare key so she could be there when he got home with a meal ready for him. He thought it a good idea and handed it over readily. There was no talk of frozen meals or of the farm. When Lilian called Susan on the telephone she was reassuring and cautious in equal measure.

'He's doing well, Susan, but he's fragile, I'd say.'

'What do you mean, fragile?'

'Well, he's not ready to cope on his own, for a start. I put some easy things to cook in the freezer for him but when I checked a few days later, he'd not been eating much other than beans on toast and the kitchen was a mess, all the dirty dishes piled up in the sink like the first time I went.'

'Oh, dear,' Susan sighed. 'If only he'd come home, he wouldn't need to worry about any of those things. Have you talked to him about it?'

'Yes, and it only makes him angry. He's still set on staying in the house. I've tried to persuade him to think about going back to the farm, but he won't. I don't want to bring it up again with him Susan, in case it makes him worse. It's part of the grieving process, I'm sure. It's still only a few months since Frances died. Give him time.'

'I will, thank you Lilian, you're so wise. And so kind. I don't know what Reg would have done without you.'

What indeed, thought Lilian, with his family unable to think of anything other than their precious farm. They'd not been to Beverley since she started looking after him, only too glad to let her be their dogsbody. Well, they'd only have themselves to blame if they didn't like the outcome.

As Christmas approached, Lilian stepped up her campaign. She arranged her shifts so she could be at Reg's almost every night. Her mother raised no objections, and Lilian wondered if she was beginning to consider Reg as a marriage prospect for her daughter. They were both well aware of the delicacy of Reg's position as a newly widowed man, but Lilian suspected her mother was hoping against hope she wouldn't be an old maid forever.

At the beginning of December, Lilian took the day off and went on the first bus into York to do some shopping. She bought fairy lights and decorations, tinsel and mince pies, which she knew she could pass off as home-made. She had arranged for a tree to be delivered and it was there when she got to Reg's house in the early afternoon. There was just time to put everything up before Reg got home. Lilian even found Frances's drab home-made decorations from the previous year. She remembered Frances droning on about how she wanted the house to look nice even though she had no money, and she knew Reg would be pleased to see them.

Lilian lit the fire and changed into the new red dress she'd bought in York. She put a frozen chicken pie in the oven and mince pies on the kitchen table, and she was getting a stool to stand on so she could put the star on the tree when she heard Reg's key in the lock.

Reg came in and stood still in the doorway.

'Reg? Is this…all right? Have I done the wrong thing? I wanted to make it feel welcoming for you at Christmas. I know how hard it must be. Look, here are Frances's decorations from last year on the tree…' Lilian looked at Reg and saw there were tears in his eyes.

'Oh, Lil. It's more than all right. It's wonderful. You've been so good to me, Lil…' Reg sank into a chair and put his hands over his eyes. 'I'm sorry, Lil. I can't help it. I feel so sad and yet I can't help but feel happy too, seeing you here. You've taken such good care of me, and it all looks so lovely…and you look so lovely too… Oh, come here, Lil.'

Lilian went over to the chair and his outstretched hand, and he pulled her towards him and into his lap. She gasped with the shock of it, but she didn't stop him gently pulling her face towards him for a kiss.

Chapter 9

The doorbell rings persistently at seven o'clock and I jump out of bed in in a blind panic. It's the police, come to arrest me. I rush through my plans in my head as I pull on a dressing-gown. They'll all be for nothing if I don't have any prior warning. If they arrest me will they let me come home after questioning? How do these things work?

As I make my way down the stairs the telephone starts to ring. I let it go to the answering machine and open the door. There are at least a dozen people on the step. They're holding notebooks, cameras, phones, even a microphone, and they all speak at once, cameras flashing.

'Dr Templeton, tell us about the body.'

'Did you kill him, Dr Templeton?'

'Was Harry Johnson your lover?'

'What happened to your husband? Did he kill Harry?'

'What have the police said to you, Dr Templeton?'

I blink in the morning sun, stutter 'No comment,' and slam the door, retreating as if it were on fire, and almost run to the kitchen, to get as far away as possible from the vultures on the doorstep. When the reporter said the story would be published today, I'd only thought of the print version. It didn't occur to me it would be online, and so early as well. I don't know who those reporters are, but I'm sure they're not all from the local paper. I realise they're not going to go away in a hurry and look in my bag for DI Twist's card. Like it or not, I'm going to have to ask for help.

'Hello?' She sounds much wider awake than I feel. I suppose police inspectors have an early start.

'DI Twist? It's Lilian Templeton here.'

'Good morning, Dr Templeton. How can I help you?'

'There's a crowd of reporters on my doorstep and I don't know what to do. They're asking questions about Harry, and it's all rather frightening. I don't know what to do, Inspector.' The shock has been enough to make my voice quiver without any effort on my part, and I think I sound close enough to tears to convince her of my helplessness.

'Close the curtains and don't answer the phone, Dr Templeton. You can either sit it out or we can move you again for a few days, whichever you prefer.'

'Which will make them go away quicker?'

'It's hard to say, but in my experience, they generally decamp more swiftly if there's no one in the house.'

'Could I go back to the Beverley Arms? I was comfortable there before.'

'I think somewhere outside Beverley would be wiser. We'll find you a hotel out of town. It should only be for a couple of days. I'll hold a press conference and tell them we're investigating various leads, but historic cases can take time to solve and they'll have to be patient. I doubt they'll think it worth hanging around for long.'

'Thank you, Inspector.'

'Pack a bag, Dr Templeton. Someone will be with you in half an hour.'

As I go up the stairs I wonder if the police will search the house again while I'm away. Even if they do, they won't find anything suspicious. And they could easily look through my bag before I leave. I can hardly pack a ginger cake and a bottle of vanilla essence. That would definitely arouse suspicion. No, safer to leave them where they are. It's the same principle as concealing a book in a library. No one will think anything of their being there. I'm pleased I moved the other things to the allotment. There'd be no way of hiding them in plain sight.

I pack enough for a couple of day s away and stay upstairs until there's another ring on the bell and I hear

Sergeant Carter calling through the letter box.

'Dr Templeton? It's Sergeant Carter here. Please let me in.' When I open the door, I see the reporters have taken a step back, and he comes in quickly and without fuss.

'Good morning, Dr Templeton. A bit of a commotion, isn't there? Don't worry, we'll soon have you out of here. I've told them you're leaving and there'll be a press conference at midday.'

'What will you say to them?'

'Well, it's up to the Inspector, but my guess is she'll say the investigation will take some time and there have been no arrests. It's easier for us to get on with our job if they leave you alone, so she'll say what needs to be said to make it happen.' I don't find this too reassuring. It sounds as if the comments will be more about giving the police a break than clearing my name, but I suppose it's the best I can hope for.

'Thank you, Sergeant. What happens next? I hope you're not going to tell me to rush to your car with a sheet over my head?'

'Not quite. Unless you'd prefer a sheet?'

'I think not.' I give him a wan smile.

'In that case, give me your bag, hold tight to my arm, and we'll go together. And whatever they ask, don't say anything. Is that clear?'

'I hadn't planned on saying anything, I can assure you, sergeant.'

'I mean it, Dr Templeton. They know it's their only chance, so they'll bombard you with questions, even if it's only for a matter of seconds. And you won't like some of them. It's important you don't react.'

'Yes, sergeant, I understand. My lips will be sealed.' He gives me a quick grin, takes my bag and opens the door.

I keep my lips tightly shut as promised, although the sergeant was right to warn me. It feels like passing through a tunnel of chimpanzees having a disco, with the questions and shouting and flashing of cameras all bursting out in front of my face. When the car door slams shut, I find I've been holding my breath and I don't care where they take me, as long as it's away from this maelstrom.

***

Sergeant Carter drives to a small hotel not far from Beverley. It's out in the fields, and he takes care to ensure no enterprising reporter has tried to follow us. I'm registered as Mrs Venables. The girl on reception doesn't pay any attention to me as I loiter by the display of leaflets for local attractions while he checks me in, and I try to hide my face. I don't know if the media have found a picture of me, but it's best to be careful. I can hear Sergeant Carter explaining that I'm recovering from an operation and don't want to be disturbed. He arranges for me to have meals in my room and escorts me upstairs.

Once in the room he tells me he or DI Twist will be in touch soon and he hopes I'll be comfortable. I'm still in shock and can't do much more than nod and thank him. Then he goes.

It's not yet nine o'clock, and I realise I've not had anything to eat or drink since I woke. I find I'm hungry despite everything, so I call down and ask for some breakfast. I unpack my few belongings and find the room is spacious, with a view across the countryside. There's a comfy chair and a desk. I'll be all right here for a few days.

When the food arrives, I put on the television and find a news channel. It's too soon for DI Twist to have held her press conference, but I want to know if the story's there. I spend some time watching the latest about American politics and natural disasters around the world, and then the announcer says it's time for the national news, and I sit up and pay attention.

There's a story about the queen, and then my house comes up on the screen and there's a reporter telling the whole world about the mysterious body found in a garden in Beverley. The shock of it almost deprives me of my power of hearing, but I focus hard, knowing it could be another half hour before the story comes around again. The reporter tells everyone my name and that I'm not available for comment, and there's a glimpse of me saying as much at my front door. He then says the body has been identified as Harry Johnson, a man who went missing over forty years ago and that the police will be issuing a statement later in the day. Then they switch to the bypass story, which seems to have gone on for days now.

I mute the television and lean back in my chair. I suppose I'd better phone Joanna. She's bound to hear about it from someone at work or through social media, even if she doesn't see it herself. I've never done much on my phone other than send texts and use the BBC news app, but there's no avoiding the fact it will be everywhere by now. I'm glad I don't have to look at any of it, and hope Joanna is able to stop herself. I dig my mobile out of my handbag, thinking it will cost too much to call her from the hotel phone, and someone could listen in if I do. I know she'll be busy teaching, but I leave a message telling her not to worry and that I'll call this evening. Hopefully, I'll have something more reassuring to tell her by then.

As the news stories play silently round and round in turn on the television, I consider what to do next. Despite myself, my thoughts wander, and I drop into a doze, lulled by the flickering images on the screen. I'm jolted out of it by the telephone ringing. Only the police know I'm here, and I'm not surprised to hear Sergeant Carter's voice on the line.

'Hello, Dr Templeton. You've settled in all right, I hope?'

'Yes, thank you Sergeant.' I know he's not called to enquire after my wellbeing, and I wait for him to elaborate.

'DI Twist asked me to confirm to you that there'll be a press conference at midday. It's likely to be on the local news, and she thought you might like to see it.'

'Thank you, sergeant, that's most helpful.'

'We'll be coming to see you this afternoon. At around three o'clock. The inspector wanted you to know.'

'Thank you, sergeant, I'll see you later.' There's not much else to say, and I put down the phone first to save him having to.

I remembered to bring my library book with me, so I don't have to subject myself to daytime television, and the time passes tolerably until shortly before noon, when I switch on the news. It's the national stories first, but then they switch to the familiar local news station, and I steel myself for the worst.

It's strange seeing someone I know on the television, and it takes me a moment to recognise DI Twist. She's at one of those long tables they use for these occasions, with Sergeant Carter and a man in a uniform with a little crown on it, who I assume is her boss. He speaks first and then hands over to her.

'We've been able to confirm the identity of the body as Mr Henry – or Harry – Johnson. Mr Johnson went missing in nineteen seventy-four. His body was well-preserved, and we were able to identify him through his

DNA.'

'Who was it matched with? Does he have a family full of criminals?' There's a smattering of laughter at this, but DI Twist doesn't look amused.

'I can't answer that question, as I'm sure you realise, due to data protection laws. It's not in the public interest to know how we identified Mr Johnson, only that we have done so. If anyone has any information about Mr Johnson's activities or acquaintances at the time of his disappearance, we would urge them to get in touch with us at the Beverley police station or on the number which should appear at the bottom of your screen.'

'What about the owner of the house? Is Dr Templeton a suspect?' My stomach twists. What will she say?

'We are looking carefully into the events of May and June nineteen seventy-four, and Dr Templeton has been able to help us with this. We are pursuing several lines of inquiry but we are not yet in a position to make an arrest.'

'Has anyone been taken in for questioning?'

'No. We'll issue a statement to the press if the situation changes.'

'What did Mr Johnson die of, inspector?'

'I'm not at liberty to say. In fact, I've given you all

the information currently at my disposal. Given the historic nature of this crime, the investigation is likely to take some time.' The questions start up again, but DI Twist exchanges a look with her boss who nods, and the three of them get up and walk away, leaving a somewhat deflated room of reporters behind them.

I turn off the television and stare out of the window while I mull it over. She didn't tell them to leave me alone personally, but she did tell them to leave the case alone. I have to admit she was helpful. There seems to be a chance the reporters will move on to more interesting matters for a while. Until she has something new to tell them, at least.

I realise there was no mention of Reg. Does this mean they've decided there's no connection? Or perhaps they've already got the information they need about him. I get out my phone and connect to the hotel wifi. I find the news programme on the TV catch-up service and watch the interview again. Yes, she asked for information about Harry, so they must be finding that hard to get hold of. And if that's the case, and they didn't mention Reg, perhaps they've got some leads on him already. Like Susan.

Chapter 10

Noise. It seemed as if the only sense working was her hearing as Lilian stood in the corner of the playground, wishing she could be anywhere but here. Without siblings or cousins to play with, her early childhood years had been spent in happy seclusion with her mother. Even her father had been a shadowy figure, out at work or golf, or reading his paper and 'not to be disturbed'. As a result, Lilian was completely unprepared for the company of other children, and while she had coped in the orderly classroom, the playground was another matter entirely. She only just managed to stop herself putting her hands over her ears, sensing this would not go down well if anyone were to notice her. Not that this seemed likely. The others were all too involved in their games to notice one little girl standing on her own under the big chestnut tree.

'Come and play!' Lilian jerked with surprise. She'd been looking up at the branches, wondering if there were any squirrels about, and hadn't seen anyone coming. A girl from her class. She couldn't remember her name. Lilian couldn't remember anyone's name and wasn't sure that she needed to. She didn't think there was anyone here she wanted to spend enough time with for it to be worth it.

'Come and play!' It was a command, not a suggestion, and Lilian found herself being dragged across the melee to a bench, which had been pressed into service as a jail. This looked interesting, thought Lilian. Still too stunned to speak, she waited to be enlightened. She didn't have to wait long.

'This is the jail, and Robert's in it 'cos he's a robber. I'm the sheriff and you can be my deputy.' The girl turned to Lilian as she said this, bestowing upon her the most beautiful smile that Lilian had ever seen. Framed by blond curls, she looked like Lilian's favourite doll, the one she'd been given for Christmas after gazing at it in the shop window for weeks.

'That's not fair! I want to be the sheriff,' said the boy behind the bench. 'And anyway, why should she be your deputy? What's your name?'

Lilian realised she would have to get her tongue to work after all.

'Lilian,' she said. Then, feeling braver, 'What's yours?'

'I'm Robert and this is Frances. She lives down my

road and she's very bossy.'

'No I'm not! My mum says I just like to have my own way. That's not being bossy,' Frances informed him. She turned to Lilian, 'I like your name. It doesn't sound like a boy's name. But it's a bit long. I think I'll call you Lil. You can call me Fran if you like, that's what my brothers call me. I've got four of them. Two are at this school and two are at the big school and I can fight them all. I can fight my sister too if I want to, but I don't 'cos she's nice. Let's pretend the prisoner's escaped. Robert, you have to run away, and we'll catch you.'

Arguments forgotten, Robert darted off, with Frances in hot pursuit. Lilian's hand was unceremoniously grabbed, and she found herself running and shrieking with unexpected delight across the playground.

Lilian never understood what drew Frances to her that day. Maybe she just needed another person for the game and Lilian was available. Whatever the reason, they stuck like glue, and by the time their differences became apparent, they were best friends. Lilian sometimes wondered if she would have ever made any friends at all if it hadn't been for Frances. She was naturally introverted, aloof even, but Frances had cut through all that like a knife through butter. Frances's games were never dull; she had too many brothers to be satisfied with the other girls' role play activities. Frances liked cowboys and Indians, spies and detectives, having absorbed such games from an early age. Lilian had a good imagination, nurtured by years of playing on her own and a precocious love of books, and she could make colourful contributions to Frances's scenes of combat and espionage. Frances was not an insensitive child, and her natural sense of kindness allowed Lilian to relax her guard and enjoy herself in the playground.

The classroom was another matter. This was Lilian's domain, and she quickly established herself as the brightest child in the class. Lilian didn't care about the stickers and gold stars the teachers handed her so freely, but Frances longed for them with a passion. Lilian would often give hers to Frances at the end of the day. It didn't matter to Frances that she'd not earned them, she just loved the glamour of wearing them and showing off at home. Later on, they would do their homework together, Lilian explaining patiently to Frances anything she didn't understand, and submitting to her attempts at beautification when they were done.

'Come on, Lil, let's do your hair like Rita Hayworth. We just need to curl it properly. Come here and let me try. Then you can make mine look like Marilyn Monroe.'

'All right, but you'll have to show me a picture.'

'Oh, Lil, when are you going to be allowed to go to the cinema? When you're a hundred?'

'If I'm lucky,' smiled Lilian, flicking through the magazine. 'Look, Frances, we could make you look just like Marilyn, you've even got her smile. Leave mine, I'll only have to take it all out again before I go home.'

'All right, but at least let me have a go at you with the make-up. That's quicker to get on and off, and you've got to get some practice in for when you get a boyfriend.' Frances seated herself on the dressing table chair and handed Lilian the hairbrush.

'A what? There's no way that's happening. I've got far too much work to do for school. I'm only here now because Father thinks I'm helping you with your homework.'

'And so you are, Lil. We're at home, aren't we? And I'd say getting you to agree to a bit of beauty treatment is extremely hard work!'

These sessions always took place at Frances's house.

They had been in and out of each other's homes since the first year of primary school, but soon after they moved up to the high school, Lilian knew this would have to change. She was helped by the fact that Frances's big sister had a plentiful supply of make-up and hair accessories that she was happy to share, while Lilian's home contained very few items of this nature. It wasn't long before they had fallen into a routine of spending time in Frances's house rather than Lilian's, and Lilian was glad Frances never asked her why she wasn't invited back. She wouldn't have known what to say. How do you tell your best friend you don't feel safe in your own home? And that you don't want to put her in danger?

As O-levels approached, Lilian knew life was about to change. Frances was going to leave school. She couldn't wait to get a job, earn enough to buy the clothes and makeup she hankered for, and get a boyfriend. Lilian's mind was full of problems at home, not to mention her studies. She had set her sights on becoming a doctor and was working as hard as she could to get high grades in her exams. There would be more of the same next year when she was in the sixth form, and she knew she would see less of Frances, although her friend had very different expectations.

'You'll still come round, won't you, Lil? I'll want to hear all the gossip from school, and I'll have lots to tell you about work. And we can go out at the weekends. We'll both have handsome boyfriends before we know it! It will be such fun to do nice things together instead of mounds of horrible homework.'

'I'll still come round if you want me to, but you'll meet lots of new friends at Woolworth's, and I expect they'll have more time for having fun than me. I'll have lots of work to do for A-levels and I'll need to spend more time with Mother now that Father's gone.'

'Oh Lil, of course you will. I'm sorry, how could I be so insensitive? How is your mum? I've not seen her since the funeral, and that was – what? Six months ago? It seems like ages to me, but I don't suppose it feels like that for you and your mum.'

'I don't know what it feels like, to be honest. So much has happened, it's been hard to take it all in, and Mother's in a daze most of the time. I don't know how she gets herself to work some days.'

'I can't imagine your mum working. Whenever I think of her it's in your old kitchen with a batch of cakes or biscuits. I used to love coming to your house when we were little. Your mum's cakes were much nicer than the ones in my house.' Frances got up and gently eased Lilian into the chair. She picked up the brush and started to smooth Lilian's straight brown locks, curling the ends gently around her fingers as she did so. 'You've not said much about how things are in the new house. It must feel strange. Not just the house, being just the two of you as well. I can't imagine what it must be like.'

'It's not too bad I suppose,' Lilian sighed. She let Frances carry on brushing, finding herself soothed by the long, smooth strokes. 'It's always been the two of us in many ways. Father was always out or reading his paper. It was a shock for Mother of course, but if I'm honest, I don't miss him much.'

'Oh, Lilian, how can you say that? I'd be devastated if Dad died. I can't imagine this house without him.'

'No, well, your dad's different,' said Lilian sharply. 'Your dad wouldn't go gambling all his money away and leave you and your mother alone and penniless with no home to call your own when he died. Your dad's different from mine in more ways than you can imagine. And sometimes I feel so guilty, because...' Frances had stopped brushing. Lilian looked at her in the mirror and could see that she was in danger of showing more of her feelings than was wise. She needed to change the subject.

'The house is tiny, of course, but I've tried to make it nice. My bedroom's so small you can touch all the furniture without moving from the bed, and there's only room for one of us at a time in the kitchen. Mother keeps saying how we should be grateful there's an inside toilet, but I'm afraid I can't get excited about that.' Lilian smiled at Frances in the mirror and saw her friend's face lighten again. 'Go on, carry on brushing. It feels lovely.'

'All right.' Frances picked up the brush again. 'You said you've tried to make the house nice. What have you done?'

'Oh, just a few bits really. I found some rugs and blankets from the old house and used them to brighten up the furniture in the front room. And there are some pretty cushions as well. They help to make it look better. We spend most of our time in there so it's worth making it as homely as we can. It's where the fire is, so I do my homework there; my room's too cold in the evenings.'

'What about the garden? You and your mum have always loved your garden, haven't you?' Frances was gently teasing Lilian's hair into small curls and arranging them around her head. Normally Lilian would have objected, but she didn't have it in her tonight. It was a relief to share her troubles with someone after keeping her thoughts to herself for so long. Staying cheerful for her mother had been a strain and even though Frances could talk all day if she fancied it, she was a good listener.

'It's hardly a garden. More like a yard. There's a bit of grass and the rest is paved. I brought a tiny greenhouse, so I've got a few favourite plants. Mother said we'd dig some beds and plant containers with herbs, but that was a long time ago. I don't think she's got the heart for it now.'

'I suppose that's natural. Maybe you'll do it, Lil. You're the cleverest person I know. I'm sure you'll sort it all out in the end. Maybe even help her get back into a lovely big house again one day, with a proper garden. You're easily clever enough to be a doctor or something like that. Look at how well you do in science. And they earn lots of money, don't they? I bet you'll grow up and whisk your mum off to a lovely house one day. There, look at yourself, Lil, don't you look gorgeous?' Frances held up a mirror so that Lilian could see the back of her head, which was now covered with small curls, pinned into place in an almost floral cap, from which flowed a gleaming curtain of glossy brown hair.

'It looks lovely, Frances. And do you know what? You're right. I will be a doctor one day. And I will earn lots of money. And I will definitely find my mother the house she deserves. I think I even know the one she'd like.'

'Oh Lil, you are funny. How can you know that? But you are wonderful too. Your mum's lucky to have you.' Lilian could see tears in Frances's eyes, and knew that it was she who was the lucky one.

Chapter 11

They arrive at three o'clock as promised and DI Twist suggests we go for a walk around the grounds. Apparently they're quite extensive and we're not likely to meet anyone, least of all reporters.

'I'm hopeful that after this morning's conference the press will decide it's not worth their while to hang around,' she says. 'The local papers may try to contact you, but I'm confident the nationals will go home for now. We'll keep an eye on your house, and with luck you should be able to go back tomorrow.'

'Thank you, inspector,' I say, and for once I mean it. I should have anticipated this level of press interest, I know. Although there's not much I could have done to mitigate it. I would have been better prepared for it perhaps, but as it's turned out I've appeared shaky and vulnerable, which is no bad thing.

'As you may have guessed, we've not had much information on Harry Johnson other than through his sister,' DI Twist says as we walk along a path crossing a manicured lawn. 'We're hopeful of getting a response in the next few days, but I suspect he'll turn out to be the sort of man people didn't want to admit to knowing.'

'Really?' I'm not sure what else to say, since I've only confessed to a limited knowledge of him.

'Would you agree with that assumption? Given what you know of him?'

'I couldn't disagree with it I suppose, but to be fair there was no proof of his being a crook, even though there was a lot of talk.'

'No smoke without fire, as they say. Not a popular saying, but one which all too often turns out to be true,' says DI Twist.

'I daresay.' I'm trying to sound non-committal, but I'd love her to think the worst of Harry. The blacker he's painted, the more likely she is to judge him worthy of a sticky end at the hand of persons unknown.

'Shall we sit down for a while? There's a nice view from this bench.' DI Twist indicates a seat at the end of the garden which overlooks the fields beyond. It's closer to an instruction than an invitation, and I sit. DI Twist positions herself in the middle, and Sergeant Carter perches at the far end, notebook in hand. So, this is where the interview begins. The rest was small talk, although no doubt he's recorded it anyway. I sneak a look at DI Twist. She's gazing into the distance, the usual vague expression on her face. I suppose she's an auditory learner as they put it, not a visual one. At any rate she doesn't seem bothered about seeing my face, and I wonder what this signifies.

'We've been talking to Reg's sister, Susan,' she says, without any further preliminaries. 'Her account of the months leading up to your marriage largely tallies with yours.' Largely? I wonder what this means, but don't want to ask.

'She also told us she bumped into you in town yesterday. For the first time in years, she said. Quite a coincidence.' I know what DI Twist thinks about coincidences, but this was the genuine article, and I feel bound to say so.

'Yes, she's only moved to Beverley recently to live with her daughter. I don't think she'd been there for years, so it's no surprise we've not seen each other before.'

'She told us how unhappy she was when Reg refused to go back to live on the farm. She still seems upset about it now.'

'Well I don't know why she should be. She got married herself soon afterwards, didn't she? To a farmer.

I'd say that's a coincidence if you're looking for them. So it all worked out fine in the end. I don't know what all the fuss is about.'

'She seemed to think your marriage was rather hasty. She'd wondered if you were expecting until Reg put her straight. It would seem she regarded Reg as quite a catch, having a good job and a house of his own. Did you always have your eye on him, Lilian? Was Frances's death a golden opportunity for you?'

'What do you mean?'

'Well, there you were, on the shelf as you put it, living with your mother, no prospect of marriage. And there was Frances, pretty, vivacious, always with a man at her beck and call. Were you jealous of her? Married to a good-looking man with a home of her own? And did you maybe see it as your turn when she died? Had you had your eye on Reg for a while, Lilian?'

'No, I had not!' I stand up in indignation. 'I was a doctor, for goodness sake. I had a healthy income of my own and could have bought a house whenever I wanted. I didn't need Reg. I was perfectly happy living with Mother. And I didn't need to go hunting for a husband. I could have had one any time; all I had to do was to snap my fingers.'

'Oh, yes?' DI Twist looks up at me from the bench. 'And who would you have been snapping your fingers for, Dr Templeton? Harry Johnson, perhaps?'

'No one in particular, but there was more than one junior doctor who'd have liked to see me outside work. And definitely not Harry. As I said, we went out once or twice, but he really wasn't my sort. What would a respectable physician like me want with a person like that?'

'Calm down, Dr Templeton. It was a simple question. Please sit down.' I do as she says, irritated with myself at having risen to the bait. I know she's trying to rile me in the hope of my giving something away, and I need to exercise some control. She pauses to allow me to settle myself, but I know she'll be at it again before too long.

'We're hoping to speak to one or two of Reg's friends about his relationship with Harry. Have you remembered anything more about it since we last spoke? Did Reg say anything specific about any plans they might have had together? Or whether there was anyone else involved? A third party we've not yet come across, perhaps?'

'No, I wish I could help you more, Inspector. As I've

said, he didn't introduce me to his friends. There were a few at the wedding, but I'm afraid I can't remember their names.'

'Not to worry, Susan has remembered one or two, and we've asked the estate agency for records of who was working there at the time. We'll find someone to help us before long.' Good luck with that one. There was never any dodgy plan involving Reg and Harry. They liked to go to the pub and the races together, and Reg was as carried away by Harry's stylish clothes and his fast cars as the girls were, but there was never any serious talk of them working together, never mind on anything illegal. It was a good story at the time, and it's still working well forty years on.

'We're now looking into Frances Blake's death. What can you remember about that?' It's an abrupt change of tack, and I'm taken off guard.

'Frances? What's she got to do with anything?'

'We're investigating anyone and everyone with a connection to Harry Johnson. He was connected to Reg, and Reg was connected to Frances. So we investigate her too. I'm not going to justify every line of inquiry to you, Dr Templeton. Please could you answer the question?

I'm tempted to say I won't answer anything I don't want to if I'm not under arrest or caution, but it would be asking for trouble.

'I'm sorry, Inspector. What was the question again?'

'What do you remember about the death of Frances Blake?' she asks patiently. I'd be irritated by now if I was in her shoes, but she's absorbed in some cows in the far field, looking at them as if they're the most fascinating thing in the world.

'Not much, other than it being so unexpected. I remember hearing about it at the hospital. She was brought in for a post-mortem, because it was an unexpected death. It was a great shock, particularly with her being my friend.'

'Yes, it must have been. So you weren't involved in the post-mortem yourself? You didn't see her medical records?'

'Oh, no, it wouldn't have been ethical, with my knowing her personally, even if I had been a pathologist, which I wasn't. She didn't have any medical issues though, that I do know. At least I assume not. I never asked her, but I'm sure I'd have known if she had. We were at school together, you know.'

'Would you say you were her oldest friend?' DI Twist asks.

'I suppose I must have been. Although she kept in touch with other girls too.'

'And what about you? Were you in touch with any other pupils from the school?'

'No. Most of them left after O-levels, and I stayed on and then went away to medical school. Frances was the only one I still spent time with when I came home for the holidays, and I wouldn't have seen her either if she hadn't been so persistent about it. We didn't have much in common by that time, but she liked to see me. For coffee or lunch, evenings out too, before she got married.'

'What about your other friends, Dr Templeton?' What on earth has this got to do with anything? Stick to the plan, Lilian, stay calm, be helpful, don't ask awkward questions.

'I'm in touch with a few people from medical school, but largely through Christmas cards. I was always too busy working and looking after Joanna and then Mother to spend much time with other people.'

'Coming back to Frances's death. Did you hear

anything about the post-mortem? In the hospital, I mean. Rumours of any kind.'

'No, what sort of rumours might there have been?'

'We've spoken to someone who worked there at the time who remembers there being some disagreement about the cause of death. It's rather vague though, and the hospital haven't been able to locate all the paperwork yet. I wondered if you'd heard anything.'

'No, I didn't. As far as I'm aware it was very clear cut. A heart attack. What else could it have been?'

'That's what we're trying to ascertain. We're still tracking down people who worked there at the time, and we're hopeful of finding out more within the next few days.'

'Well, I would expect the post-mortem report to have been straightforward enough. It was a heart attack, and that's that.' I know saying it won't make it true, but I can at least give myself hope that they won't dig anything up. 'I don't remember any rumours, although I was preoccupied with Mother at the time, and I've never been one to gossip. If there had been talk, I wouldn't have heard it anyway.'

'Very well, Dr Templeton, thank you for your help.

We'll be gathering more information about Frances Blake over the next few days as well as continuing our investigations into Harry Johnson and your husband. We'll have more questions for you in due course.'

'Perhaps I'll have moved back home by then,' I say, making polite conversation as we all rise from the bench and head back towards the hotel.

'Perhaps.' She gives me another of her non-smiles. 'There's no need to come with us, Dr Templeton. Why don't you stay here for a while and enjoy the fresh air?' Once again it feels like a command even though it's put as a suggestion, and I think it best to do as she says.

I sink back onto the bench with a sigh. So many questions about Frances. I didn't expect all this. But I didn't expect them to identify Harry. Or to be so interested in Reg. Maybe I should have read more detective novels in my time, then I'd be better acquainted with their methods. Who could they have talked to from so long ago at the hospital? Who had reason to suppose Frances's death wasn't a heart attack? What did they suspect it was? And were they right? I know these questions are going to torment me until the police tell me more, and there's absolutely nothing I can do about it.

Chapter 12

It wouldn't be long now. Out in the yard, before picking some parsley to go in the omelette she was planning for supper, Lilian scrutinised her monthly bank statement, even though she knew what it would say. She'd made enough surreptitious visits to estate agents to estimate that she only needed another thousand pounds. It had taken five years' saving, not to mention all the years of training, and she was nearly there. She'd been to look at the house a few times, walking along the road and then over the Westwood. She'd peeped over the fence and spied an old lady out in the garden a few times. She'd even spoken to her once, to say what a nice day it was. The garden was badly overgrown. She supposed it was too much for the old woman, and hoped when the time came, she'd be easily persuaded to sell up.

Lilian hugged herself as she thought of her mother's face when she told her. Not only the excitement of moving to a house with a big garden, but *that* house. The very one! It would be perfect. Lilian knew they could have moved to a better property before. Her salary would easily have covered the rent. But she'd wanted the Barn

House, and no other house would do. She owed it to Grace. All the problems of the past fourteen years were her fault, and she was going to put it right at last.

Lilian was increasingly worried about her mother. So much so, she nearly told her of the plan in the hope of cheering her up a little. But she resisted the temptation to do so. She wanted to wait until she could take her out there, walk her down the road and say, "Look Mother, it's yours!"

In the meantime, they must carry on coping as best they could in the poky terraced house near the railway. There weren't many trains going through each day, but you could hear every clack of the wheels over the rails, not to mention the drunks on their way back from the local pub. It was less than half a mile from their old home, but they could have been on another planet as far as her mother was concerned.

The only place which felt like home was the front room. Lilian had done her best to make it cosy, with a bookcase, pictures on the walls and colourful blankets on the chairs. There was a home-made rug in front of the fire, and Lilian always kept them well stocked with wood. It was her one extravagance. However deflated she felt, a fire could always cheer her up.

Outside was no more spacious than indoors. The yard was barely twelve feet square, and Lilian had needed every ounce of resourcefulness to make the most of it. She'd bought cheap pots over the years and filled them with herbs and geraniums, liking the combination of scent and colour. She kept two fold-up chairs under the stairs for the rare sunny days on which her mother could be persuaded to sit outside. And there was her greenhouse. Only a tiny one, but Lilian's most prized possession. She had to choose her plants with care. Where she had once had a dozen different orchids, she now had a precious pair, and other plants were carefully selected for their beauty or rarity. At the back was her faithful friend, Mr Monk. Even though he was the cause of all their troubles, he had also been her saviour, and she couldn't bring herself to get rid of him. She had surrounded him with cacti and other prickly plants, so there was no danger of her mother touching him, and she never worked in the greenhouse without long sleeves and gloves. There wasn't any real danger to her mother, Lilian knew; she would have been thrilled if Grace's depression had lifted for long enough to allow her to be interested in the contents of the little glass structure.

Lilian wondered idly if she would ever need to use Mr Monk again. He'd certainly got her out of trouble once, even if it hadn't ended as well as it might have done. How was she to know about the gambling debts? She'd have it all put right before long, anyway. Mr Monk was for emergencies only. Lilian couldn't imagine anything that bad happening again. She was clever and practical, and she believed she could solve anything life threw at her. Maybe she should get rid of the plant. But not yet.

Lilian took the parsley inside and started chopping. Omelette was one of the few meals she could make without mishap, and she allowed herself to think about her plans for tomorrow. She had the day off, and she would have a lie-in and a morning in the garden with her library book. She was meeting Frances for lunch, and then she had some shopping to do in the afternoon. Lilian sometimes wondered why she kept up her friendship with Frances. Perhaps it was because Frances was the only friend she had, because it certainly wasn't based on anything they had in common. Lilian didn't have a need for friends, and those who had made an effort in the past had soon slipped away through lack of encouragement.

Except Frances.

***

Lilian drummed her fingers on the table and wished she'd brought her book with her. Frances was always late. She didn't know why she was surprised or irritated, she should have learnt by now. She'd already told the waitress she would wait for her friend twice, and gave in the third time, asking for a lemonade so as to have something to occupy her while she waited. At last Frances rushed in, all flap and apologies.

'I'm so sorry, Lil, what must you think of me! A customer came in just as I was about to go off, and there was no one else free so I had to deal with him, and he wouldn't make up his mind. I mean, how important can it be whether your socks have got stripes or spots on? I ask you!' Frances sank into her seat with her usual drama, fully expecting to be forgiven. Lilian did, as always. It would have been too much bother not to.

'Not to worry. It gave me a chance to sit down for once. Now, what would you like to eat? My treat.' It was always Lilian's treat. There hadn't been much change in Frances's purse since she married Reg. You'd have thought two salaries went further than one, and it did nothing to improve Lilian's views on the downside of married life.

'Oh, thanks Lil, you're a doll.' At least Frances was good at thanking her, thought Lilian, and it made a change from sitting at home on her own. She decided to perk up and try to enjoy herself, even if the conversation centred on Frances's woes, as was the usual pattern. Food ordered, Frances sat back in her chair with a big grin on her face.

'Guess what?'

'What?'

'We've found a house!' Frances almost squealed with excitement, and a few people turned in their seats to see what the fuss was about.

'That's wonderful news, but there's no need to let the whole restaurant know.'

'No, sorry, Lil, but I'm so excited. I couldn't wait to tell you, but I knew if I started before we'd ordered I wouldn't be able to concentrate on the menu.'

'Well, you can tell me all about it now. Where is it? Did you decide to go outside Beverley in the end? Don't tell me you've found somewhere you can afford in town?'

'It's not in the middle, but it is Beverley. On the edges, more like Molescroft, I suppose. It's going cheap because the old lady who's in it now hasn't had anything done to it for years. It needs loads of work and modernising, but we'll do it gradually. Maybe we'll let Harry help out for once!' Frances giggled at the thought, but barely paused for breath before blurting out her story.

'Anyway, Reg heard about it at work. He was asked to go and value it, and he thought it might do for us as soon as he saw it. He got one of the other agents to look at it too, he said it all had to be above board. We couldn't let the old lady think we were taking advantage, could we? She's ever so sweet, Lil. She lost her husband a while back and now she can't cope on her own so she's going to live with her son. Anyway, the price was just low enough for us, with a huge mortgage of course, but we'll manage somehow. Oh, Lil, it's so exciting! We're hoping to move in before the end of September. You'll have to come and see it. You'll be our first visitor!'

The food arrived and Frances paused at last. After a mouthful or two, Lilian asked, her heart in her mouth, 'And does it have a garden?'

'Oh, yes, it's huge. It's rather overgrown. The poor

old lady hasn't been able to keep up with it on her own. And there's a big grassy area full of wildflowers. It's almost a field to be honest. And best of all, it backs onto the Westwood. You can see the trees and the cows, all the way up to the Black Mill.'

'It sounds wonderful. Does it have a name?' Lilian hoped Frances was too full of her story to wonder why she would ask such a question. Frances nodded vigorously, chewing frantically so she could answer.

'Yes. It's so nice to have a name rather than a number, don't you think? It's quite sweet really. It's called the Barn House.'

Lilian didn't choke. She didn't have any food in her mouth. She'd known what was coming anyway. Statue-still, she could hear a rushing sound in her head. She thought she was going to pass out. She couldn't faint, she couldn't stand the fuss. She made herself pick up her fork and take a mouthful to give herself time. Thankfully, Frances had not yet run out of steam.

'I asked why it was called that, as it doesn't look like a barn. And Mrs Tapping – the old lady – said it wasn't because of the house. It was because of the barn. The house used to be a farmhouse – some bits of it are really old, and others are added on more recently - and there was a barn opposite, but it's been knocked down now. I suppose it was where the two newer houses are over the road. I'd have preferred one of those to be honest. Much less work to do on them. But there's no way we'd have been able to afford it. Are you all right, Lil? You're looking a bit pale.'

'No, I'm fine,' Lilian said. 'It's a bit hot in here don't you think? I'll go to the ladies and splash my face. I won't be long.' And it might give you time to eat something while I'm at it. Frances had barely touched her meal, she was so busy talking. So busy crashing a wrecking ball through Lilian's wonderful plans.

***

She didn't go shopping. She didn't know afterwards how she got out of the restaurant or what she said to Frances. It must have been all right though, as Frances never said anything about it afterwards.

Lilian didn't even think about which direction she was going in when she walked onto the street. It was still hot, but she thought there might be a breeze if she went up the hill to the Black Mill, so she walked down Wood Lane and up onto the Westwood. Lilian had read somewhere about the colour combination of blue, green and white being intrinsically calming, and she found her heart slowing down at last as she walked onto the grass and saw the blue sky and scudding clouds above her. The wind caught her hair as she walked up the hill and she started to feel in control of herself once more. The Black Mill loomed in front of her, far more intimidating than its origins should suggest. She liked it, though. When they were young, she and Frances had made up stories about the prisoners locked inside and their dramatic rescues. They had been thrilled when they discovered Dick Turpin had been arrested and held prisoner in Beverley, and for weeks afterwards their games had featured a wide range of highwaymen. They had been badly deflated on discovering the mill really was no more than what its name suggested – an old windmill.

Oh, Frances. Her only friend. Not much wanted perhaps, but faithful and well-meaning. And part of her memories of a happier, more innocent life. What was she going to do? Lilian sank onto the narrow bench encircling the mill and looked back towards the minster. It was her favourite view of the town, along with most other people, she supposed. It took several minutes for Lilian to gather

her scattered thoughts, and even then, her mind was blank with shock. How could this have happened? If only she'd been able to get a mortgage instead of waiting until she had enough saved. But she'd need a man to co-sign the application, and she had no one to ask. Lilian pushed her anger away. It wasn't helpful. She needed to think.

Lilian spent half an hour on the bench and another hour striding around the Westwood before she felt her brain was working properly. She knew she had to think logically, scientifically, and she ordered her thoughts in her mind as meticulously as if she had been recording a delicate experiment in the laboratory.

First, what needs to happen? I need to get the Barn House. I've known it for years, I've planned for it for years, it has to happen. Lilian briefly considered buying a different house, but she knew it wouldn't work. She didn't have enough money for one thing, and her mother was getting worse by the day. She couldn't wait much longer to move her out of their cramped little home. It would have been different if she were a man, she could have borrowed money, but she wasn't a man. She only had enough – nearly enough – for that particular house, in its run-down state. And anyway, it was the one she wanted, the one her mother needed to get better. It was her fault – perhaps not entirely her fault, but Lilian blamed herself anyway – that her mother was in this state. It was up to her to put it right, and there was only one way to do it. The Barn House.

She needed to think of a way to stop Frances and Reg buying it. Could she tell them? Ask them to let her have it instead? Lilian might have been able to bear the humility entailed in such a conversation, but she didn't for a minute believe Reg would do anything other than laugh at her. Frances might want to help, she was a kind girl, but this was her big chance. She couldn't stand living at home with her parents any longer and she would be devastated to know she was hurting Lilian and her mother in this way.

She could go around to the house and ask the old lady – Mrs Tapping, was it? – if she could buy it instead. But she didn't have all the money yet, and why would the old lady wait for her when Reg and Frances were ready right now?

Lilian had the situation straight in her mind, but she still didn't have a solution when she got back home, tired and thirsty and unable to take another step in the heat of the day. Her mother was still out, and she supposed she'd have to go and do the shopping. She'd completely forgotten about it until she got the milk out for her tea and saw how little was left in the bottle. She opened the back door to let in some fresh air. There was some shade in the yard now, and she stood in it for a minute, gazing into space and wondering what the solution to her problem might be.

Lilian's eye fell on the greenhouse. She had so looked forward to having a bigger one in the Barn House garden. There was room for six little greenhouses like the one she had now, although one big one would do. She'd made such plans for that garden. Well, plans for her mother to have plans. It would restore her to her old self, she knew it would. She could give up work – Lilian earned enough for them both – and concentrate on the garden. They'd do the house up gradually, take their time, but the garden would get their attention first. Grace would look after the roses and Lilian would raise all sorts of wonderful plants in her greenhouse. She might even have a separate locked section at the back. She'd seen one in a big greenhouse in a stately home garden once. It had been for poisonous plants, so children wouldn't touch them by accident. She wasn't planning on children, but she wouldn't want her mother to come to any harm.

Lilian's thoughts stopped. Mr Monk. She'd enjoyed the dark humour of giving the plant its name when she first grew it all those years ago, and it still made her smile. Monkshood, wolfsbane, aconite, whatever you wanted to call it, it was growing in her greenhouse, ready to be picked and crushed and soaked and strained and baked in a cake to die for.

Chapter 13

How close are they to the truth? Will I be going to prison? I consider these questions as calmly as I can now I'm back in my own home. How much longer will it be my home, come to that? Another question to add to the list. The police have connected Harry to Reg and both of them to me. They don't know what happened to Reg yet and they don't have a cause of death for Harry. So far so good. But…they're looking into Frances. Did anyone have doubts about it being natural causes? I didn't hear anything at the time, but that doesn't mean it wasn't happening. And if so, how long before they connect her death and Harry's? And might they go even further back? It will depend on how they view me. So far, the questions have led from Harry to Reg and then on to Frances. If they start asking questions about me, who knows where they'll end up?

I decide there's no need for immediate action, but I must be ready to leave at any time. It would also be best to be prepared for the house to be searched again, and this time with poison in mind. If I want to remove the little bottle and the cake, I must do it now. I could leave them at the allotment with the other things. I think long and hard about this and decide to take the bottle out of the house. If I need the cake, it's likely to be at short notice and I won't have time to retrieve it. And if they do suspect something, liquids could easily be a focus. It might be best to remove that particular item.

There's no time like the present, so I cycle over to the allotment and put the bottle in the cracked pot with the other things. While I'm there I tidy up the beds and pick some late fruit and vegetables. Mother would have been pleased to know that I still come here, and I realise that the only thing left to do in settling her affairs is to transfer the allotment registration, which is still in her name. It's not worth bothering now, and I like the idea that she still owns this little patch of ground. The sun's shining and there's a crisp autumnal breeze in the air. The exercise is invigorating, and this is something I'll miss when I'm gone. The thought snags my brain, and I realise I've accepted I'll be leaving. I'm not sure if this is good or not, and stop digging, leaning on my spade to consider the question.

If I know I'll have to leave, why not go now? All the arrangements are in place. The house is already in Joanna's name and I'll leave her enough to be well provided for. I know she'll be all right. It might have been different if Mother had still been alive, but now that's she's gone there's nothing to keep me here. The idea of travel, finding somewhere new, is starting to appeal.

So what's stopping me? Perhaps a part of me isn't as ready to go as I thought. I love the house, the garden, my life here. I realise I'm torn. I'm ready to go but I don't want to leave. It doesn't make sense, but there it is. Let's wait and see how things turn out. I doubt whether they'll get enough evidence to charge me with anything, and when the case is dropped, I can make the decision in my own time.

I return to my spade and put the fruit and veg into my backpack. I'll drop it off at the women's refuge on the way home. I can't risk the police seeing it and asking where it all came from, and I don't like to see it go to waste.

***

I don't think I'll ever be able to hear a doorbell again without expecting to see a policeman on the step. At least it's not reporters, one must be grateful for small mercies.

'Good morning, Dr Templeton.' Polite as always, at

least before she comes into the house, DI Twist is looking particularly smart this morning. She's wearing a crisp white shirt under a navy suit with chunky gold jewellery at her neck and wrist. Her hair is decidedly less wispy than usual, in a sleek French plait rather than her customary untidy bun. I wonder if she has another press conference later in the day. Or maybe someone's given her a makeover.

Sergeant Carter is looking his usual preppy self. I don't suppose he'd have the nerve to try anything different. I wonder who will be asking the questions today as we settle ourselves in the living room.

'Do you have any further news, Inspector? About when the work in my garden will be resumed?' It's a little old lady preoccupation; I don't want to show an unhealthy interest in the case itself.

'Yes, we do, as it happens. We've spoken to the council and they say they can send the workmen back in around two weeks. They'll be in touch in due course,' says Sergeant Carter, clearly pleased to be able to impart some good news.

'But that's not what we're here to talk about,' says DI Twist.

'Oh? Doesn't it mean the investigation is closed?' I can't help myself from hoping this might be the case, even though I know it's highly unlikely.

'No, it doesn't. We've been speaking to various people and some new questions have emerged which we need to follow up with you.'

'I'll do my best to help, Inspector. I hope you know that by now. I simply want this whole unpleasant business to be over.'

'As do we, Dr Templeton, as do we. As you are aware, we've been looking into the death of Harry Johnson, the disappearance of your husband, and the death of Frances Blake. It seems remarkable to me that three people with whom you were intimately acquainted died – or disappeared – within a period of less than a year. Doesn't it strike you as strange?'

'I believe I've made it clear, Inspector. I wasn't intimately acquainted with Harry Johnson. Be that as it may, no, it has never struck me as strange. Frances's death was tragic, but I've not thought about Harry for years. And Reg's disappearance was extremely traumatic. I wasn't in any state to make connections to other people, and I never have. Life is full of tragedy and unexpected events, and some of them happen to occur close together. I never saw any significance in it, and I don't see any now.'

'We're not so sure, Dr Templeton. As I said to you before, we're looking into the possibility of Frances Blake's death not having been a heart attack after all. We're finding it hard to get hold of some of the people we need to speak to, but if there is any hint of it being from unnatural causes, we will have to consider a connection to Harry Johnson's death.'

'Well, I can't think why you would, but I suppose you have your methods.' I can hardly tell her how to run her investigation, but I don't like the way this is going.

'Quite. Now, moving on to Frances Blake and the circumstances surrounding her death. We've spoken to Susan Fanshawe again, and she has told us that she overheard rumours at Frances's funeral about Frances seeing another man. 'Fancy man' are the words she remembers being used. Is there anything you can tell us about that?'

'No, I can't. I'm shocked at the idea. Whatever made them say that, I wonder?' I'm thinking as quickly as I can. Might I be able to put this idea to good use? Open up another fruitless avenue for them to pursue?

'Mrs Fanshawe didn't have any more details. Apparently, the girls who she overheard stopped talking as soon as they saw her, and she didn't like to ask them. They were at Frances's funeral, after all. And then she didn't see them again. It wasn't something she wanted to dwell on, and she forgot about it until now.'

'I should think she didn't want to dwell on it. It would have been dreadfully upsetting for poor Reg. Although I don't suppose they'd have said such a thing without reason.'

'No, indeed. We found one of the girls - she's retired now, of course – who worked with Frances in the men's outfitters, and Sergeant Carter went to see her.' She nods towards him, a signal for him to continue with the questions.

'Oh, yes, I remember her working there. I think she quite enjoyed it, especially the gossip with the other girls.'

'Yes, that's what Mrs Barrett said,' agrees Sergeant Carter. 'She's the lady I've been talking to. I asked about the rumours and she told me Frances had often gone out for her lunch. The other girls brought their own sandwiches in. It wasn't common to go out, they couldn't afford it. So when Frances started going out once, and sometimes twice a week, tongues started to wag.'

'Maybe she was meeting Reg? He worked in town as well. I don't suppose they thought of that, did they?'

'No, they knew it wasn't Reg, because they asked her one day. Apparently, she gave them a wink and said no it wasn't him; she could see him any day of the week at home. And when they asked who she was meeting, she said…' Sergeant Carter consults the notes on his screen. 'Let me see now…ah yes, she said, "That's for me to know and you to wonder".'

I can't stop myself from gasping. I know all too well who Frances was meeting for lunch, and this is a gift I can't ignore. Sergeant Carter looks up sharply and DI Twist turns her head slowly towards me, breaking off from her contemplation of my bookshelves.

'Does that mean something to you?' she asks.

'Well, yes it does, Inspector. That phrase. It's what Harry Johnson used to say. Every time someone asked him a question he didn't want to answer, it's what he'd say. It was his catchphrase, everyone knew it. Reg even said it once or twice when he was talking about Harry.

Oh dear.'

'Oh dear what?'

'Well, do you suppose it was Harry she was seeing? Surely not, she always seemed so happy with Reg. At least, mostly happy, I suppose.'

'What do you mean by that?' DI Twist is sitting up straight now, and the sergeant has returned to note-taking duties.

'Oh, nothing much, they had the usual problems, I suppose. You know, the sort of thing you mentioned the other day, Inspector. The difficulties young couples can experience when they're first married. I didn't think they applied to me and Reg, but they may have done to Reg and Frances. Money, for instance. He'd taken out a big mortgage on this house and they were struggling financially. Frances would have liked to give up work and have a baby, but they couldn't afford it. And she didn't like the amount of time Reg spent with his friends.'

'Do you think she might have been seeing Harry Johnson?'

'Well, it had never occurred to me before, but she was a bit secretive in the weeks before she died. She didn't seem to have time to meet me very often. I'd hardly seen her at all during those last couple of months. Maybe she was seeing someone else. Maybe it was Harry – who knows? He was certainly a charmer and she was an attractive woman. Maybe they were both just having a bit of fun.'

'It's unlikely she'd have been able to marry him, though. His sister suggested he'd found someone who he was planning to be with permanently.'

'Oh, I don't know. Divorce was getting easier in those days. Frances was the flighty sort, and she was used to getting what she wanted. If she'd decided to get out of her marriage, she'd have found a way.'

'You seem very certain of that, Dr Templeton.' Have I gone too far? Best not to look too obvious.

'I don't know about certain. I'm simply trying to make sense of what you've told me, Inspector. I don't know anything definite about what Frances might or might not have done. I only know the phrase was one Harry liked to use. Maybe I'm putting two and two together and making five. I'm sorry, I'm not trying to do your job for you.' I give a little laugh, hoping it won't look as if I'm trying to put ideas into their heads.

'Oh, I wouldn't worry about it, we're always open to suggestions, aren't we Luke?' She gives her sergeant a smile that reaches her eyes for once, and I wonder if there's more than a professional relationship between them.

'Oh yes. All ideas gratefully received,' he replies.

'While we're on the subject,' she says, turning back to me. Oh, yes, what subject? 'Was Reg the jealous type?' Oooh, yes, I think he might have been.

'I used to think he was possessive. He didn't like Frances going to work, although she had to for the money. And he was pleased when I agreed to stop when I got pregnant. He liked the idea of having me at home, cooking his dinner and ironing his clothes. And he was never keen on my spending time with Mother.'

'How do you think he would have reacted if he'd found out later on that Frances had been seeing Harry around the time she died?'

'Oh, dear. It would have been hard for him. Even though she was dead, he still saw her as his wife. He mentioned her a lot, even after we were married. I didn't mind. I understood his need to talk about her. It was all so recent, and I knew he was still grieving for her.'

'How angry do you think he would have been?'

'I don't know, Inspector. I do know I took care never to mention my dates with Harry, even though it was over before I started seeing Reg. It wasn't a conscious decision, but I knew it would cause trouble. I can't put my finger on why I knew, but I did. Does that make sense?'

'Yes, it does. We often have strong feelings which we can't rationalise at the time, but which turn out to have been justified. We'll have to consider this information in the light of the inquiry.'

'Have you asked all your questions for today, Inspector? All the comings and goings these last few days have quite worn me out, and I think I need a rest now.'

'Yes, I think we're finished for now. Oh, yes, just one more thing.'

'Yes?'

'I don't suppose you have any records of your work shifts and holidays from that time? The hospital is having difficulty locating them.'

'No, Inspector. I wish I did. I'd love to know when someone was able to sneak into my garden without my knowing and put a body there.'

'Yes, exactly. There may be other ways to identify some dates. Maybe holiday photographs? Or perhaps a diary? I don't suppose you kept a diary then?'

'No, I didn't keep a diary. I'll look for photographs, though. I took some on all our holidays. I'll see if I can find any with relevant dates on them.'

'Thank you, Dr Templeton, that'll be helpful. We'll be in touch soon, no doubt. Please don't stand up, I know you're tired. We can see ourselves out.' I hear the front door close behind them and sink deeper into my chair.

A diary. No, I don't keep a diary. Oh, I used to, from my twelfth birthday, when Mother gave me a fat leather five-year diary with a lock and key. I had longed for it for months and wrote in it faithfully every night, buying a new one every five years. It was my best friend. I told it everything. About Mother, about Frances, about Him. I'd not been able to sleep until my day was on its pages, and even when I married Reg, I wrote in it every night. Telling him I didn't need much sleep, waiting until he was snoring, and hiding it under the spare room floorboards every night. And then he found it. I've never written a diary since, and I never will.

Chapter 14

Lilian found it was easier to plan Frances's death than she had anticipated. Frances had been kind to her in the past and Lilian had grown used to seeing her, but she'd not felt close to her for years. She briefly contemplated life without her only friend. She couldn't identify anything about Frances which she would miss once she was gone. Maybe she wasn't the friendship kind. She had lived with other students at medical school and shared with junior doctors at the hospital. It wasn't enough to make them friends, and Lilian knew it. She also knew the others had stayed in touch, attended each other's weddings, gone on holiday together. She had taken part in none of this and felt neither excluded nor overlooked. She simply hadn't been interested. Did this make her a psychopath? Lilian had only spent a short time on the psychiatric ward during her training, and she didn't feel qualified to answer the question. She couldn't dismiss it though. Did it matter? Probably not.

Lilian knew from experience how to make the mixture, and it wasn't difficult to get the house to herself. Coming back from a night shift, she had breakfast with her mother before saying goodbye as Grace headed off to her cleaning job in the hotel. Instead of going to sleep, Lilian retrieved her supplies from under the bed. She knew she couldn't use her mother's cooking implements and she had cycled into Hull a few days ago to purchase new ones, visiting three different shops in the process. If everything went according to plan there would be no investigation of Frances's demise, and certainly not one involving Lilian, but she liked to be thorough in her preparations.

Lilian set out the saucepan, jug, sieve, and pestle and mortar. She found an old spoon her mother wouldn't miss and tipped the dregs out of a small bottle of vanilla essence. Although the day was warm, she put on trousers and a long-sleeved shirt, which she buttoned tightly at both wrists and neck.

Lilian went into the yard and opened the greenhouse. The plant was tucked away right at the back. She didn't think her mother would venture in here, but she had always thought it best to keep it out of sight. She picked up the plastic gloves which lay on the shelf by the door and put them on, ensuring they covered her shirt cuffs. A new pair of scissors was in her hand , and she cut three strong stalks from the plant, stuffing them into a plastic bag before leaving the greenhouse.

Back in the kitchen, she laid the plants on the newspaper-covered table and surveyed the scene before her, making sure nothing had been forgotten. Lilian didn't ask herself if she wanted to go ahead with it. She didn't question whether she was doing the 'right thing'. She knew what she was doing wasn't right. But it was necessary. She'd considered all the options, and this was the only solution. She put on the face mask she'd picked up in the operating theatre the previous week. It wasn't strictly necessary, but it was as well to be prepared, and the mask was easier to breathe through than a scarf. She took a deep breath and turned to her task.

Lilian cut up the stalks into smaller pieces and placed them in the mortar a few at a time. She ground down heavily with the pestle, adding more pieces as they gradually turned to pulp. When the mortar was full, she tipped the contents into the saucepan of water which was coming to the boil on the stove. Picking up the spoon, she swirled everything around until it was well mixed. She left the saucepan to bubble away and went outside, where she tidied up the small yard and the greenhouse to pass the time while the liquid absorbed the contents of the plants.

Once the hour was up, Lilian strained the mixture into the jug and left it to cool. Now was the time for a nap. She set her alarm for midday and allowed herself to rest. When she awoke at twelve o'clock the mixture was sufficiently cool for her to pour it into the vanilla essence bottle. She knew she couldn't afford the risk of anything being contaminated by the plants or the residue, so she wrapped everything up first in the newspaper and then in a large plastic bag from the hospital. This went into the rucksack that she took to work. She'd go for a bike ride later and find a bin in one of the surrounding villages to put it in.

Lilian scrubbed the outside of the vanilla essence bottle harder than she'd ever scrubbed anything before and took off the gloves and mask. It was a strange feeling, looking at the little bottle. It seemed so innocent. And familiar. As she looked at it, Lilian felt a sense of calm descend upon her. The first step was complete.

***

It was hot. No surprise in July, but Lilian would have preferred a cooler day. She'd decided to make the cake that morning while her mother was at work. It was easier to do it while she was out than to explain why she was baking on a hot Saturday morning. She put on a pair of thin plastic hospital gloves as the cake cooled before pricking it all over with a pin. She then added the mixture from the little bottle, watching it trickle into the holes with satisfaction. The kitchen filled with the aroma of ginger, and she realised with dismay that her mother would smell it when she returned. She'd want to know where the cake was, and Lilian couldn't tell her she was taking it to Frances, it was far too great a risk. She realised she would have to make another one.

Sighing, she reflected that at least it would give her something to do while she waited for the first one to cool. Familiarity with the recipe made her deft, and by the time she turned out the second cake – on the table, not the counter, to avoid confusion – the first one was ready to go. Putting on her gloves again she wrapped it in greaseproof paper and then in a plastic bag from the supermarket. She put the cake in her largest handbag and left it ready by the front door.

Lilian decided she'd had quite enough of the kitchen for one day. Leaving the second cake to cool, she tucked the vanilla essence bottle away in a cracked pot in the greenhouse. It wasn't an easy job making it, and she thought it might be worth keeping. You never knew when such things might come in useful.

***

It was no cooler in the afternoon, and the bike seat chafed Lilian's legs as she pedalled her way to Frances's house. It was further out of town than Lilian remembered, or maybe it hadn't been so warm on her previous visit. The handbag slung over her shoulder didn't make things any easier, bumping against her thigh and trying to twist round in front of her. By the time Lilian reached Frances's door she needed a comb, a cool drink and some shade. The first was in her bag – one of the benefits of never sorting out its contents – and she assumed Frances would be able to provide the rest.

Lilian rang the bell. Frances had told her Reg would be going to the races with Harry today, and Lilian hoped fervently that she hadn't decided to spend the afternoon shopping or with her mother. Since Frances didn't have much money and her mother hadn't seen her since she moved house as she didn't like Reg, these possibilities were remote, but Lilian knew better than to assume anything. Fortunately, the hot weather had encouraged

Frances to stay at home, and after only a short wait she came to the door.

'Lilian! What a surprise! What are you doing all the way out here?'

'Oh, I was making a cake for Mother, and I remembered you'd said you were on your own today. I thought it might be nice to make you one too and bring it over.'

'That's so kind of you. And when it's so hot as well. Come in, I'm in the garden. There's a big shady tree and I'll get you a cold drink. It's water or squash, nothing more exciting I'm afraid. Or would you prefer tea?'

'Squash would be lovely, thanks. Oh, and here's the cake.' Lilian pulled it out of her bag and handed it over.

'Oooh, it's very well wrapped. I don't suppose you wanted crumbs in your bag, did you?' Frances chattered on as she led the way into the house. She was wearing a bikini underneath what Lilian judged to be a hastily pulled-on sundress, and she looked like a model in a magazine. Lilian marvelled at how easy it was for someone with good looks to make even clothes from Woolworth's look special.

'I've drunk so much squash today I'm surprised I

don't look like an orange,' said Frances, as she poured two glasses and looked in the freezer for ice. 'And I'd die without ice on a day like today, wouldn't you, Lilian?'

'Oh…yes, I suppose I would,' said Lilian, distracted by the garden outside. It had been dark the last time she'd been here, and she hadn't been able to see it. This would be her first chance to look at it properly. She knew she should offer to unwrap the cake, but she couldn't. She had to think of another way.

'Don't be shy about eating the cake, Frances. I made it for you and it's best when it's fresh. There's plenty for Reg as well so dig right in.'

'Oh, yes, I will. It was so sweet of you to make it.' Frances picked up the bag and took out a plate. 'Will you have some too, Lil? Ooh, it looks delicious, and it smells so warm and gingery – lovely!'

'Not for now, thanks, I had a piece with Mother after lunch and I'm still a bit full,' Lilian said.

'All right, maybe I'll tempt you to a slice later on with a cup of tea. You can stay for a while, can't you? Please say you can. It's lonely out here when Reg is away, and I get so bored.'

'That would be lovely,' said Lilian and she followed

Frances outside.

Lilian couldn't fathom how Frances could be bored when there was so much to do in this garden. Two unkempt flower beds bordered a path leading away from the house, and she could glimpse what looked like an overgrown lawn, or maybe a field, through a honeysuckle-covered archway at the end. She was itching to get her hands on a trowel and a pair of secateurs, and she knew her mother would have loved to put it all to rights. She kept these thoughts to herself and sat with Frances on one of the two deckchairs positioned on the weedy patio outside the back door. Frances sighed as she sank into her chair.

'Ah, this is the life, isn't it Lil? Sunshine, iced drinks and the best ginger cake in Yorkshire! You're a real pal coming out here today. I was feeling a bit down, and you're cheering me up already.'

'Were you? What about?' Lilian couldn't imagine why Frances should feel sad, and she didn't much care either, but she knew she ought to ask.

'Oh, it's Reg. He doesn't seem to remember we're married half the time. He's off with his friends more than he is with me. Late back after work, at the pub with his mates. It's not as if I don't work as well. You don't see me down the pub with my mates, do you? No, it's back home to have his tea on the table for when he doesn't get in.' Lilian watched as Frances paused for long enough to take a sip of her drink and a mouthful of cake. How much would she need to eat? It hadn't taken too long before, but she supposed the mixture could have been of a different strength. She hoped one slice would be enough. Even Frances might find the weather too hot for two pieces of cake.

'Mmm, this is gorgeous, Lil, you're a genius. Anyway, look at me today, for instance. It's a lovely day, we could have gone for a nice walk together, or a picnic, but he's off with Harry. Said he's going to make his fortune at the races. Huh, lose it more like, I reckon.'

'It must be hard getting used to married life,' said Lilian. She wanted Frances to have time to carry on eating, and she racked her brains to think of something to say. 'Have you seen much of Reg's family since the wedding?'

'No. They don't like me. They wanted him to take over the farm, but now he's married and living here they know it won't happen. They live miles away, past

Driffield. They think Beverley's the other end of the earth and I'm one of its wicked women, luring away nice farmers from their families.'

'What a shame,' said Lilian. Eat, eat, she willed in her head. 'I've always thought one of the nice things about getting married must be getting a new family, but perhaps it's not always the case.' She was prattling, talking nonsense, but she had to keep going to allow Frances time to eat the cake.

'My friend from medical school, Mary her name was, did I ever mention her to you?'

'Did you who?' asked Frances. Lilian ears pricked up. This didn't make sense, but she knew she mustn't let Frances know she had noticed.

'My friend Mary. I shared with her in my second year and she got married at the end of the third year, and…'

'Lil.' Frances slurred the word, but it was enough to stop Lilian in her tracks.

'Yes? Oh, Frances, are you all right? You don't look too good. Is it the heat, perhaps?'

'Yes, heat…feel a bit dizzy…'

'Here, let me take you inside. It's cooler in there, you'll soon feel better.'

'Sounds good,' said Frances, although she could hardly get the words out. 'Can you... help me up, Lil?' Lilian heaved her out of her deckchair and half carried her into the kitchen, where she sat down heavily on the first chair she came to.

'Sorry, Lil, don't feel well,' she said. 'Might be going to ...' and she vomited onto the kitchen floor. 'Sorry, Lil, so sorry,' she kept saying, and Lilian was glad she'd thought through her plan so often and so precisely. She couldn't have done what she needed to otherwise, with Frances sitting on her chair looking so sad and pathetic. Even if her resolve had faltered, the plan was in progress now. It was too late to go back. Lilian grabbed the washing up bowl from the sink and put it on Frances's lap.

'Here, just in case it happens again.' She rather hoped it would. The less food in Frances's stomach the better. She didn't want a pathologist finding ginger cake in there. She watched Frances dispassionately for a minute or two before realising she ought to show some concern. She fetched her a glass of water, although it didn't help, and in the end, she knelt next to her, holding her hands around the bowl, and murmuring comforting assurances that she'd feel better soon.

After less than twenty minutes, Lilian realised she had to take Frances upstairs. Although she didn't want a mess on the bed, she needed Frances to be able to walk. There was no way she'd be able to carry her up if she was unconscious.

'Come on, Frances. It looks like the sickness has stopped now. Let's get you upstairs. You'll feel better if you have a lie-down. Maybe you can sleep it off. I think it might be heat stroke. A good long sleep in a darkened room should do the trick.' Frances was too weak to speak but she nodded woozily and allowed Lilian to support her as they went down the hallway.

Even though Frances could moreorless stand, the stairs looked like a mountain to Lilian as they stood at the bottom, Frances swaying heavily against her shoulder.

'Come on now, up we go,' she said. But Frances wobbled against her even as she took her first step, and Lilian knew this wasn't going to work.

'I think you might need to crawl, Frances. You'll feel steadier that way. Look, I'll help you. Like this.' Lilian took Frances's hands and put them onto the third step. She bent her legs and put her knees on the bottom step.

Moving her friend's limbs as if she were a puppet, Lilian slowly manoeuvred her up the stairs. Frances was almost a dead weight by now, but Lilian kept talking in an effort to keep her awake. She would have given anything to stop and rest halfway up but didn't dare to for fear of Frances nodding off.

At last they reached the top. Frances showed signs of wanting to collapse, but Lilian forced her, still on her hands and knees, to the bedroom.

'Here we are, Frances. We need to get you on the bed now. Can you feel it with your hands? Now, straighten those knees and we'll have you up and on it in no time.' Lilian put on her most encouraging hospital voice as she pulled Frances up, planting her hands on the bed. Frances slumped with her head on her arms on top of the covers and Lilian saw she had no strength left in her. She went around the bed and climbed on top, then, before Frances could slip off again, she put her hands under her armpits and heaved. She managed to get the top half of Frances onto the bed, then went back round to the other side and lifted her legs up.

Lilian sank to the floor, leaning against the bed and panting. She gave herself half a minute to recover, then got up to look at her friend. Allowed to rest at last, Frances had regained some awareness of the situation.

'Don't...... feel .... good, Lil,' she panted. 'Do.... you think.... I need.... a.... doctor?'

'Don't be silly, I *am* a doctor,' Lilian said, smiling down at her. 'Don't worry, I'll take care of you.'

'Yes, you.... will. You'll.... take.... care....' she murmured as her eyes closed and her breathing started to rasp. Her face was ashen and her skin clammy from exertion and the effects of the poison. Her blonde curls stuck to the skin around her face and to her neck. It wouldn't be long before she lost consciousness.

'I'll fetch you a damp towel, Frances; it will help to cool you down,' Lilian said. She went into the bathroom and stood by the window for a while, breathing slowly. It overlooked the garden, giving her a view across the Westwood beyond. The empty deckchairs below her looked inviting, and she imagined how it would be to sit out there having tea with her mother. She could see roses along the untidy borders and fruit trees in the field beyond. The scene both calmed her and gave her the strength she needed to finish the job.

Lilian took her time finding a towel and then ran the

water in the sink for a good two minutes to make sure it was nice and cold. She wrung the towel out several times, so it didn't drip. Only then did she walk slowly back to the bedroom. It was over.

Lilian checked Frances's pulse. It was there but fading rapidly. She took the towel downstairs and hung it on the washing line to dry. There was nothing mysterious about a towel hanging on a line. She took the rubber gloves from her bag and wrapped the cake up again. She scrubbed the plate and washed up her glass, searching in Frances's cupboards for the right places to return them.

With the cake back in her bag, Lilian looked round the kitchen. Yes, everything was as it should be. She left the door to the garden open. Anyone coming to the house would assume Frances had been outside with a cold drink, had too much sun and gone inside to lie down. She hesitated, wondering if she should go back upstairs. No, best to get away sooner rather than later. She couldn't risk Reg coming home early from the races. That would spell certain disaster.

Lilian got back on her bike and was startled to see it was little more than an hour since she had arrived. The day was too hot for cycling any further than necessary, but she knew she had no option. Lilian headed towards Walkington. It was only a small village, and she knew this would enable her to check that no one was looking when she put the cake in the bin. The heat was to her advantage. No one wanted to be out and about in this, and they were all in their gardens and cool houses.

It was a downhill ride back to Beverley, and as Lilian sailed across the Westwood, she felt a familiar sense of release. The first part of her plan was complete, and all she had to do now was wait to be told of the sad news of Frances's death. She rather thought the cause would be found to be a heart attack. But for now, she would go home, put on the kettle and have a cup of tea with a nice slice of ginger cake.

Chapter 15

How long can this go on for? After a lifetime of handling pressure at work I would have thought I could handle this, but my nerves have frayed a little more as each day passes and I wait for them to come back with their questions. Even sitting on Mother's bench hasn't helped. My mind runs round in jagged circles, going over and over my plans and wondering whether I'll need them. First I'm convinced they'll find out everything, and then a minute later I'm certain there's no way they can. Even if they have their suspicions, they can't find proof, and without proof they can't arrest me.

Inertia doesn't help. I'm scared to go out again for fear people will say something, stare, maybe even shout at me. The story isn't on the television any more but I know if I dared to look on social media, I'd see a torrent of abuse and theories. Can I ever show my face in Beverley again, even if they don't arrest me? No smoke without fire, as DI Twist says, and it would take more years than I have left on this earth for the gossip to die down.

I try to keep busy in the garden, which - apart from the far end – looks tidier than ever before. I read and watch documentaries on the television. It surprises me how much there is to learn about the world, and it distracts me from my anxieties. Joanna calls every night, and despite my protestations, she is planning to come up for the weekend.

'Enough's enough, Mum,' she said last night. 'I can't bear to think of you shut up in the house on your own. It must be driving you mad. I promise I won't make you go out if you don't want to, but at least I can cheer you up with a game of Scrabble.'

'As long as you don't think I'm going to let you win,' I told her.

'No need, no need – I can beat you on my own, thank you.' She always makes me smile. I'm going to miss her when I go. It's hard not to listen to the voice in my mind telling me to leave now. I have a feeling in my bones that the police are busy unearthing things I would rather stay buried and that if I'm clever, I'll make my getaway while I can. But I would like to see Joanna one last time.

It's only two days after I come home from the hotel, but it feels like a week. It's Friday, and I'm looking forward to Joanna arriving later tonight. The sheets are all clean, but I wash them to give myself something to do, and hang them outside in the breeze, so they'll smell fresh on her bed. I may even iron them, if only to impress her. She knows my views on ironing sheets. I'm on my way to see if they're dry when the doorbell rings. They're back.

'Good afternoon, Dr Templeton,' says DI Twist. 'May we come in?' I don't bother with pleasantries; they've been here too many times for it now. We troop into the living room and sit in what have become our accustomed places.

'How is the investigation going, Inspector?' I ask hopefully. 'Are you any nearer to finding out what happened to Harry Johnson?'

'We don't have the full story yet. It's been hard to find people who knew him other than his sister, and we've reached a dead end at present. That's not to say we're giving up. We're currently following new leads regarding Reg and Frances.'

'I don't understand, Inspector. Why are you asking about Reg and Frances? What have they got to do with Harry's death?'

'We're looking into them because there's one common connection between them all, Dr Templeton.

You.'

'Me? Because Harry's body was found in my garden? If you've reached a dead end, isn't it because someone you've not found out about is responsible? I've been thinking it over, Inspector, and if you ask me, one of his dodgy contacts killed him and put him in my garden when I was at work. Maybe Reg helped them and then had to disappear to escape from them. Have you thought of that?'

'We have considered the possibility, as it happens. We are detectives after all.' She shoots a small and genuine grin at Sergeant Carter, and I wonder if this is a private joke between the two of them, or maybe my doddery old woman act is working after all.

'As I said, we are still pursuing our inquiries and it would be remiss of us not to include you in them, as I hope you understand. Even if only to clear your name. Don't you want that, Dr Templeton?'

'I certainly do. But I don't like the implication that I had something to do with it. It's all very distressing. I've not looked at those places online where people make horrible comments about these things, but I'm sure there are plenty of people saying I should be arrested. Or worse.'

'That's as maybe. The fact is you haven't been arrested. You won't be unless we suspect you to be involved in the death of Harry Johnson. Or someone else.'

'Someone else? Who else do you think I might have killed?' She ignores the question, turning instead to her partner.

'Sergeant Carter? Would you like to take over here? You're the one who's most up to date with this side of the investigation.' She sits back in her chair and takes out her notebook and Sergeant Carter turns towards me.

'Yes, we're interested in the deaths of certain members of your family, Dr Templeton,' he says.

'Oh, yes, and which members might they be?'

'Your father and his brother,' he says. I stiffen. I can't help it. I suppose I should have stopped being surprised by the lines of inquiry they think to take, but this is one I would rather they had left alone.

'We understand they both died of heart attacks. Rather suddenly. Is that correct?'

'I can confirm my father's death, yes. He died unexpectedly when I was fifteen, and yes, it was a heart attack. I didn't know about my uncle before then. It was only when my father died that Mother told me his brother had also died suddenly of the same cause. The doctors supposed it must be a hereditary condition. Mother often reminded me in case I'd inherited it, and I've had regular tests because of it.'

'And do you have a problem with your heart?'

'No, I don't, as it happens. These conditions quite commonly pass down the male line, you know.'

'You seem to have known a lot of people who've died of similar causes,' says the sergeant.

'I don't understand.'

'Your father, your uncle, Frances. All dying suddenly and unexpectedly of heart attacks as adults. Have you never thought it strange?'

'No. Why should I? My father was much older than Frances, and I never knew my uncle, so I didn't make that sort of wild connection. I don't know what you expect me to say about it.'

'You might be interested to know that despite extensive questioning of people working at the hospital at the time, and examination of the records, there is no evidence to suggest Frances died of anything other than natural causes.'

'Yes, I am interested. And pleased, in the light of your earlier comments. But not surprised.'

'We've carried out similar inquiries into the deaths of your uncle and father. This was more complex as they died so much longer ago.'

'I should think it was. And I've no idea why you should ask about them anyway. What else would they be due to?'

'That's the thing, Dr Templeton. It's been suggested your uncle died from poisoning.'

'Poisoning? What kind of poisoning?'

'We've spoken to the son of a young pathologist who was working at the hospital at the time. He worked abroad for most of his career but came back when he retired. Dr Ward died some time ago, but his son works at the hospital now, so we were able to trace him quite easily. He has all his father's old papers and he dug them out for us. Dr Ward kept meticulous notes of every post-mortem he observed during his training, including that of your uncle.'

'How interesting. And what did his notes say?' I keep my voice steady and feel a strange combination of fear and curiosity.

'It appears your uncle died under tragic circumstances, but I suppose you know the story yourself.' Sergeant Carter looks at me questioningly.

'No, I don't as it happens. My parents rarely spoke about their families. They moved to Beverley when they got married and I got the impression their parents hadn't approved of the match. I never met any other members of my family.'

'Really?' The two detectives exchange glances, but I can't see why this should be of significance.

'It seems your uncle, John Templeton, was engaged to be married when he died. It was in nineteen forty-three and he was home on leave from the air force. He'd been a teacher before the war and became something of a hero. Did your parents never speak of him?'

'No. I really don't know why not, but there it is. What happened to him, Sergeant?

'He died, less than a month before the wedding. He'd gone out for a picnic on the moors with his fiancé when he fell ill.'

'Oh dear, what was wrong with him?' It won't do any harm to reinforce my ignorance of events, and I adopt a suitably shocked expression.

'They didn't know at first. His fiancé described his mouth and tongue starting to tingle and his feeling nauseous. They packed up the picnic and started to head for home, but he got worse, slurring his words and becoming breathless. She left him and ran to the nearest road, where she flagged down a passing car. The driver called an ambulance when he found a phone box, but by the time they arrived the poor man was dead.' Sergeant Carter pauses, and I suppose he's waiting for a response.

'I'm sorry, sergeant. It's all rather a shock, hearing about the death of my uncle in such detail. I don't know what to say, other than it sounds like a heart attack. Was that the diagnosis? I presume a post-mortem was carried out?'

'Yes. The symptoms described by the fiancé tied in with heart failure, and the post-mortem showed nothing different, so that was the agreed cause of death.'

'Yes, I understand. And this young pathologist - I'm afraid I don't remember his name - what did he have to say about it?'

'It appears Dr Ward thought some of the symptoms were incompatible with a heart attack. He was a keen botanist and he recognised them as typical of aconite poisoning.'

'I'm sorry - what poisoning?'

'Aconite. It's the name of a plant. It's a Latin word, from the Greek meaning 'without dust' and 'without struggle'. It was used to poison arrows and kill wolves in the past, hence its other name, wolfsbane. It's also known as monkshood, because of the shape of the flowers.'

'You've certainly done your research,' I say, and he blushes, although I didn't intend it as a compliment.

'Dr Ward thought there might be more to Mr Templeton's death than met the eye, and he went to visit his fiancé and asked where they'd been when he fell ill. She described the place to him and after some hunting, he found it. He also found a bunch of flowers which she said John had been picking for her when he fell ill. One of them was aconite.'

'He only had to touch it to die?' I take care to sound shocked and horrified.

'He might not have been so severely affected if he hadn't had an open wound on his hand. He'd cut himself the day before and the injury hadn't had time to heal. Once the poison entered his bloodstream, he didn't stand a chance.'

'How dreadful,' I say. 'What did Dr Ward do? Did he ask for a blood test?'

'No, the poison leaves the system within twenty-four hours. It was too late. Dr Ward was a young doctor, hoping to get on in his department. He didn't want to cause trouble, and what good would it have done anyway? John Templeton was dead. Knowing it was an accidental poisoning rather than a heart attack wasn't going to bring him back.'

'No, I suppose it wasn't,' I say, and I find myself blinking back the tears. It's hard to hear the story told with such clinical precision. Even after all this time, I can't stop myself from thinking how different things would have been if John Templeton had chosen different flowers to gather for his beloved.

'Are you all right, Dr Templeton?' DI Twist has noticed, and I turn it to my advantage.

'Yes, thank you. It's a terribly sad story, isn't it? That poor girl. I wonder what happened to her. Did you find out?' I try not to hold my breath as I wait for the answer.

'No, Dr Ward didn't mention her name. We're trying to find out more about her, but we've not had any luck so far.' Good. That's one thing at least.

'I still don't understand what this has to do with anything.'

'It raises the question of poisoning. Harry Johnson's body showed no apparent sign of trauma and the pathologists have struggled to suggest a cause of death. However, the stain on his jacket might be vomit, which would be consistent with aconite poisoning. And we also have to consider Frances Blake's death in the light of this discovery. If one death from poisoning can be diagnosed as a heart attack, why not another? And on the same topic, what about your father? Another heart attack. Maybe his death wasn't so clear-cut either.'

'This is ridiculous! My father was under a lot of stress. It's not surprising he had a heart attack. He left huge debts, and I dread to think what pressure he must have been under. One person might have been accidentally poisoned, and you decide half the heart attacks in Beverley are poisonings too! You may as well check all the heart attacks in the last forty years and reopen their autopsies. Is that what you're going to do?'

'We're not interested in all the heart attacks in Beverley. Only those of people who knew you, Dr

Templeton. Which leads us to your plant collection. I seem to remember you saying you have a number of rare plants in your greenhouse. We thought it might be a good idea for us to have a look at them.'

'To see if I've got this…what do you call it…wolf thing in there? Go ahead, look if you like. I daresay you ought to have a search warrant, but I won't insist on it. Go on – help yourselves!' I stand up and indicate the door to the kitchen.

'Neither of us would recognise the plant, but we have an expert in the car outside who we'll send in, if you don't mind. Purely to set everyone's mind at rest.'

'Please do, but I can assure you he'll only find a rather splendid collection of orchids. I hope he enjoys looking at them.' Sergeant Carter leaves the room and then comes back into the house with a man who I assume is the 'expert'. They disappear in the direction of the kitchen and I turn to DI Twist.

'Does this mean you're going to arrest me, Inspector? I'm starting to feel hounded, I must admit.'

'No, Dr Templeton, we're not going to arrest you. Our investigations are progressing, but we don't have anything definite. Assuming you're telling the truth about the contents of your greenhouse,' she smiles.

'I really have nothing to do with any of this, you know,' I soften my voice and try to sound conspiratorial. 'There's nothing I want more than to help you find out what happened to poor Harry, but I worry all these questions you're asking about other people are diverting your investigation. There must be people out there somewhere who knew him. Who knew what he was up to, and who might have killed him? Shouldn't you be looking for them instead of worrying about strange plants?'

'Don't worry, Dr Templeton. We're exploring every avenue, including anyone and everyone who knew Harry Johnson. Please be patient with our questions, and hopefully it will all be over soon.' She looks towards the door as the two men return, Sergeant Carter giving her a shake of the head as he enters the room.

'We'll be leaving you now,' she says. 'Thank you for your help.' She follows the others out of the front door, and I watch them walk down the drive.

I have to get outside. And I need to do something to keep myself busy. I can't sit still. I take the sheets and pillowcases off the line and fold them meticulously, concentrating fiercely on the seams, getting them all perfectly in line. I set up the ironing board and iron them until not a single crease remains, then put them on the bed in Joanna's room. I go back out and cut a few late roses for her room. I can't stop there, I never can, and I carry on pruning, weeding and tying back stray branches. After an hour's activity my mind is ready to process what has happened. And I can't deny it. They're getting close. Closer than they can possibly imagine.

***

'Mum!' Joanna's out of the car and running up the drive, her coat flapping in the breeze and a scarf flying off her shoulders.

'Now, that's what I call a big hello,' I say, when she releases me from her arms and I've enough breath to talk. 'There's no need for a fuss, you know. I'm quite all right.'

'Really?' She looks at me critically. 'I don't see how you can be, not with everything that's been going on.'

'Oh, I'm always happy if I'm in my own home. It was only when I had to stay in hotels that I felt strange. And I'm even happier now you're home. Shouldn't you get your things out of the boot? And take the key out of the ignition? You don't want it stolen, do you?'

'Oh, Mum, no one's around to steal it, don't be ridiculous,' she says, but she makes her way to the little car, nonetheless. It takes three journeys to bring everything in. When trouble strikes, Joanna cooks, and it looks as if she's been at it for days.

'I brought lots so we can just heat it up and enjoy ourselves relaxing with a glass of wine,' she says, emerging from the boot with two casserole dishes. 'Grab the cake tin, Mum. I know baking's the one thing you can do in the kitchen, but even I need a break from your ginger cake now and then. I've made chocolate brownies and lemon drizzle. Oh, and did you watch the Bake Off this week? Wasn't that carousel pie amazing?' She chatters on without the need for much in the way of response, and I can already feel my cares receding as I put the kettle on to boil.

***

The weekend passes in a daze. I know this will be the last time I see Joanna, so I try to treasure every second. I often envy the pupils in her classes. She would never brag, but I've seen some of the letters they write to her after they pass their exams, and I'm convinced Frances would have done better at school if she'd had Joanna as a biology teacher. She looks very much like Mother at the same age, and it's always been a blessing. I don't know how easy I'd have found it if she'd looked like Reg. She's not like Mother on the inside, though. She's like me. Strong, able to cope with anything. She'll find it hard when I go but I know she'll be all right.

The relief I feel in seeing her doesn't last long. We have to talk about the case, and although I don't tell her about the most recent questions I've had to face, the fact that it's not closed is enough to cause her concern. She pulls the details of the last few days out of me as we sit in the living room after supper, knowing I've only given her the bare bones over the telephone.

'It's not good enough, Mum,' she says. 'Here you are, an elderly lady on your own in an intolerable situation. How you can set foot in the garden at all, I don't know. And don't pretend it's not been difficult for you. I can tell you're not your normal self.'

'Oh yes, and how can you tell that, may I ask?'

'By looking at you! You're slobbing around in your oldest clothes, you've not put your make-up on, your hair's a mess. If it weren't for the situation you're in, I'd think you were starting to let yourself go.' She's right of course, but it's not because of the strain. I've not dared to look any different while she's been here in case the police come back. I suppose it was inevitable she'd notice. At least there's a reasonable explanation for it, so I have to agree with her.

'I suppose you're right. I've not felt myself at all. I've been putting on comfy clothes because it seems easier. And there doesn't seem much point in makeup or a smart hairdo when I'm hardly going out. I'll try harder, I promise.'

'Oh, Mum, I didn't mean it that way.' Joanna's instantly apologetic. 'You carry on wearing whatever you want. I'm not surprised you want to wear comfort clothes and hide away with this whole suspicion thing hanging over you. I'm only glad you're not on any social media. I've had a look at some of the comments and they're horrible. I've closed my accounts now. People were starting to work out who I was and post disgusting comments.'

'Oh, Joanna, I had no idea. This is dreadful.'

'It's all right, Mum. I can handle it. And the police have been helpful. They've given me good advice about what to do.'

'The police? Have they been talking to you? What for?'

'Oh, come on, Mum. Of course they have. I lived in this house for over twenty years, they were bound to ask if I knew anything about...well, about it.' I'd not thought of that. I've been so wrapped up with my own fears and plans I never gave a thought to the possibility of the police contacting Joanna.

'Have they asked you lots of questions?' I keep my voice even, but I dread what she's going to tell me.

'No, they haven't. Although they called me yesterday and I think they might have done then, only I said I was coming up for the weekend. They asked me to pop into the station while I'm here. They offered to come to the house, but I thought you'd probably had enough of them by now.'

'That was thoughtful of you. Yes, I'd prefer never to see them again, but I suppose it's unlikely.'

'And what about afterwards? When it's all over? Will you want to stay here, knowing what was in the garden all that time? With people gossiping about it? You know it'll take years to die down.'

'Oh, Jo, I don't know. I've been thinking about it, obviously. You know I don't care about what other people think, but it has been awkward going into town, and I haven't liked it. It's my home and I never thought I'd want to leave it, but now I'm on my own, I have started to feel differently. Maybe it's time to move on.'

'If I let you,' Joanna grins at me. 'It's my house now, don't forget.'

'Yes, I know, and it's my rent keeping you going, don't you forget, young lady.'

'I won't, don't worry. But seriously, if you do want to move, I can easily sell up and buy somewhere else for you to live in under the same arrangement. Let me know when you decide, and I'll talk to the solicitor. It could be hard to sell in the immediate future. I might try and give that bit of the garden back to the council. It was bought from them in the first place wasn't it, by the old woman who wanted a pond?'

'Yes, it was. It's a good idea. Something to consider, but perhaps not yet. Let's concentrate on having a lovely weekend.'

'You're right as always, Mother. And before you ask, yes, I'll watch 'The Day of the Jackal' with you, I know it's your favourite.'

It passes all too quickly, as always. Joanna goes to the police station and comes back with a puzzled expression, saying they asked questions about the house, as she'd expected, but also about her childhood and the rest of the family.

'I told them there wasn't much, apart from you, me and Gran. They were asking about your father and your uncle. I said all I knew was they both died of heart attacks, and they said that might be up for discussion. What on earth did they mean?'

I have to explain the whole of yesterday's interview, when I was hoping to avoid it, but it doesn't change things. She's intrigued but not unsettled, believing the police are on a wild goose chase and it will all be over soon.

'And when it is, let's go on a trip together, Mum. It's half term soon, and maybe we could go somewhere sunny, sit on a beach for a while. Would you fancy that?'

I tell her I would, and she says she'll start looking for some options online. But I know that although I'll be going away soon, it will be on a very different sort of trip.

Chapter 16

Claggy, sticky, crumbling. Lilian's first memory was of the feel of soil between her fingers. She must have been very young, because she was sitting down at the time, and the recollection was bonded to an image of red buckle shoes that she found in photographs of herself at the age of two. Later memories were more detailed, but they never prompted the same intensity of feeling as that first awareness that here was something special. Something that could make things grow. All her memories had one thing in common, however. The warm, loving, calming voice of her mother.

***

'How was your first day at school, darling?' Lilian could only just hear her mother's voice through the folds of her coat, in which she had buried her face. She had rushed out of the building and straight into Grace's arms, desperate for the scent and feel of her and the sound of her voice.

'It was good.'

'I can't hear you, Lilian, not if you talk to my coat,' her mother laughed. She pulled Lilian in front of her and held her by the shoulders. 'Here, let me look at you. No,

it's the same Lilian. You've not turned into a monster.'
Lilian giggled. Her mother always checked to see if she'd
changed overnight, and it made her feel as if she were
back home already. School had been good, but so many
new people in one day had exhausted her.

'Can we go home now?'

'Of course we can. I've made a special cake for tea.'

'Will Father be there?'

'No, darling. He's still at work and he'll be back late
tonight. We'll go down to the allotment after you've
eaten. There's still some rhubarb left, and the
blackberries are ripening nicely.'

'I don't like their prickles,' said Lilian, as they turned
towards home. 'I'll pick the rhubarb and you pick the
berries.'

'All right, it's a deal. Now, tell me about school. Did
you make any friends?'

'Yes, I did. My friend is called Frances. She has four
brothers and a sister. She plays good games, but she can't
write her name like I can. Miss Spencer said I'm very
good at writing.'

'That's lovely, dear,' Grace stopped at the kerb. 'Eyes
right, Lilian, eyes left. All right, quick march!'

'You forgot eyes right again, Mother.' Lilian was proud of her road drill and didn't like to leave anything out.

'So I did, clever girl. Anyway, tell me more about your friend. Frances, is it?'

'Yes. She has yellow hair like Sally-doll. And blue eyes like you. She says she's going to call me Lil and I can call her Fran, but I think I'll call her Frances.'

'You must call her whatever you think best. Did she say where she lives?'

'No, but she has to share a bedroom with her big sister. And she has cousins. What are cousins?' They were at the house now, and Lilian waited for her mother's answer as she opened her handbag to find the key.

'They're relatives. Family members.'

'What does that mean?' Lilian didn't have any idea what her mother was talking about.

'Well...if I had a sister or a brother and they had a child, that child would be your cousin. Here, let me help you with your coat.'

'And do you?' Lilian wriggled her arms out of her sleeves and bent down to unbuckle her shoes.

'Do I what?'

'Have a sister or a brother?'

'No, I don't.'

'And does Father have one?'

'No, he doesn't.' Lilian saw an unfamiliar expression cross her mother's face. Many years later she understood what it meant, but her four-year-old world could not furnish her with an explanation.

'So I don't have any cousins.'

'No, we've got a little family, just you and me and Father. But there's a big cake in the kitchen for tea, do you want the first slice?'

***

'Mother, why doesn't Father come in the garden with us?'

'Oh, he has other interests, Lilian,' Grace carried on digging holes for the bulbs and tossed some weeds into the wheelbarrow as she spoke.

'What, like golf, and work?'

'Work's not exactly an interest. Your father has to go to work to earn money to pay for our house, our lovely garden, our food, our clothes, everything. He works hard, and he plays golf to relax.'

'What do you do to relax?' This was a new concept to

Lilian. She'd not thought of grown up life as being divided into work and play, and she was already assessing how she spent her own time.

'I don't do anything to relax. I don't have to go to work, and everything I do at home is a pleasure.'

'Everything? Even scrubbing the floor?'

'No, maybe not that,' Grace smiled as she straightened up from the flowerbed. 'I suppose the housework is like my work, and the gardening is my relaxation.'

'Even though it's probably the hardest work, especially when we're cutting back the roses.'

'Yes, even though it feels like hard work sometimes, it's what I love best.' Grace looked round the garden as she spoke, and she sighed with pleasure. 'And I think I've made a decent job of it, if I say it myself. Even at this time of year, it's pretty. But I do love it best in the summer, when everything's properly out.'

'Why do we have the allotment as well? Couldn't we grow the fruit and vegetables here? There's plenty of room.'

'I know. It's to do with the war, when we were made to use every inch of land for food. We got the allotment so as to grow more, but when it was all over, I told your father that it was time for some colour in our lives; I wanted the garden to be beautiful, a work of art, not a cabbage patch. We kept on the allotment for food, so now we have the best of both worlds.'

'Which do you like best? The garden or the allotment?' Lilian loved the colours of the garden, but she had always found her greatest satisfaction in growing and picking her own food, and she took a great pride in harvesting the produce grown on her own little patch. She had her own bed in the garden as well, but somehow flowers were less rewarding.

'Oh, the garden, every time. I only keep the allotment on so that your father doesn't make me grow vegetables here. But don't tell him that, he's just pleased it saves money on the grocery bill, and he's never had to spend money buying me flowers.' Lilian thought this sounded a bit sad, and that maybe it would have been nice for her mother to have been bought flowers, but she changed the subject instead.

'I know what I want for my birthday. If you'll let me.'

'If I'll let you! Whatever do you mean?'

'What I really want is a greenhouse, but you might

think it would spoil the work of art.'

'A greenhouse! What makes you want one of those?

'I'd like to try growing special plants. Ones that need warmth all year. Maybe an orchid. I read about them in a book from the library. I could buy the plants or seeds with my pocket money. And I could grow some seedlings for you in there as well, if you'd like.'

'Well, Lilian, what a wonderful idea. Of course you can have one, as long as your father agrees. You'll be reaching double figures, it's quite an occasion. You'll be well on your way to growing up, so you should have a grown-up present, and a greenhouse sounds very grown up to me.'

***

Lilian closed the greenhouse door and took the watering can back to the shed. Her plants were all moist and happy, and she was particularly pleased with her new orchid. She liked to think of herself as a specialist with exotic plants, and she was ready for a new challenge. She had recently read a book about poisonous species from the library, and she thought this might be an interesting new avenue to explore. She would look for more on the subject next time she went, and she was already planning which ones to buy with the tokens she was expecting to receive for her birthday. Lilian was a proper teenager now, almost fourteen, and starting to make plans for the future. She had made up her mind to study botany when she left school; her teachers said she was clever enough for university, and a future with plants was all she wanted. Maybe she could work in a nursery, or even one of the big gardens. Her secret dream, rarely admitted even to herself, was to work at Kew, in London.

A watery sun shone in the late winter afternoon. Lilian allowed herself to dream a little, and she was pleased to smell her mother's famous ginger cake as she pulled off her boots at the kitchen door.

'Is that you, Lilian?' her mother called. 'I was just going to call you in. The kettle's boiled and there's cake on the table.'

'Mmmm, I can smell it,' said Lilian. 'Should I take some in to Father?'

'No, I'll take it. He's not in a very good mood, and he might not be too happy at being interrupted when he's reading his paper.' Lilian didn't ask what the matter was. Her father's moods were part of her life, and she had learnt to keep her distance as much as possible. She felt a sudden surge of resentment. It wasn't fair, the way he treated her mother sometimes.

'Why is he so grumpy? You'd think he'd be happy with such a wonderful wife waiting on him hand and foot while he reads the paper and plays golf all weekend.'

'Lilian! Don't talk about your father that way.'

'Why not? You should meet Frances's father, he's completely different. He's 'Dad' for a start, not some Victorian patriarch. And he's nice to people. He tells jokes, he hugs his family, he listens to people talking about their day. He doesn't get cross over nothing and refuse to talk to his family for days on end. I wish I had a father like that.'

'Stop it, Lilian. We'd be lost without Malcolm. He provides for us both, and that's what matters. I can't think what's come over you. It must be your hormones. Everyone says teenagers are difficult, but I thought you were different. I must have been wrong.' Grace swept out of the room, leaving Lilian to pour her own tea and cut her own cake. She sat at the kitchen table, waiting for the heat to leave her flushed cheeks. What her mother said was true. Malcolm did provide for them, but shouldn't there be more to family life than that? She didn't want to fall out with her mother, though, and she jumped up to hug Grace as soon as she came back into the room.

'I'm sorry, Mother. I didn't mean to upset you.'

'I know you didn't.' Grace hugged her back and sat down at the table to pour her own tea. 'I know your father's not the most affectionate of people, but he's all we've got, and we must love him as he is.'

'I suppose so.' Lilian paused and cut a slice of cake for her mother. 'Mother, can I ask you something?'

'Of course, darling, what is it?'

'It's a bit embarrassing.'

'Don't worry, I'm a grown woman, I'm sure I can take it,' Grace smiled as she took a bite of cake.

'It's just that, well, I think I might need a bra now, and... well, other things too. Things for...well, for...I think they're called my monthlies.'

***

Lilian had been what was known as a late developer. Most of the girls at school were wearing a bra for at least a year before she needed one. Frances was way ahead of her, and she filled Lilian in with the details, so she knew what to expect when her body began to change, even though she found it difficult to talk to her mother about it.

Lilian was ready for her body to fill out, ready for her 'monthlies' as everyone called them. She wasn't ready for Malcolm.

The changes were so cleverly insinuated that she barely noticed them at first. A smile when she walked into the room. A 'how was your day, dear?' which had to be answered for fear of being rude. She saw her mother being first surprised and then pleased at Malcolm's new interest in her. She could almost feel her relief at seeing them getting on better. What Grace didn't see was what went on in the living room while she washed up the supper dishes.

'Go and get your new plant book, Lilian. I'd like to know more about what it is you're so interested in.' Insisting she sit next to him on the sofa. Positioning himself right in the middle of it so she had to squeeze in beside him, one thigh pressed beside his, the other against the armrest. Then one day he was sitting in the armchair when she came in.

'Come over here, Lilian. Come and sit on my lap while you show me your book. It'll be cosier. I'll let you have a look at my newspaper while we're at it. There's an article here I think you'll be interested in.' The voice was friendly, coaxing, and she could see no room for refusal. He wasn't interested in her books, of course, and there was plenty he could get up to behind his newspaper, securely hidden should Grace come in early with his coffee.

This went on for months. Lilian didn't know what to do. She knew how angry he could get, and she didn't dare refuse to continue. She couldn't bear his hands on her, running over her stockings and creeping under her school shirt. She tried to position herself so his options were limited, but it was impossible to protect all of her body at once. After two months, she could stand it no longer. It was the time of her monthly, she was feeling queasy and out of sorts, and perhaps this was why she found the courage to confront him.

'I'm not sitting there with you any more,' she told him. 'And you can't make me. I don't care if you shout at me, and if you do then I'll tell Mother what it's about. And if you won't talk to me again, fine. I'm going to sit here, on my own, and read my book.' She planted herself in the opposite chair, opened her book and glued her eyes to its pages, not daring to meet his stare. She turned a page, two. Silence. She had to look up in the end. He was behind his newspaper, ignoring her.

Lilian was jubilant. Her father was a nasty, dirty old man, but she had stood up to him and everything was going to be all right now. Lying in bed that night she tried to work out how soon she could leave home. She knew she could get a grant for university. She wouldn't have to ask him for money. She'd only started her O-level courses, so she had nearly four years left. Longer than she would have liked, but she'd just have to put up with him.

Lilian was dropping off to sleep when she sensed a change in the air. Her bedroom door was well-oiled, so it hadn't creaked when Malcolm eased it open. She turned over, widening her eyes in an effort to see in the darkness. She had hardly got her bearings before there was a swift movement, a weight on the bed, a hand over her mouth.

'Don't,' he whispered. 'Just don't. Because if your mother finds out about this, I'll tell her it was your idea. I'll divorce her and you'll both be out on the street. So just don't.'

***

Never again would Lilian allow herself to be in such a position of helplessness. She would learn to take control of her life, to solve any problem which arose, no matter how great. She would demonstrate resourcefulness, resilience, daring and a readiness to break the law if necessary. But that came later. At fourteen she was shocked and intimidated into silence. She didn't know much about the laws of the land, but she fully believed in Malcolm's power to put her out on the street with her mother. And she was convinced he would do exactly that if she refused him or told anyone what he was doing to her. Even if she had dared to do the latter, she doubted whether anyone would believe her.

Every night as she lay waiting in dread for his arrival, she would pray. She'd learnt about God in school, and even though the family didn't attend church, she didn't see why it should stop her. Lilian prayed for one thing and one thing only. For Malcolm to die. If he died, the house and his money would come to her mother, and they'd be all right. She knew they would. She'd get a job as soon as she left school. Maybe her mother would too. Whatever happened, they'd have the house, and he wouldn't be here. Lilian prayed before he came, and she prayed again after he left. Please God, let Malcolm die.

Lilian's sleep was suffering as well as her nerves, and

concentrating in school became harder. She couldn't afford to let her marks slip or her mother would start asking questions, and she couldn't risk that happening. Besides, she needed good grades if she was ever going to get into university and escape from her father.

She never had any trouble staying alert in biology lessons. Although plants were her favourite, all aspects of the subject fascinated her, and now they were studying the human body, she wondered if she might prefer medicine to botany. There was plenty of time to decide, and she already looked forward to the day when she could devote herself to the subject she loved best.

Today they were being introduced to genetics. Lilian already knew something about it from her plant books, and the teacher was pleased with her answers in class. They had been told to read the next section of the book to themselves and be ready to answer questions. Lilian began to read the passage. It was about dominant genes, and eye colour was used as an example. The book explained how everyone has two genes, one from each parent, and how if they are different, the dominant gene will determine the colour of the eye. It seemed logical to Lilian and she looked up, wondering what Miss Harris would ask, but before the teacher could begin, Frances raised her hand.

'Miss Harris, I don't understand. What's a dom...dom...'

'A dominant gene? That's what I'm about to ask the class, Frances. Listen carefully and you may learn something.' Lilian loved biology but she thought Miss Harris was unnecessarily harsh on Frances. She gave her friend's hand a squeeze under the table and whispered, 'Don't worry, I'll help you with it later.' Frances gave her a grateful smile, trying to avoid the teacher's gaze as she asked one of the other girls to explain.

'Yes, that's right, Dorothy. I'll draw it on the board to make it easier to understand. Brown is the dominant gene over blue when it comes to eyes. Remember, everyone has two genes, one from each parent, so if a person has a brown and a blue gene, their eyes will be...?'

'Brown,' someone called out.

'Yes, good. See, here's a capital B for the brown gene and a small one for the blue. Here's the father in our family. The mother also has one of each. Here she is, next to him on the board. Now, when these parents have a child, the child can have two brown genes, two blue or one of each. Do you all understand? Frances?'

'Yes, Miss, it's easier now it's on the board.'

'Good. Now who can tell me the outcomes of the different combinations? Lilian?'

'Two blue would give the child blue eyes, and one of each would mean their eyes were brown. So, if they had four children, you'd expect three of them to have brown eyes.'

'Er, yes, you would. Very good, Lilian. And if both parents had blue eyes then so would their children, as they would all have two blue-eye genes. Parents who both had two brown genes would only have children with brown eyes. I'll put all three examples on the board so it's clear for everyone to see. I want you all to copy this into your books.' As she started adding letters and colours to the board, Frances turned to Lilian.

'You're so clever, Lil, how'd you work it all out?'

'It's easy once you understand it. I've read about it before, only with plants, which helps.' They concentrated on their diagrams for a while before Frances spoke again.

'D'you know, Lil, I'm starting to get it now. I've been thinking about my family. My mum has blue eyes and my dad has brown. I've got blue eyes and so has Ted, and the others all have brown like dad. So he must have one of each gene. It all makes sense now. I'm going to tell Mum about it when I get home. I think she'll be interested.' Lilian nodded absently. Frances's words, innocent and enthusiastic, had triggered a thought in her own mind. She knew the colours of her parents' eyes as intimately as Frances did. They both had blue eyes. And Lilian's were brown.

***

Lilian did nothing at first. She spent that evening going over and over it in her head. She knew she was right. At least one of Grace and Malcolm was not her parent. Now she understood why she had been brought up in such carefully preserved isolation. She knew her parents had moved to Beverley around the time she was born, and she had never seriously questioned why they weren't in touch with their wider families. Now she knew the reason - or at least she thought she did. She was illegitimate. Her parents' families were ashamed of her. And of her parents. They had moved here so no one would know. Lilian wondered if she'd been told the truth about her parents' wedding anniversary. It must have been after her birth, not before. Or perhaps she was a love child? Born to another woman after her father's philandering? Perhaps a young girl who couldn't keep her on her own? Or maybe she'd been adopted? But if she was, then why the secrecy, the separation from family? Lilian's thoughts went round and round in her head until she could bear it no longer. She would have to ask.

She couldn't imagine broaching the subject with her father. It would have to be her mother. She would get her on her own at the weekend while Malcolm was playing golf. They usually had a good three hours then, sometimes longer if he stayed at the club for lunch. She would ask her on Saturday.

When the time came, Lilian found she was trembling. She had never considered herself to be the nervous sort, but now the time had come, she was bursting with pent-up emotion, not only over her parentage, but from Malcolm's nightly visits. She had decided it would be easier to talk if she wasn't looking directly at Grace, so she made her a cup of tea and suggested they sit on the garden bench to drink it.

'That's a lovely idea, Lilian. It's such a warm day for the time of year. Let's put on a scarf though, I don't want you to catch a chill.' Lilian didn't think a scarf would stop her shivering with nerves, but she wrapped one around her neck and carried the cups outside. They sat side by side on the bench, her mother smiling into the sun.

'Mother. There's something I need to ask you.'

'Yes, dear? What is it?'

'It's about…' Suddenly, Lilian didn't know how to begin. Should she say anything at all? She was desperate to know, but terrified of upsetting her mother.

'Lilian? What is it? You can ask me anything, you know. I won't be angry, or upset, you know I won't.'

'I know.' Lilian took a deep breath and let it out again. 'We had a biology lesson the other day. Miss Harris was teaching us about genes.'

'Jeans? Whatever was she talking about…Oh, you mean genes in your body, not denim. Sorry, Lilian, go on.'

'She was using eye colour as an example. She put a diagram on the board to show what colour eyes children would have if their parents had blue or brown eye genes.'

'Yes? We didn't learn about this sort of thing when I was at school. It sounds very interesting, but I'm afraid I won't be able to help you if there was something you didn't understand.' Oh dear, Lilian had hoped once she'd got this far, her mother would realise what the problem was, but she was clearly going to have to spell it out for her.

'The thing is, Mother, you and Father both have blue eyes, don't you? And I have brown eyes.'

'Yes, that's right.'

'But Mother, Miss Harris told us that if two blue-eyed people have a child, he or she will have blue eyes. It's impossible for them to have a child with brown eyes.'

'No, Lilian, she must have got it wrong., My parents both had brown eyes and I've got blue. So you don't have to have the same eye colour as your parents.'

'No, it doesn't work that way. Brown is like a winning sort of gene. You get one gene from each parent, and if they're both blue you have blue eyes. If you get one of each then the brown gene wins and your eyes are brown. So your parents must have had one of each and passed their blue ones to you. D'you understand?'

'I think so, but what are you trying to say?'

'You and Father must both have two blue eye genes, yes?'

'Yes.'

'So where did my winning brown eye gene come from?' There was a silence. Lilian looked sideways at her mother. Grace was staring into the distance, apparently oblivious to her surroundings and to Lilian.

'Mother?' Lilian gently touched her mother's knee. 'It's all right, whatever it is. If I'm adopted, just tell me. I won't mind, honestly.' Lilian suddenly found herself hoping this was the answer. It would be simple, safe. But she knew it wouldn't be. Grace was only twenty years older than Lilian, and who adopted babies at that age?

'No, Lilian, it's not that.' Her mother spoke as if from far away, and Lilian wondered where her mind was taking her.

'What, then?' She couldn't keep the impatience out of her voice. 'Please tell me, Mother, I think I've a right to know.'

'I suppose you do. I always thought I'd tell you when you turned eighteen, when you became an adult. Malcolm would never discuss it though; he'd never want you to know at all. He'd be furious if he found out.' Grace paused and turned to look at Lilian. 'Look, Lilian, I'll tell you the truth about your past, but you have to absolutely promise me you won't tell your...Malcolm. Do you promise?'

Lilian heard the slip of her mother's tongue and thought she might know what was coming. She nodded firmly and waited for Grace to continue.

'Malcolm isn't your real father, Lilian. He's your stepfather, and also your uncle.'

'But how can he be both?'

'I can explain if you stop interrupting,' her mother said with a faint smile. 'The first thing to tell you is that we didn't move here from West Yorkshire. We both came from a village near Bridlington, much closer than we wanted you to think. We told you we were from further away to make it easier to explain our not seeing family. And we didn't want you to go looking on your own.'

'But why not?'

'Let me tell this in my own way, Lilian. You'll understand soon enough. In nineteen forty-three I became engaged to be married. His name was John. We met at a New Year's Eve dance and fell in love almost immediately. People did in those days. He was in the air force and was home on leave. He had two weeks left and we spent most of it together. He was a science teacher before the war, but his real love was for plants and gardening. We had that in common, and he came around to the house to tidy up the garden for my parents. They thought he was wonderful too, and even though I was so young, they agreed to us becoming engaged.' Grace paused and set her teacup gently on the ground under the bench. She straightened her back as she sat up again, as if steeling herself for the next part of the story.

'John came home for two weeks' leave in June. We started to plan the wedding. We'd decided on September, if he could get the leave. And we started looking for a house. John had been teaching in Beverley before the war and wanted to come back here afterwards, so we looked for a house here. We found one. It was rather run down and in Molescroft rather than Beverley, which made it cheaper. And it had a huge garden which backed onto the Westwood. We both fell in love with it. John had some savings put by and my parents said they'd help out. The owners liked us and agreed to wait until we could afford the deposit. We were so happy.' Grace's voice quivered, and Lilian knew the happiness had not lasted for long. She refused to let herself interrupt, waiting with well-concealed impatience for her mother to continue.

'John's parents were happy about the marriage too. They were kind people, but they were worried for me. They knew what the life expectancy for fighter pilots was like, and they didn't want me widowed so young. But we didn't let ourselves think about it. We lived in the moment and made our plans. What else could we do?' Lilian couldn't help herself, the question popped out of her mouth as if of its own accord.

'Did he die, Mother? And were you pregnant with me? And did you have to marry...Malcolm?'

'Yes, that is what happened, but not in the way you might suppose. Malcolm was John's brother. I knew him by sight before I met John. We both used to travel to work on the bus to Bridlington, and I noticed him looking at me several times. I knew he liked the look of me, but I wasn't interested in him. I knew a bit about him. He was an accountant and he'd not been able to join up as he had flat feet. He was embarrassed about it and jealous of the attention John got when he was home. It all made him rather cross, and it didn't make him very approachable, at least not to a young girl. Anyway, when I became engaged to John, he was very unhappy about it. He sulked, I suppose, but we barely noticed him, we were too wrapped up in ourselves.'

'What happened?'

'As I said, John was home on leave in June. We went for a picnic one day, out in the fields on the way to Bridlington. It was a beautiful day, we were in the middle of nowhere, and we...well, we...' Grace stopped, blushing, and Lilian couldn't prevent a giggle escaping her.

'Oh, Mother, I'd never have thought it of you! Are you saying that was when you... started me? I know how long it is from June to March and what can happen in that time.' Grace couldn't help laughing too.

'All right, Lilian, yes, we started you.' She sighed deeply. 'Oh, it was the happiest moment of my life. I've not thought about it for years; I've not let myself, because of what happened next.' Lilian knew better than to ask what this might have been, and waited.

'I was tidying myself up a bit, comb, lipstick, that sort of thing. And John said he wanted to give me something to remember the day by. There were lots of wildflowers around and he started picking them. I said I wouldn't be able to remember for long as they would die, and he said I'd have to press them in a book when I got home and then I could keep them for ever. I was laughing at him running around looking for different colours. He picked a beautiful bunch. There were all the usual ones, cornflowers, poppies, cowslips, buttercups, and one I'd not seen before. It had lots of flowers on a tall stem, a bit like bluebells in colour, but a deeper shade, as I remember. They had a funny shape, almost like little faces peering out from under tall hoods. That bunch of flowers has stayed in my mind, I can't get rid of it. I suppose it was the last thing I saw before my world fell apart.' Grace stopped to pick up her teacup. Lilian knew there couldn't be more than dregs in it, but she didn't interrupt with questions. The rest of the story would follow when her mother was ready.

'He was just about to give me the flowers when he collapsed. I don't know where they went. He'd gone a horrible grey colour, and when I helped him to sit up, he was shivering. He was sick soon after and said he felt a bit better. I said we should go back to the bus stop and get home, and we started walking, but he wasn't able to take more than a few steps. He buckled at the knees and couldn't get up again. I said I'd go for help and for him to rest. I ran to the road and eventually stopped a couple in a car. They went to the nearest phone box and called an ambulance while I waited by the road to show them where he was. It took forever for the ambulance to come, with me wanting to go back to him the whole time, although I knew I couldn't, or they'd never have found him. By the time they got to him, he'd died. They did a post-mortem because of it being so sudden. They brought him all the way to Beverley so the doctors there could look at him. They said it must have been a heart attack. He didn't have a history of heart problems, but they said it sometimes comes out of the blue, and there was no other explanation.'

'Oh, Mother.' Lilian reached her hand over and Grace squeezed it tightly.

'It was dreadful. The funeral, everything. It's all a blur now. Then, a few weeks afterwards...'

'You found out you were pregnant,' Lilian finished.

'Yes. Oh, it's not something I'm proud of now, but I was desperate. I went after Malcolm. I knew he'd been wanting me for himself, even while John and I were courting, and I took advantage of him. I told him I realised I'd chosen the wrong brother. He fell for it. His parents didn't, and nor did mine. They all tried to tell him to hold back, but he was so thrilled to have me that he agreed to get married quickly. I said it was the only thing that would make me happy. I starved myself so I wouldn't show, but I couldn't hide it on our wedding night. He was furious. He knew the baby – you – would arrive too soon after the wedding for decency to be preserved as he put it. And he could tell it was his brother's, by the size of me. It had to be, Malcolm and I hadn't been passionate about each other the way I was with John.'

'What did he do?'

'He said we had to make the best of a bad job. He took me to both our parents and told them what had happened. He said he was ashamed of me, but we were married now, and he wouldn't desert me. But they all agreed we couldn't stay in the village, because everyone would be gossiping about me and he would look like a cuckold. I still don't know what that is.'

'And that's when you came to Beverley?'

'Yes. He knew he could get work here and there wasn't much time if we were to get settled before you arrived. He said we had to have a new start, away from our families. They could tell the village what they liked.

He told them to say we'd gone to London so there wouldn't be too many questions. They agreed. I was heartbroken. I couldn't imagine never seeing my parents again. But I was young, and still grieving for John. I didn't know what I wanted other than to be safe, and for you to be safe too. I had to agree with Malcolm. I had no choice.'

Lilian couldn't imagine such a situation. But maybe she could. After all, wasn't Malcolm still getting exactly what he wanted right now?

'So my father was my uncle John? And Malcolm's my uncle?'

'Yes, that's right. I'm so sorry, Lilian. It's not an easy story to have to hear. I don't know what I'd have told you if I'd had more time to prepare. Maybe there was no other way to explain it all.'

They sat quietly for a few minutes, still holding hands. Lilian finally broke the silence.

'I suppose at least one of John and Malcolm's parents must have had brown eyes?'

'I suppose they must have. I never noticed.'

Chapter 17

It's getting dark when Joanna leaves. She's waited as long as she could, and I suppose she'll have missed any traffic by now. She offered to stay another day, saying the school would give her compassionate leave, but I told her not to. It wouldn't have made it any easier to say goodbye, and perhaps it's best to get it over with.

'Drive safely,' I tell her. Not because she won't, but to give me something normal to say. 'Text me when you get there, so I know you're safe.' She looks at me in surprise.

'You don't usually say that, Mum. You must be getting soft in your old age.'

'Maybe I am, or maybe I just don't want to lose you to some daft teenage driver.' I'm feeling uncharacteristically emotional, and I have to cough to stop the tears gathering in my eyes. 'Off with you now, you need some sleep before you face the rabble in the morning.'

'Don't remind me.' She smiles her sweet smile, so like Mother's, and it's all I can do not to gather her my arms and keep her with me forever. I resist the temptation, thanks to her opening the car door and giving me a quick hug before getting inside.

'Bye Mum, see you at half term - be good!'

She's gone.

***

The house seems quiet the next morning, and I start to feel restless. I know I've seen Joanna for the last time, and it's not unlike the feelings I had when Mother died. I don't suppose many people do know when they're seeing their family for the last time, and I'm not sure if it's a good thing or not. At least I was able to make sure Jo will have happy memories of this last weekend.

It's not long before they're back again. I knew they would be, and I've been steeling myself for what's bound to be coming next. I only hope they won't arrest me yet. I want a day or two more to set everything up perfectly for my departure. It's the afternoon this time, and there's a determined look on DI Twist's face when I open the door.

'We'd like you to come with us to the station, Dr Templeton.' I hadn't expected this, and my heart starts to hammer against my chest. Not now, it's too soon.

'Am I under arrest, Inspector?'

'No, if that were the case, we'd have said so by now.

We simply want to ask you some questions in a more formal setting. The DCI has nominated you as a significant witness and we need to undertake an official interview in a place where it can be properly recorded. It's voluntary, of course.' She leaves the sentence hanging in the air. It's voluntary, but what happens if I say no? It's best not to try to find out.

'I understand, Inspector. I don't suppose I need to call a lawyer, do I?' I make it sound like a joke, but I do want to know.

'You're perfectly welcome to contact one if you wish, but you're not under caution or arrest.' And it would look as if I had something to conceal if I did ask for one.

'I'll be fine,' I say. 'After all, I've got nothing to hide. I'll get my coat and handbag. I won't be long, Inspector.'

I'm grateful as always for the house's location at the end of a quiet road, and no one sees me getting into the car. Even though it's unmarked, it would be easy to see what's happening. Those two have an air about them that shouts 'detective', and the last thing Joanna needs is to see me splashed all over social media again. The police station car park is quiet too, and I think I may walk home afterwards. I could do with the exercise.

The interview room is stark, as I'd expected, but not frightening. The table has a recording machine on it, and I can see a small camera high up in the corner, facing in my direction. DI Twist and Sergeant Carter sit opposite me, and he presses the button on the recorder, stating our names, the date, and the time. DI Twist opens a file and gazes at what I assume is a list of questions. It looks rather long.

'Dr Templeton, you've been helping us with our inquiries concerning the body found in your garden on Monday the ninth of September. We are here now to interview you so your answers can be recorded formally. Thank you for agreeing to come along to the station today. Is there anything we can get you? A cup of tea, a glass of water?'

'No, thank you.'

'Just let us know if you need anything later on. We'll be going over some of the ground already covered in our discussions with you at your home, so please don't be surprised if it feels like we're asking you questions you've heard before. This will be to confirm your answers and to give you the opportunity to tell us anything which has recently come to mind. Do you have any questions?'

'No, it all seems clear to me.'

'Good. You are not under arrest and you are free to leave at any time. Can you confirm that you understand this, and you are happy to proceed?'

'Yes,' I say. It's much more formal than previous interviews, and I suppose I should have expected this, but I feel nervous, nonetheless. I reassure myself they've no evidence of anything and sit up straight in my chair, trying to look confident. DI Twist is back in her old habit of looking anywhere but at me. It must have been much more interesting for her when we were in my house. There's not much to look at on the walls in here. I wonder when she's going to carry on and get a surprise when Sergeant Carter abruptly takes over.

'Our investigation into the death of Harry Johnson has led us, as you are aware, to consider the disappearance of Reginald Blake and the death of Frances Blake. We have also looked into the deaths of John and Malcolm Templeton because of their similarity to Frances Blake's death. As a doctor, what is your view on the theory that John's death might have been caused by wolfsbane poisoning?'

'I've not considered it. You mentioned it the other day, but I didn't think any more about it. Why should I?'

'You've told us of your interest in rare plants. I'd have thought you'd have an opinion.'

'Wolfsbane isn't a rare plant. It's an interesting one, because of its medicinal properties, but it's not rare.'

'Meaning it could have been in the fields where John died?' the sergeant asks.

'I suppose so. I hadn't thought much about it.'

'When Malcolm Templeton died, the doctors assumed a genetic weakness?'

'So I believe. Mother certainly did.'

'And yet there was no evidence found of a heart defect at either post-mortem,' he says, looking at his notes. 'It seems to have been a case of assumption based on lack of evidence.' Sergeant Carter sounds rather disapproving, and my professional pride is piqued.

'I'd say the previous family history was evidence in itself,' I say. 'I think you're being rather harsh on those doctors, sergeant. We're not miracle workers, you know.' I expect a smile from him at this, but I don't get one. He's too busy turning over the documents in front of him, while DI Twist seems to have found something to look at outside the window.

'We've located the hospital report of your father's death,' he says. 'I gather you were at home with him on the day he died.' I feel my stomach clench. Why was that in the file? It must have been in the ambulance crew's report. The pathologists wouldn't have known or cared who was in the house at the time.

'Yes, I was.'

'There seems to have been no direct police involvement. Is that right?'

'Yes, it is. Why would there have been?'

'We routinely look into any sudden death, that's why,' DI Twist says, turning her gaze on me.

'They must have decided it was natural causes very quickly then, mustn't they?'

'Clearly they did, but we're not inclined to be quite so trusting now,' she says. 'So we'd like you to tell us about that day. Where was your mother, for example?'

'She was out shopping. She was at the market and she had some other errands to run. My father - Malcolm, that is - was reading his paper in the living room. He'd been playing golf all morning and he'd said he was feeling rather tired. He didn't usually get tired. Maybe it was a sign of the heart attack to come,' I say pointedly.

'Where were you? Didn't you hear any noises coming from the room to indicate he might be unwell?'

'No, I didn't. I was outside all afternoon. We'd let the garden go a bit over the Christmas holidays, and I had decided it was time for a good tidy up. I didn't hear a thing until Mother got home and found him. She called me in at once to tell me what had happened.'

'What were you doing in the garden? I wouldn't have thought there was much to occupy you in January,' says Sergeant Carter. I suppose he's learnt about gardening from his granddad. Great.

'I was cutting plants back, clearing the leaves, tidying the greenhouse and so on. It was a sizeable garden. There was always a lot to do.'

'How did you get on with your father?' he asks.

'What can that possibly have to do with anything?'

'Answer the question, please,' says DI Twist. 'Did you get on well? Was there friction between the two of you?'

'We got on as well as most teenage girls do with their fathers, I suppose. I wasn't a daddy's girl if that's what you mean. I wasn't spoilt or indulged. We didn't have a great deal in common and he was often out of the house, so I was closer to my mother. Does that answer your question?' DI Twist has been watching me closely. What can she see? Don't be silly, she can't know about anything I'm not telling her.

'Tell us about Frances,' she says, and the abrupt change of subject takes me by surprise.

'What about her?'

'You said you'd known her since school, she was your best friend. Did you like her?'

'Of course I liked her. She was my friend. What do you expect me to say?'

'People often grow out of their childhood friends,' she says. 'It's rare, I've found, for friendships made at the age of five to continue beyond the end of school. Why do you think yours lasted so long?'

'You're right in a way, we didn't have much in common, but that was probably part of the attraction. Frances needed my help while we were at school, and she still liked to ask my advice when we grew up. She was the only person I knew who was interested in clothes, makeup, having fun. She cheered me up.' These are probably the truest words I've said to the detectives.

They've taken me off-guard and I hope I won't regret them.

'Why did you need cheering up?' asks the sergeant. For the first time today there's a softer tone to his voice, and I remind myself to be careful.

'We had a difficult time in the years following my father's death. My mother found it hard going back to work and having to move house. I enjoyed my evenings with Frances. They distracted me from my responsibilities at home.'

'Did things change when she met Reg?'

'Yes and no. We were still friends, but she found it harder to find time to see me. Reg wanted her at home with him, and they didn't have much money for socialising. I treated her to lunch every now and then.'

'Her death was very sudden. Had you seen any warning signs? You're a doctor after all, one might have expected you to pick up any early indications of a heart condition.'

'I suppose there were times when she said she was tired. In the middle of the day, when you wouldn't expect it. I just thought she was finding it hard work running her own home as well as working full time. You're right though, it might have been a sign of a weak heart. I only wish I'd thought of it at the time. It might have been prevented if I had. Oh dear, what an upsetting thought.'

'Don't blame yourself, Dr Templeton, it's much easier to spot these things with the benefit of hindsight.' Sergeant Carter gives me a small smile. There's no similar response from DI Twist, who follows up swiftly with her own question.

'Going back to the possibility that John Templeton died from wolfsbane poisoning, what do you have to say about the theory that Malcolm and Frances died from the same cause? That it was accidental in John's case, but deliberate for the other two?'

'It sounds preposterous to me,' I say firmly.

'And what about the theory that Harry Johnson was poisoned in the same way?'

'Even more ridiculous. Whatever reason would you have for thinking that?'

'Two reasons, Dr Templeton. Firstly, the stain on his jacket which our pathologists believe is vomit. One of the symptoms of aconite poisoning is vomiting, as I expect you're aware.'

'I don't know anything about the symptoms, only

about it being fatal. And there are hundreds of reasons why he might have had such a stain. I don't think that sounds like proof of anything.'

'The second reason is his connection to you.' She looks straight at me, those baby blue eyes boring into mine.

'And why is that a reason, may I ask?' I'm trying to maintain my dignity along with my composure, but it's increasingly hard not to let the anxiety creep into my voice. They're making far too many of the right connections. But they don't have any evidence. I'm not under caution. I'm not under arrest. If they had proof, I would be. I take a mental deep breath and tell myself I can do this.

'Tell us more about your father, Dr Templeton. Did you have a grudge against him? A reason for wanting him out of the way?'

'Of course not. We weren't close, but that's hardly a reason to want him dead.' But she's not interested in my father any more, and changes direction like a hound tracking a fox.

'What about Frances? And Harry? Did something happen to turn you against them too?'

'No, why should it? Nothing happened to turn me against anyone.'

'And did you really not put two and two together when you heard about John's death? I would have thought a plant expert such as yourself would have recognised the symptoms of aconite poisoning. When did you really find out about it? Are you sure it wasn't before your father's death rather than afterwards? And are you sure you've never grown wolfsbane in that greenhouse of yours?'

'That's absolutely absurd. John died of a heart attack, not from poisoning. I've never grown that wolf plant in my life. And what possible reason could I have for murdering any of them anyway?'

'Let's take Frances first, shall we? Maybe you weren't as chummy with her as you'd like us to believe. You were very quick to get together with Reg after she died. Maybe you and Reg had fallen in love and decided to bump her off so you could get together.'

'That's a ridiculous suggestion. I barely spent any time in his company before Frances died.' She ignores my protestations, and ploughs on regardless.

'Maybe Reg liked the look of your salary to help him

out with his mortgage. He was off at the races the day Frances died. Maybe you sneaked over and poisoned her.'

'This is outrageous. You certainly have a good imagination, Inspector, I'll give you that.'

'And maybe Harry found out and blackmailed Reg. Perhaps you and Reg killed him together.'

'And what possible reason would we have for doing that?' It's alarming to hear her mention blackmail; she's clever, even if she isn't on the right track. Yet.

'Maybe Reg disappeared in case the police came calling. Maybe he was planning to return. How long did you wait for him, Lilian, before you realised he wasn't coming back? Before you accepted he'd found someone else?'

'I don't know what to say. This is all ludicrous.'

'Is it?' says DI Twist. 'Well, maybe it is, and maybe it isn't. Either way, there are too many coincidences in this case. And I don't like coincidences.'

'Even if it were true, what evidence do you have? For any of it? You've searched my greenhouse already. There are no poisonous plants there, and there never have been. You can search my house if you like, there's nothing there either.'

'We don't think you're foolish enough to keep evidence of murders from forty years ago,' says DI Twist, the slightest hint of a smile on her lips. 'And whatever we may think of you, Dr Templeton, we do not consider you to be a fool.'

'Thank you, Inspector.' There's a pause, and I decide it's time to finish this conversation. 'Thank you for sharing your theories with me today, it's been most instructive. However, I had nothing to do with anyone's death, natural or otherwise, and I suggest you direct your enquiries in a less…fanciful direction. I hope you've asked all your questions now, because unless you have a reason to detain me, I intend to leave.' I get up, gather my coat and bag, and wait by the door for Sergeant Carter to open it for me.

'Goodbye, Inspector. I expect you'll be in touch again once you have the evidence you need.'

I march out of the room with my head held high, but the shaking starts as soon as I leave the police station. At least it's on the right side of town, so it's not too far to walk home. And I need the exercise. They've not got it right. But they nearly have. They've got close enough to be suspicious, but not the evidence they need to arrest me. And it all happened so long ago I don't suppose I'm considered a risk to the public.

The exercise does me good, and when I get back, I change into my walking shoes and go out again, onto the Westwood this time. I know the garden won't bring me its customary peace today. The sun is edging towards the horizon, and I sit on a bench where I can see it sinking behind the racecourse. The clouds are turning, shades of pink, purple and grey against the blue of the sky, and I wonder if I will ever find a place I can love as much as this. I was convinced it was time for me to go this morning. I was ready to leave the house, the garden, Joanna. But now, up here, looking at the sky stretching for miles around me, I know I can't take the final step. What on earth is stopping me? Is it the place? The knowledge that when I leave here, I'll be leaving Mother? Or is it the familiarity? Am I scared of starting anew, away from everything I've always known?

I don't have to do it. Not yet. They won't find any evidence. They'll give up in the end. I'll see Joanna again. I'll put my garden to rights. I'll never need the package in the allotment, I'll be able to live here forever.

Chapter 18

Lilian would never forget the day when her mother shared the story of her background. There was too much information for her to absorb immediately, and it was a few days before she felt she had a proper understanding of events. Writing in her diary each evening, she found that by putting the facts and her responses into writing, she was able to grasp the implications of what her mother had told her. The fat little book with its lock and key had been her confidante for nearly five years, and she now began to pour out her heart to it in earnest. With no one to confide in – she knew Frances could not be told – it was only through her nightly scribblings that she was able to come to terms with her new world.

Once enough time had passed for her to get her thoughts straight, Lilian found an enormous sense of relief in discovering Malcolm was not her father. She welcomed the idea that her love of plants had come from both her parents, and she knew that one day she would ask her mother for more details about John Templeton. It also meant there was no reason to feel ashamed of her nightly prayers for Malcolm's demise. She knew it wasn't right to want someone dead, but at least she was no longer wishing it on her own father.

Most intriguing was Grace's account of John's death, and her description of the flowers he had gathered moments before. She noted that Grace had not touched the flowers, they had been left abandoned in the fields, and therefore wouldn't have been seen by the ambulance crew. She immediately recognised Grace's description of the blue flowers with their strange, hooded faces. It was monkshood, so called because of the cowl-shaped flowers. She seemed to remember it had another name, and on checking her reference books she found it was also known as wolfsbane or aconite. It was an interesting plant with healing properties, but it could cause death if it entered the bloodstream or was ingested. If John had a cut on his hand, simply touching the plant could have been enough to kill him. The symptoms were similar to those of a heart attack, and the poison left the body's system less than twenty-four hours later. Lilian doubted anyone would have looked for it anyway.

Lilian spent a long time thinking about monkshood. She decided it would be interesting to grow some in her greenhouse, and she sent off a postal order to the seed catalogue. When the seeds arrived, Lilian was dismayed to find it could take a year or more to sprout. She didn't know how much she would need, but she was sure it would be more than a small shoot or two. She didn't think she could wait for a year. The situation with Malcom was intolerable, and now she knew there was a solution, she was impatient to execute her plan. She had money saved up from birthdays and Christmases, and she decided to spend it on some seedlings. If she took good care of them and kept them in the greenhouse, they should grow quickly enough to give her a sufficient quantity to work with in a matter of weeks rather than months.

The seedlings arrived with strict instructions to wear gloves when handling them. Lilian put the pots at the back of the greenhouse where there was no chance of anyone coming across them by accident. She found an old sheet and set it up over the plants to give them the shade they needed and watered them every day to maintain high moisture levels. Lilian gave the seedlings plant food every week to accelerate their growth, and she monitored them anxiously almost every day. There were three pots, each containing three seedlings. Lilian wanted to be confident of at least one plant growing successfully, and she reasoned that even if they were small, if she had plenty of plants, she would only need a little of each in order to carry out her plan.

There was encouraging progress within a month. Two of the seedlings had died but there was at least one healthy plant in each pot. One was growing with particular vigour, and Lilian named it Mr Monk. It helped her to feel she wasn't alone in her enterprise, and she even found herself talking to it. She wondered if talking to plants was an early sign of madness, but decided it was more likely to be a symptom of loneliness. On the other hand, loneliness wasn't behind her plan, and maybe she was a little bit mad after all. After another month, Lilian removed the weaker seedlings from each pot to allow the stronger ones space to grow. She was pleased with their progress, especially Mr Monk, who was still the tallest of the three. By the end of the Christmas holidays she had three healthy plants, and she decided the time had come to act.

Lilian had read that the roots of the plants would be as poisonous as its leaves and stalks. As they were still relatively small, she decided to use the two smaller specimens in their entirety and to cut some but not all of the stems and leaves from Mr Monk. If she got the strength wrong, she might have to start all over again, and she thought it would be best to have at least one plant in reserve. Lilian knew monkshood was poisonous, and it could also be used for homeopathic purposes, but she didn't yet know how to turn it from a plant into a potion. She had ordered a book on homeopathy from the library, and it arrived in early January. The process was quite simple; the challenge lay in acquiring the necessary equipment and finding a place and time when she would be uninterrupted in order to make it.

Lilian had asked for gifts of money with which to buy plants for Christmas, and this had not aroused suspicion on either Grace or Malcolm's part. Once the school term started, she made short detours every few days to buy a pestle and mortar, a jug, a sieve and a plastic bowl. She took a spoon, a small saucepan, a knife, and an empty jam jar from the kitchen and put everything under the bench at the back of the greenhouse. She had decided this was the best place to make the mixture. She often spent hours in there, so with luck no one would come looking for her. Now she needed some means of cooking. Lilian's family had never owned a tent, but she had looked in the windows of the camping shop in town a few times and had seen a prominently displayed camping gas stove. It was advertised as the 'must have' item for the outdoor life. Lilian decided it was her 'must have' item too. She had just enough money left to buy one. She was ready.

Lilian's experience in the greenhouse almost put her off cooking for life. Nervous from the start that someone would come looking for her, she knew she shouldn't be lighting the stove indoors, and was terrified of the greenhouse exploding around her. Praying she wouldn't need to use it, she filled a bucket with water and put it next to the bench, thinking of Frances's mother's saying: 'Prepare for the worst and hope for the best'. She was certainly hoping for the best today. Lilian had also taken great precautions to avoid poisoning herself. Her long shirt sleeves were tucked into her gardening gloves, the collar was buttoned at her neck, and she had covered her face, highwayman-style, with one of her mother's scarves. Lilian filled the jug with water and poured some into the pan. She set it on the gas stove and realised she had forgotten to bring matches. Cursing inwardly, she removed the scarf and gloves and went to find some. Her mother was busy cooking and barely noticed as she walked through the kitchen and into the living room, where she found some on the mantelpiece. Thank goodness Malcolm was out playing golf, or she'd have had some explaining to do.

Back in the greenhouse, Lilian's nerves were no better than before, but she lit the gas without further ado before putting on the gloves and scarf again. As the water heated up, she chopped the plants and roots, checking constantly on the pan as she did so. It was hard work, her hands sweaty inside the thick gloves, and clumsy with the knife. She finally had the plants cut into small pieces and she put them in the mortar, where she ground them up with the pestle until the whole lot was a brownish-green sludge. She added it all to the boiling water and watched anxiously whilst straining her ears for the sound of her mother approaching. The half hour that Lilian had decided it needed seemed to last for ever, but she made herself wait, despite her impatience for it to be done and her fear of the greenhouse exploding. Once the time was up, she turned the gas off with a sigh of relief and realised she needed to leave the mixture to cool before decanting it into the jam jar. At first, she thought it best not to put it outside in the cold air in case her mother came out, but she decided it was worth the risk for the time it would save. She set the pan down carefully behind the greenhouse and realised there was a very simple way of preventing her mother from coming outside. Leaving the gloves and scarf in the greenhouse, she went into the kitchen.

'Any chance of a cup of tea, Mother?' Although it wasn't over yet, she was exhausted from the strain of making her potion.

'I was wondering if you'd like one, dear. I was about to come out and ask but you've saved me the trouble. You've been busy out there. What have you been up to?'

'Oh, this and that, watering the plants, tidying up the greenhouse. I don't know how it gets into such a state, but it does. There's no time for sorting it out in the summer so it's good to get it done now.'

'I suppose it is. Have you finished?'

'Not yet, but I was desperate for a drink. I'll finish it off in a minute.' Lilian sat back in her chair, watching her mother put tea leaves into the pot.

'Would you like a piece of cake, dear? It's ginger, it'll warm you up a bit.'

'Yes, please.' Lilian paused, a solution to what she

hoped was her final problem starting to grow in her mind. 'It's one of Father's favourites, isn't it?'

'Yes, that's right.'

'Would you teach me to make it? I'd like to be able to make at least one cake in my life and it might as well be one we all like.'

'Of course, dear.' Lilian could see Grace trying to hide her surprise. She had never shown an interest in cooking before, and she knew her mother would see this as a good sign. 'I'll teach you this afternoon if you like. They keep for over a week, so it won't matter us having two.'

'Lovely.'

***

A faint green in colour, it didn't smell of much. Lilian still felt it was best to use a cake with a strong flavour, just in case. Malcolm might have a good sense of taste, and it would be a shame to fall at this final hurdle. She cut a thick slice from the cake she had baked the previous day with her mother, put it on a plate and pin-pricked its surface, trickling the mixture over it and watching it sink in. She flipped it over so the tiny holes couldn't be seen and added a cake fork to the plate. She put the kettle on, made a cup of tea, and took both cup and plate into the living-room. Malcolm looked up.

'Lilian, what are you doing here?' Malcom looked over the top of his newspaper, clearly none too pleased to be interrupted.

'I thought you might like a cup of tea and a piece of cake. Mother taught me how to make it yesterday. I thought maybe you could tell me if it tastes as good as hers does.' Lilian smiled as sweetly as she could as she put the tea and cake on the table beside Malcolm's chair.

'Oh, all right then.' Malcolm lifted his paper again, indicating that Lilian was expected to leave him in peace. A thank you would have been nice, but Lilian's purpose wasn't to garner praise. She left the room, crossing her fingers and praying he wouldn't forget about it. She made herself walk calmly back to the kitchen. She returned the cake to its tin, put on her gardening shoes and gloves, and went outside. Malcolm might call out for her and she needed a good excuse for not going to his aid. She hoped it would all be over by the time her mother returned from the shops, but if she didn't and Malcolm was still alive, she needed an alibi of sorts. She wouldn't hear anything from the garden.

Lilian put the mixture back in the greenhouse. She found she couldn't sort out her own thoughts and now it was over, her hands wouldn't stop trembling. She felt a strange mixture of euphoria and terror. She didn't want to let herself imagine what would happen if it didn't work and Malcolm somehow found out what she had tried to do. She had to keep busy, distract herself with hard physical activity. She decided to cut back the climbing roses and the dead wood from the honeysuckle. This was a conveniently time-consuming task, and once it done, she noticed all the leaves lying on the lawn. Her mother would be pleased if she raked them up, so she did that as well. Her watch showed it was an hour and a half since she had left Malcolm. He hadn't come to find her, so that was a good sign. She reckoned her mother would be back in half an hour and she wanted to remove the teacup and plate if she could, so she went back inside. As she approached the living room door, Lilian stood still, listening intently for any sign of Malcolm being in a state where he could harm her. All she could hear was the ticking of the clock in the hall and the chatter of children cycling past on the pavement outside.

The door was ajar. She pushed it open, holding her

breath as she did so. Malcolm was slumped in the chair. The newspaper was on the floor with the cake and the plate. She didn't feel for a pulse; his vacant, open eyes told her all she needed to know. The cup of tea sat untouched on the table. It must have been stronger than she'd realised. He'd barely moved. Lilian picked up the teacup and hurried back to the kitchen for her gloves. She collected every crumb from the carpet and put the cake and the plate in the greenhouse with the rest of her equipment. She'd have to dispose of them all, but that could wait. She washed and put away the tea things and went back out into the garden.

Chapter 19

I feel different when I wake up. It's late, past nine o'clock, and I've slept better than I have in weeks. I know it's because I've made the decision to stay. I thought I was ready to go, I made my plans, everything was in place, and still is for that matter. But I wasn't ready for it. I know now I'll see Joanna again; I'll make the garden beautiful again, I'll live here for as long as I want to. Maybe I will move, who knows? But it will be when I'm ready. Maybe I'll find somewhere smaller, near to Jo. I can decide whenever I want to.

I take my time getting up and have a late cup of coffee in the garden. The doorbell rings as I'm drying the mug. I sigh and make my way to the front of the house. I thought they'd leave me alone for a day or two. Surely they can't have found out more in the short time since I was at the police station?

'Susan! What are you doing here?' I can't help myself. I know I sound rude, but I'm amazed and delighted to find someone other than detectives on my doorstep. It makes me giddy, and I forget my manners.

'I'm sorry, Susan, I didn't mean it to come out like that. I just thought you might be someone else, and it gave me a surprise seeing you there. Would you like to come in?'

'Yes please, that would be nice.' She's looking rather hot and sticky, even though the day isn't especially warm. She must have walked here from her house in town, and I suppose she's not used to more than the short distance to the shops. She's clutching her knitted bag and wearing one of her usual shapeless garments, with the customary sandals on her feet. At least she won't have got much in the way of blisters.

'Come in, Susan, would you like some coffee? The kettle's not long since boiled.'

'Thank you, Lilian, I don't much go for coffee, but a cup of tea would be nice.' There's something different about her, and as she talks, I realise it's her voice. It was rather loud and strident the time I met her in town. She wouldn't stop jabbering on the whole time I was with her, but today she seems subdued, and I wonder what's the matter with her. The kettle needs filling, and we sit at the kitchen table while it comes to the boil. I expect her to start chattering straight away, but she's silent, fiddling with the handles of her bag.

'It's lovely to see you, Susan, but it's a long way for

you to have come. Did you want to talk about something in particular? Is one of the family poorly? I'd be happy to advise, but you'd be better off seeing your GP if there's something wrong.'

'No, it's not the family. It's something else.'

'Yes?' There's a pause before she bursts out with it.

'It's about Frances.'

'Frances?' I'm taken aback. What on earth could Susan want to talk to me about Frances for?

'Yes. The day she died. Were you here, Lilian?'

'Here?'

'Yes, did you come to the house that day?'

'No, why would I have done?'

'Maybe she called you to ask for help when she started to feel ill. Or maybe you just came to see her. You were her friend, after all.'

'Well, I didn't. Why are you asking such a strange question, Susan? If I'd been to see her then I'd have said so.'

'Someone saw you here.' Her voice is firmer now, and she's looking me in the eye with an unexpected and unsettling hint of challenge.

'Whoever would say such a thing? It's not true,

anyway. I think someone is trying to stir up trouble, Susan.' I'm thinking as fast as I can. Maybe someone did see me. Neighbours are limited in number on this road, but there are a few. I realise that even though I didn't see anyone, someone could have seen me. Out in their front garden perhaps, concealed behind a hedge.

'This lady seemed very certain. She said she saw you and she's thinking about going to the police. I told her not to do that just yet. I said I wanted to ask you about it first. You were so kind to Reg when he was depressed, and I wanted to know what you'd have to say about it. In case there's a simple explanation.' When she says this, I know there's only one possible course of action, and I have to act quickly.

'You did the right thing, Susan. Look, the kettle's coming to the boil. I'll make the tea and we can sort it out properly. Would you like a piece of cake to go with it? I've a nice ginger cake in the tin. I had a slice earlier, and it's delicious, I can promise you.' Susan's distracted by this domestic talk, and she nods her head vaguely.

'Will you do me a favour and put the water in the pot when the kettle boils? The tea caddy's next to it, if you don't mind warming it first?'

'Of course.' She looks pleased to have something to do, and as she crosses to the counter where I've put the teapot, I whip behind her back and snatch up the washing up gloves and a plate. Then I go into the pantry to get the cake out.

'I don't know about you, but I like to make tea with leaves, don't you?' I call out to her, hoping to keep her attention on her task.

'Oh, yes, I've told my daughter it tastes better with leaves, but she likes to use tea bags. They're not the same, are they? Do you know, Lilian, she didn't even have a strainer in the house when I moved in with her, what do you think of that?' She's warming to her theme as I'd hoped she would, and this gives me time to put on the gloves before cutting a fat slice of cake and putting it on the plate. Mother's old sleeping tablets are on the shelf and I take three from the container. She's adding the tea to the pot as I come out with the plate, and I put it on the table.

'Oh, thank you, Susan, you're such a help. Here, you sit down, I'll bring everything over and find some cups.' With my back turned towards her, I add more water from the kettle and crush in the tablets, giving it all a good stir before taking the pot to the table. Susan won't drink her tea until it's had time to brew, I know that much, so I take my time finding a jug for the milk and getting a cake fork out of the drawer.

'What an enormous slice of cake! I shan't be able to eat all that, Lilian!' She's right there, but not because of its size.

'Oh, I'm sure you can manage it, Susan, you'll have a long walk back to town after all. You'll need a bit of energy then, won't you?' The tea must be ready now, and I pour us both a cup.

'I suppose I will,' she says, looking at the cake with anticipation. She takes a sip of her drink and sighs with pleasure. 'Now, that's what I call a nice cup of tea. And it's a real treat to have home-made cake. My daughter never bakes. It's all shop bought with her. I suppose she has the children to look after, they keep her busy enough.'

'Do you not bake yourself, Susan?' As I ask the question, she takes a big forkful of cake, and she has to chew for several seconds before she can answer.

'Yes, I love to bake but I've not got used to her kitchen yet, and I don't want to look like I'm taking over.

Oooh, this is gorgeous, Lilian. Where did you get the recipe?'

'It was my mother's. I don't go for cordon bleu cooking, but I can at least make a decent ginger cake.' She takes another bite as I'm talking, and I know it won't be long now. I put plenty in it this time, knowing if I needed to use the cake, I'd want it to be quick.

'Anyway, this lady I was telling you about. The one who said she saw you on the day Frances died.'

'Yes, what a strange story. What did she say, exactly?'

'She came up to me at the Women's Institute. My daughter made me join. She said it would be a good way to make some friends in the town, and she was right, they're a lovely bunch of ladies. Anyway, this woman came up to me this morning and asked if I was the sister of Reginald Blake.'

'More tea?' I interrupt the flow with the pot in my hand. If she pauses to drink more, she'll hopefully eat more too. She's not looking ill yet and I need it to happen soon, or I'll have to start thinking of answers to her questions.

'Lovely,' she says, and takes another bite of cake.

Good. 'Aren't you going to drink your tea, Lilian? Look at me having a second cup and you've barely touched yours.'

'Oh, I don't like it too hot. Joanna's always teasing me because she says I drink it luke-warm like a child. Go on, Susan. Tell me about this woman.'

'I thought it was because of the story in the newspaper, you know. A few people have asked me about it. They only want a bit of gossip and I don't say anything to them. I don't want them talking about me to the papers, thank you. But this lady was different. She said she was interested because she'd lived in that road a long time ago. This road, that is.' I need to talk so as to stop the flow and give her time to eat more. Why isn't she showing any signs yet?

'Oh, really, what was her name? I might have known her. It wasn't Barbara Michaels was it? She used to live over the road a long way back and her little girls played with Joanna. They were such good friends and it was a shame when they moved away.' She's had time to eat two more mouthfuls. It must start to take effect soon.

'No, I don't remember her name. But Lilian, she said she remembered Frances, and she said how sad it was when she died. She said what a shame it was that the doctor hadn't been able to help her, and I asked her what doctor did she mean? She said she'd seen the nice young lady doctor from the hospital cycling up the road that afternoon. She recognised you because you'd treated her little girl in the casualty department. You were really kind, she said, and she remembered you because there were so... so few...' At last.

'So few lady... doctors,' she says, starting to droop in her chair.

'Are you all right, Susan? You don't look very well.'

'Feeling a bit hot,' she says. 'Feeling a bit...' She suddenly vomits over the remains of her cake.

'Oh, Susan, you must have got overheated walking all that way here. Maybe I should have given you a cold drink instead of the tea. Would you like to lie down on the sofa for a minute or two until you feel better?'

'Good idea,' she says, and I help her up and into the living room. There's no plastic sheeting or stairs to climb today, and I hope it won't be long before she loses consciousness. She'll have drunk enough of the sleeping tablets to help her drift off, especially when combined with the poison. Her skin's clammy already, her eyes are glazed when she lies down, and I can hear the beginning of a rasp in her breath.

'I'll get you a cold flannel and a glass of water, Susan,' I say, and she nods weakly as she closes her eyes. I go back to the kitchen and take my time making sure the tap is running nice and cold, and when I return there's no sign of movement from her. It's been the quickest of the lot, apart from Mother, of course. That's good. Not because she didn't suffer, but because I need to get away.

***

I have to get it right. There's no room for mistakes, and I know I have to act quickly. Even though no one's likely to miss Susan for a few hours, the police could come calling at any time. I open my laptop and book a ticket on the first flight I can find to a country with no extradition treaty. I don't want to speak to more people than necessary at the airport, so I check in immediately, print out the boarding pass and put it in my backpack with my passport.

Upstairs, I pull my suitcase down from the wardrobe and pack quickly; mostly summer clothes, but a cardigan, sweater and raincoat too, just in case my plans change. It will be nice to wear smart clothes again, I've had enough of looking a frump, even if it has helped me to cultivate a suitable image for the police. I pick up my book from the bedside table and take the envelope of cash from the desk. I empty my purse of all unnecessary items, which I leave on the kitchen table with my mobile phone. I don't bother clearing up. There's no need, and I find it amusing to think DI Twist will have the evidence she wants at last. A final glance at Susan reassures me that she's lying still, and her breathing is shallow. There's no doubt she'll have gone before anyone has time to find and treat her. Such a shame about the woman at the WI.

It's a while since I've driven the car, I prefer to use my bike, but it fires up readily enough when I turn the key. I do a quick check – backpack, suitcase, keys. I'm all set. I pause the car on the drive and close the garage door behind me, then pull out onto the road without a backward look. I thought I didn't want to leave, but it turns out I can after all.

It's only a few minutes' drive to the allotments. There's no one around; it's often quiet during the day at this time of year. Retrieving the package, I leave the little bottle behind with a note attached to warn whoever finds it to take care because it's poisonous. It's done its job now and there's no need for anyone else to die. In less than five minutes I'm back on the road and heading across the Westwood towards the motorway. I find it hard to believe that I'm finally leaving Beverley for what I know is the last time, but I know I've no choice, and I can feel the weight lifting from my shoulders as I drive past the long late summer grass and grazing cattle. I'm ready to move on, I have to move on, and I smile at the thought I'll never have to see Detective Inspector Ronnie Twist again.

It shouldn't take more than a couple of hours to drive to the airport, and I know I'll have to wait there for a few hours before I can board the flight, but I'm too wound up to stop for food or anything else. The euphoria of leaving has worn off now, and I can't stop a nagging conviction that they're on my tail. I tell myself not to be silly. No one knows where Susan's gone. It will be hours, days probably, before anyone finds her. The worst that could happen is the police coming to see me, but the last interview was less than twenty-four hours ago, and it's unlikely they'll want to talk to me again so soon. I give myself a shake and focus on the task ahead. It's a while since I've been to the airport , and I'm not familiar with the parking arrangements. I'll need my wits about me if I'm to manage everything smoothly without drawing attention to myself.

***

The short-stay car park is closest, so that's where I go. I've succeeded in parking at the right terminal, which is an achievement in itself after all those signs. I'd forgotten how complicated airports are, and after turning off the engine I take a moment to think. It feels good to be sitting still, and I'm tempted to stay here for a while in the quiet gloom of the car park. My growling stomach reminds me I've not eaten since breakfast, and I know I must do something about it if I want my brain to work properly. I tell myself I'll feel much better with food inside me, and it gives me the impetus I need to get moving.

Getting out of the car and stretching my legs helps too, and I can't deny feeling a sense of excitement as I wheel the airport trolley into the terminal. It will take me a while to work out where to take my suitcase and there's plenty of time before the flight leaves, so I head first to a coffee shop, where I find a seat in a corner to eat a sandwich. A screen on the wall opposite me shows flight information alongside a news channel. I spend a minute or two looking at all the flights on display and wondering how long it will be before mine appears at the bottom of the screen. The novelty soon wears off, and I turn my attention to the news channel, which has a strip at the bottom showing what the newsreader is saying. There's the usual stuff about the economy and climate change, and then the strip changes colour and the words 'Breaking News' appear. My stomach lurches. It can't be me, can it? Not so soon? But it is me.

Breaking news from East Yorkshire, where a woman is fighting for her life after being found in a house in Beverley. Police investigating the historic death of Harry Johnson, whose body was found on the property two weeks ago, discovered the woman at lunchtime today. Detective Inspector Ronnie Twist told us that the owner of the house, Dr Lilian Templeton, is urgently wanted in order to assist the police with their enquiries. A major search is underway for Dr Templeton, whose picture is shown here.

It's a newspaper photograph, taken last week. I'm at the front door in my pyjamas looking rumpled and confused, and it's not as clear as it might be. I don't know how easy it would be to recognise me from it, but I can't afford to take any chances. There's a whooshing sound in my ears like the sea, and I have to close my eyes to make it go away. I know that I could easily lose my balance if I were to stand up right now, so although my mind is screaming at me to get out of the coffee shop as quickly as I can, to run, I don't. I open my eyes and take another bite of my sandwich as my face disappears from the screen, wait for the noise in my ears to stop, and pick up my backpack. I push the trolley away, thanking my lucky stars the shop isn't busier and the screen doesn't face the counter, and head out onto the concourse. Taking the suitcase off the trolley I look for the one place where I know I can find some privacy. A sign points the way and it only takes me a minute to find. I lock the toilet door, sit down, and breathe. Think, Lilian, think. It's just a problem to be solved.

***

I consider my options and the resources at my disposal. It's obvious, I'll have to use the contents of the package sooner than I expected. I'd thought of it as a backup for the future, but it would seem its time has come.

I'll need more space, so I move to the disabled toilet

and open the suitcase. Off come my frumpy comfort clothes in exchange for a smart suit and blouse, heels, and sunglasses. I find the Liberty scarf Joanna gave me for Christmas and tie it jauntily at my neck, apply make-up and add a squirt of perfume. It doesn't take long to comb back my hair and put it in a neat bun at the nape of my neck. At last I feel more like myself. I hadn't realised how my recent persona had been dragging me down until now. Looking in the mirror, I know I've got myself back again. I straighten my back and lift my chin in a way that I'd schooled myself out of, and I know when I walk out of this cubicle, I'll be a new woman.

I look at the suitcase and realise I can't take it with me. They'll be looking at CCTV cameras and they'll see me with it, I'm sure. The same applies to the backpack. I transfer the essentials to a plastic bag and put the backpack inside the suitcase. The toilet lock has a slot on the outside that you can turn to undo it if someone gets stuck inside, and I use a coin to twist it round. I wonder if the airport staff will realise what they've found before they call the bomb squad and almost wish I could stay long enough to watch.

I don't want to talk to anyone I don't have to, and the

urge to leave is almost uncontrollable, but I remind myself that I've transformed myself, no one will recognise me, and the concourse shop girls won't have seen the news yet. I make myself take my time choosing a straw hat and a smart and spacious reversible handbag to match my shoes. The girl in the shop doesn't look old enough to have left school, and she's busy on her phone when I walk in. I hope she's not looking at a news app. She comes over and asks if she can help me. I say no thank you and then feel mean. She looks as if she's about to die of boredom, and the length and perfection of her nails suggest she has very little to do. I try to be more friendly when I take my purchases to the counter, and she smiles and asks if I'm heading anywhere nice. It catches me off-guard and I can't think of anywhere other than Tokyo. My brain freezes. What can I say? Despite having looked at the screen in the coffee shop, I can't remember any other destinations and I can't risk saying somewhere that doesn't leave from this terminal. I have to say the first thing to enter into my head. The truth. Or almost the truth. What might have been the truth.

'Yes, Tokyo. I've never been to Japan before. I believe it's fascinating.'

'Oh, yes, I'm sure it is,' she says absently. 'Enjoy your trip.'

'Thank you.' Slowly, Lilian, slowly, don't rush. Saunter, but purposefully. Look as if you've somewhere legitimate to go. And hope she doesn't wonder what you're doing here more than six hours before the only flight of the day leaves for Tokyo. Wait a minute, there are plenty of flights to Tokyo if you don't mind changing, it's only fugitives from justice like me who need direct flights. I need to calm down, I really do.

I make my way as casually as I can to the station, resolving to get on the first train out. None of them are going anywhere useful, but they all go through Manchester Piccadilly, and I reason that I can get more connections from there. I buy a ticket at the machine and hide in a back seat behind a free newspaper to help calm my nerves. My mind's too distracted to take anything in, and I can't remember a thing I've read afterwards, but at least it's deterred any friendly passengers from engaging in conversation. Piccadilly is bustling and I feel safer in the crowds. There's a train leaving for London in ten minutes, and I put my growing skills with ticket machines to good use. A casual glance around the station confirms there aren't any policemen in evidence. Reassured by this, I walk through the barrier with my head held high and find a seat with further ado. When the trolley comes around, I ask for a coffee and a packet of biscuits, and the lack of interest in the girl's eyes as she serves me gives me the confidence to put my newspaper down while I drink it.

Staring out of the window at the passing fields, I realise I've not been able to relax at all since first thing this morning, and the stress is beginning to take its toll. I've had a lucky escape but it's not over yet. I consider my situation as objectively as I can. I've done a good job of transforming myself physically, but I didn't think to look for CCTV at the toilets in the airport, and they could pick me up there, or at the shop. I need to leave the country as quickly as I can, and I have to make sure the trail ends in London. Despite the bundle of cash in my bag, I know air travel isn't an option. Paying in cash for a flight is the sort of thing that can get a person noticed, especially if the police have put out an alert. So what can I do? When making my plans, I had considered the ferry from Hull. If the timing had been different, I might have cycled there, but the wait would have been too long.

Maybe the ferry from Calais or Portsmouth? No, that would involve crossing London and another train, and I've not got the strength for it.

My mind wanders, thinking of the different ways Joanna's travelled in her time. We didn't go on holiday much when she was young, but she caught the travel bug when she went to university and I used to love hearing her tales. I remember one story about her hitching a ride on a lorry in Italy and getting stuck in a tunnel. It still makes me smile now, thinking about her expression as she mimicked the driver arguing with the other motorists. The memory stops abruptly. A tunnel.

***

I watched a programme on the television once about people trying to evade the police. There was a cash prize at the end, and it was all rather exciting. I remember the biggest challenge was evading the CCTV cameras. The police seemed to be able to pick people up almost anywhere, and I know I will need to be clever if I'm to avoid this happening to me. There's no reason why they shouldn't track me to the train, and I need them to lose the trail here. As we approach Euston, I tie the scarf round my head and put on my raincoat. I reverse the handbag, so the brown side shows instead of the black, and I contrive to leave my hat on the shelf above the seats. The new me adopts a hunch and a quavery voice and asks a kind-looking gentleman for help getting down from the train.

'Oh, thank you, I've had a knee replacement you know, and I can't help being scared it's going to collapse under me whenever I'm on stairs.'

'No problem, glad to help.' He's not wearing a suit and he's got a little roll-on suitcase, so not a businessman, and hopefully not in a hurry. He looks as if he's leaving, so I grab his sleeve. One can't afford to have any shame in these circumstances.

'Would you mind coming with me as far as the ticket barrier? I'm feeling a bit wobbly and I'm not sure how they work. I'll be all right after that; my daughter's meeting me.'

'I'd be delighted. Here, take my arm.' I witter on about my daughter and how she's working for the NHS – it's all I can think of – until we reach the barriers. He helps me through with my ticket, and when I say I can see my daughter he departs with nicely disguised relief. Thinking of those cameras, I go into a shop and browse for ten minutes, then follow another old woman out closely enough to look as if we're together and make my way to the taxi rank.

***

It's the rush hour, and I know this will work in my favour. I've been surrounded by crowds ever since leaving the train, and St Pancras is the same. I go to the exchange bureau and get some euros. Not so many as to arouse suspicion, but enough to see me through a night in a hotel. A change in image won't hurt before I buy my ticket. There are bound to be cameras at the counter, and I need to look as different as possible from earlier in the day. I'm debating which of the clothes shops to go into when I feel a tap on my shoulder. It's all I can do to stop myself jumping three feet in the air or taking off like a hare.

'Excuse me, isn't it....?' I recognise him straight away. A doctor I used to talk to at conferences. He was always rather flirtatious, and if things had been different, I might have responded more positively, but I'd had enough of men by the time I met him. I realise I forgot to replace my sunglasses after taking them off to buy the euros. I reach casually into my bag and grab the glasses, putting them back on my nose.

'I'm sorry?' He's startled by my haughty tone, which I've based on that old woman in the television series about an abbey.

'Oh, I'm sorry, I thought for a minute you were someone I used to know.'

'Please don't apologise, it's easily done.' I give him a condescending smile and turn back towards the shops, my heart pounding again. How long will it be before he sees the news item and puts two and two together? Has he seen it already? Is he looking for a policeman right now to report me to? I need to get those clothes immediately. I walk into the first shop I see and find jeans, flat shoes, a T-shirt, and a linen jacket. Another hat would be wise, and I pick up a beret near the till. I'll look like mutton dressed as lamb, but it won't be for long, and the people in the shop are helpful in allowing me to change once I've paid. The old outfit goes into the shop bag and I decide to hang onto everything for now. If I dump the bag it could be found and matched with the CCTV pictures, which will hardly help my cause.

The machines will only take cards, and that's obviously not an option. There are two ticket counters and one has a long queue, so I go to the other one. It's for business class tickets, and I know that will be more expensive, but I don't want to wait. I march up to the desk and ask for a ticket for the next train to Paris. The young man in his smart uniform breaks off from his conversation with a similarly under-occupied colleague and pays attention.

'Let me see, Madame, I will find out if we have any available.' He taps away at his computer in what I suppose he hopes is an efficient fashion, and then gives me a smile which, in my current state of exhaustion, I find hard to resist. I remind myself to be professional and tip my chin into the air.

'Yes, Madame, we have tickets. Do you just require the one?'

'Yes, please. How much will it be?'

'Two hundred and forty-seven pounds, with an additional ten pounds administration charge. How would you like to pay?'

'In cash.' I have the money ready at the top of my bag. It wouldn't look good to be grubbing around for it. I count it out carefully and hand it over.

'Your name, Madame?' I stare at him. I hadn't

thought about him asking for my name, and it takes me several seconds to think what to say.

'For the ticket, Madame. Your name, please?' I pull myself together and blurt out the answer.

'Thank you, Madame, have a good trip.' He gives me another winning smile before returning to what must be a gripping story if his companion's gestures are anything to go by. I turn and walk away from the ticket office, debating whether to go through now or to get a coffee. My ticket only requires a ten-minute check-in and I'm starting to flag. As I head towards a cafe, I see a board with the latest news on it.

Manchester airport has been closed for two hours due to a bomb scare. And the search for Dr Lilian Templeton has been escalated. The police have reason to believe she may try to leave the country, and all ports are on high alert. If any member of the public sees her, they should call the number on the screen immediately.

Never mind the coffee, I need to get going. Now. I realise I've been putting this moment off, and I know why it is. If it works, I'm on my way to a new life. If it doesn't, I'll be in police custody within the hour. The time has come to find out, and the knowledge that it will all soon be over, one way or another, sets my heart thumping again. I can't afford to wait any longer, and the sooner it's done, the better. Back straight, chin in the air, I walk towards security.

***

When I come out of the station, I cross the road and walk into the first hotel I see. It's a good one as it happens, and on opening the door I find a well-appointed room. I sink into the upholstered chair and look out over the lights of Paris. It's nearly midnight, but the city's still busy. I wonder when I'll have the energy to explore; right now, I feel as if I could sleep for a week. I'd love a coffee but in the interests of a good night's sleep I make myself a cup of tea and take my few belongings out of the bag. Tired or not, I'll need to go shopping tomorrow, and not only for clothes. A visit to a hairdresser will be a priority, and I'll need to convert at least one of my assets.

I can't resist it any longer. I have to look at them. It's been a long time since I tucked them away in their little pouch, and I've not liked them being at the allotment all this time. I take a tissue from the box on the dressing table and lay it flat on the shiny wooden surface. I pull open the pouch's drawstring, tip the diamonds onto the tissue, and spread them out with my fingertips. I don't like to touch them too much, it disturbs their sheen. They don't sparkle, they've not been cut. I prefer them that way, it's less ostentatious. I only bought them for practical reasons after all. I'll sell three tomorrow. They'll give me enough for a long time of travelling. I can decide later where to settle down.

I think back to the day after Harry. I was less shocked by what I'd done than by how vulnerable I'd let myself become, and I promised myself I would never allow it to happen again. I wasn't naïve enough to suppose none of my murders would come to light one day in the future. I knew I should have an escape plan. Buying these little rocks each year whilst at the doctors' conference in London was my insurance. Together with the passport. I knew I needed a second one, just in case. I didn't like the idea of finding a dead child's grave like they do in films. And as I was clearing out Frances and Reg's things, a simple solution arose. It's easy to keep renewing a passport once you've got it. And a doctor is always a good person to countersign your photograph.

I put the diamonds back in the bag. Seeing them again and thinking of the travel and new adventures ahead has lifted my spirits. I decide it's time to celebrate and to toast my future endeavours. I call down to reception.

'Hello, it's room two-oh-one here. Is it too late for room service?'

'No, Madame, how may we help?'

'I'd like a smoked salmon sandwich and a bottle of champagne please.'

'Just the one glass, Madame?'

'Just the one, thank you.'

'Very good, Madame Blake, it will be with you shortly. Have a good evening.'

Oh, I will. I most certainly will.

THE END

www.blossomspringpublishing.com

Printed in Great Britain
by Amazon